Also by Daniel Serrano

Gunmetal Black

boogie down

DANIEL SERRANO

GRAND CENTRAL
PUBLISHING

NEW YORK   BOSTON

Copyright © 2010 by Daniel Serrano
All rights reserved. Except as permitted under the U.S. Copyright Act of 1976, no part of this publication may be reproduced, distributed, or transmitted in any form or by any means, or stored in a database or retrieval system, without the prior written permission of the publisher.

Book design by TexTech International

Grand Central Publishing
Hachette Book Group
237 Park Avenue
New York, NY 10017
Visit our website at www.HachetteBookGroup.com.

Grand Central Publishing is a division of Hachette Book Group, Inc. The Grand Central Publishing name and logo is a trademark of Hachette Book Group, Inc.

Printed in the United States of America

First Printing: November 2010

10 9 8 7 6 5 4 3 2 1

For my father, Hilario, this funky tune.

You with your precious eyes, you're blind to the corruption of your life.

—Sophocles, *Oedipus Rex*

boogie down

CHAPTER 1

Cemetery Hill

Cassandra was an NYPD detective, an undercover assigned to stop a monster.

The newspapers called him the Marathon Slasher. He stalked female joggers at night. He shredded their faces with a scalpel.

Cassandra's job was to lure the Slasher out of hiding. To act the part of a lonely jogger, unaware, reckless in her choice of shadowy cinder trails at dusk.

Cassandra was nervous. Undercover work was always dangerous.

Plus she had seen the photos in the case files. The scars. The grief in the victims' eyes.

Her department-issued semiautomatic was holstered inside her waistpack.

Two male undercovers shadowed her. Ghosts, they were called. Their job was to protect Cassandra yet stay out of sight. Each pretended to be a lone jogger, one ahead, the other behind Cassandra, about a twentieth of a mile, approximately one city block.

Compost in a nearby field mixed with the July heat to

deliver a sweet, disgusting smell. That summer had been a scorcher.

Cassandra spoke up: "Jennings, what's your twenty?"

They communicated using radios rigged to look like MP3 players.

"Behind you, Detective, about an eighth of a klick."

"All clear?" she said.

"Yes."

"Pace?"

"Ten-minute miles."

Cassandra glanced at her watch. "Ten-zero exactly?"

That would put Jennings thirty seconds back.

"Ten point oh exactly, Detective. Nobody's gonna sneak up on you."

Tactical teams throughout the park monitored their transmissions and tracked them on satellite.

Each jogger had a GPS chip on his or her person. Cassandra's was tied to her sneaker. A command post managed the entire set from inside a fake Metropolitan Transportation Authority repair truck, parked on Broadway, under the number 1 train.

Cassandra radioed the lead ghost: "Jones? What's your twenty?"

She envisioned Jones checking the GPS watch he had coaxed from Technical Assistance. "A block ahead of you, Detective. Ten-minute miles."

Six miles an hour. Fast for her, this late into the run. Sweat salted her eyes.

Jones called. "Approaching the bridge, Detective. Ready for Cemetery Hill?"

Runners talked about the Hill. They feared it.

It was called Cemetery Hill because the city's first native-born mayor had been buried up there. It was known as a spirit-breaker for runners, but supposedly rewarded your effort with a special view of Manhattan's distant spires.

Previously Cassandra had always been too fatigued by this point to take the Hill and had stayed on the flats. This night she wanted to push herself.

"Stick it."

"Ten-four."

Cassandra imagined the lead runner crossing the bridge that connected to the back hills. Thirty seconds later she came to the span herself. She crossed it.

Trees on either side of the trail reached for one another with their branches like laced fingers. They formed a dark canopy over the trail that enveloped all who passed beneath.

Cassandra pumped her knees. Her earphones radiated silence beneath her ghosts' heavy breathing. She bopped her head and pretended to listen to music to appear like an easy target. In her mind, she got to the Spanish part of "Diamond Girl."

The first hill rose. It quickly became vertical. Like running in sand. With boots on.

Cassandra immediately regretted her decision to take the Hill.

She felt jumpy. It was dark. A raccoon scampered from a bush and she flinched. Cassandra's heart rate was off the chart. She labored to breathe.

She glanced back and saw only shadows. She glanced again and caught the flash of a man suddenly in, then suddenly out of sight on the curved path behind.

A *running* man.

Cassandra's heart skipped. *Where did you go?*

She slowed to let the running man round the bend. He didn't.

Where are you?

She whispered into her mic. "Jennings?"

"Yeah?"

"You see him?"

"Who?"

"In front of you. John Doe running man."

"Where?"

"Just ahead of you, maybe half a klick."

Jennings cleared his throat. "Negative."

"On the Hill."

"The Hill? I thought you said, 'Skip it.'"

"What?"

Jones cut in. He could see their locations on his special watch. "Detective, it looks like Jennings didn't take the cutoff, he stayed on the flats. I'm heading back—"

Cassandra stage-whispered, "Negative. Slow your pace and stand by. Tactical units stand down."

A lieutenant inside the fake repair truck radioed.

"Detective, you have to abort. It's too dangerous. Jones, turn around and rendezvous with her. Jennings—"

Cassandra cut in: "No, Lou, please don't. If it's him, he ain't made me. Don't blow my cover."

"Detective—"

"I'm fine, Lieutenant. I have my firearm."

It got harder to breathe.

The lieutenant hesitated. "Ten-four."

Cassandra didn't waste oxygen thanking him. "Jennings, are you hauling back?"

"Fast as I can."

"Floor it."

Cassandra glanced behind. Nothing.

I saw you. I know you're back there, running man.

Cassandra touched the cherished gold ring on the chain around her neck. She said a two-second prayer and quietly unzipped her waistpack. She felt the gun and removed a small can of pepper spray.

"Jennings?"

Her feet were like buckets of wet cement.

"Halfway up the Hill, Detective. Don't see nobody."

How is that possible? The curvature of the trail was not so great; one of them should be able to see someone between them.

Cassandra glanced back.

Nothing.

When she turned to face forward the Marathon Slasher leaped from behind a tree with his scalpel out.

"It's him!"

He swung.

Cassandra snapped her head back. The blade missed her throat by a whisper but sliced the earphone wires. The Slasher swung his free hand and tore her necklace off.

Cassandra aimed the spray but the Slasher knocked her hand and the aerosol discharged into her face.

"Aaahhh!"

The sting exploded up her nostrils. It lit her eyes on fire. The can dropped from her hand.

Cassandra's eyes welded shut. She threw a wild punch.

The Slasher slapped her with a hand like cast iron. He grabbed her ponytail and yanked her off the trail into some trees.

"No!" She kicked. "Stop!" She could not see.

Her sneaker with the tracking chip came off.

Cassandra plunged her hand into her waistpack.

The Slasher threw himself on top of her. They tumbled downhill, grabbing each other.

Suddenly he was above her, scalpel high.

Cassandra jammed the gun under his chin.

"Freeze!"

He froze.

She strained to keep her eyes open. "Toss the blade!"

He hesitated.

She flicked the safety and cocked the hammer. "I swear to God!"

The Slasher tossed the scalpel.

Cassandra pressed the muzzle to his carotid. "Off me! Kiss the dirt!"

The Slasher moved slowly.

Cassandra got to her knees and jammed the muzzle into the back of his head. She forced him face-down and scrambled for the cuffs in her waistpack. She restrained his hands behind his back, then spun away to empty her water bottle into her eyes.

"Oh, God!"

She gagged, hands on knees.

There was something in her bra. She felt it.

Her special ring!

The necklace was gone, but the ring had fallen into her cleavage. Cassandra held back a sob.

The Slasher spoke to her in Spanish. "I will peel your face away and the world shall see who you really are."

His accent was unfamiliar to her. He was not Puerto Rican, Mexican, or Dominican. Cassandra's backups, Jones and Jennings, called from the running trail.

Her eyes swollen almost shut, she bent and grabbed the links between the cuffs. She put her foot on the Slasher's shoulder and yanked. His rotator cuff popped.

"¡Ayy!"

She spoke Spanish. "Threaten me again and I'll kill you."

Her ghosts ran up with flashlights and guns drawn. Jones had a finger through the laces of her running shoe.

Cassandra snatched it and pointed. "Weapon's in the bushes. Locate it for Crime Scene."

Jones searched for the scalpel. The Slasher squirmed and moaned. Blue and white lights flashed through the trees. Sirens approached.

Jennings bent toward Cassandra. "Great work, Detective. You collared the Marathon Slasher." He put his hand on her lower back. "Wanna go for a drink after the paperwork?"

Mucus dripped from Cassandra's nose. She looked into the man's face. He had been assigned to protect her.

She thought of something sarcastic to say, but heaved on his sneakers before she could get it out.

CHAPTER 2

Mother's Milk

The following morning Cassandra was in the kitchen of her house on Virgil Place, in Castle Hill, in front of the stove in her robe and slippers.

She was sore. Her face stung as if she'd fallen asleep in the sun. Her throat was irritated. But she was alive, Praise God, in one piece, and making breakfast for her son.

Yellow butter sizzled in the frying pan. The smell of it filled Cassandra's kitchen. She poured pancake batter into perfect circles.

"Jason, honey, I need you to clear the table."

The boy was playing with toy cars, as he did every morning. He did not respond. He lined the cars side by side, counted them, recited their colors in order. Then he scrambled the cars and lined them up again exactly as they had been. He counted and recited their colors again.

Cassandra interrupted before he restarted the process.

"Jason."

He stopped but did not look up.

"Please put your cars away so we can eat. Thank you."

Her son's eyes did not find hers. Cassandra stood in front of him, collected the cars, placed them in his hands.

"Go put them in your room. Wash your hands, breakfast is almost ready."

Jason slid slowly off the chair and went to his bedroom. She grabbed the spatula.

Children with autism require routine. Cassandra had learned that.

What she had never imagined was how much *she* would need these mornings with her son. Nothing could take away her guilt and constant worry about how much work kept her away from him. She was not there to attend or protect him for most of the day. That bothered her.

But their quiet time, when they ate together, that gave Cassandra great satisfaction.

Seven in the morning and already the heat was making the back of Cassandra's neck sweat. Her mother returned from the corner store with bananas and an armful of newspapers.

"Wait until you see!"

Cassandra had made front-page news.

The *New York Post* and the *Daily News* had run virtually identical full-page color photos of the Marathon Slasher as he was wheeled from an ambulance into the emergency room, hands cuffed to the sides of his gurney like Hannibal Lecter.

In each picture Cassandra was escorting the prisoner in her running gear. The gold detective's shield dangled across her chest.

Both papers featured the same headline: CAPTURED!

One ran a caption: *NYPD Det. Cassandra Maldonado hauls alleged Marathon Slasher to hospital after daring Bronx foot chase.*

Her mother read the news account. She stopped and looked up at Cassandra.

"That man tried to cut you?"

"Mom, reporters exaggerate. Want a pancake?"

"Too fattening."

"You always say no, then end up eating one of mine."

"Cassandra, you did not tell me this was gonna be dangerous."

"Want some scrambled eggs?"

"Cholesterol." Her mother went back to reading.

Cassandra told her mother that the commissioner's office had called about a press conference with the mayor.

"The mayor? Think you can get a desk job?"

"I told you, Mami, I wanna go to HI-PRO."

"What's that?"

"High-profile crimes. Celebrities. Cases that make big news."

"Out on the streets?"

"Sometimes. But not like before. No more buy-and-bust operations with drug dealers." Cassandra pointed the spatula at the newspapers. "I can't do undercover work anymore. The whole world knows I'm a cop."

"What about the hours?"

Cassandra knew her schedule had been a strain on her mother, who took up the slack in caring for Jason. It was only the three of them now. Cassandra's recent stint at Missing Persons had given her a predictable 8:00 A.M. to 4:00 P.M. schedule. No overtime, and she was home in the evenings to care for her son. Her mother feared a return to old ways.

"I don't think I'll work so much overtime when I get

my promotion. It comes with a raise. I can still keep coming home at a decent hour. You'll keep your evenings."

"I'm not complaining."

"I know, Mami. Egg white omelet?"

"Uy, no. Don't taste like anything." Her mother pointed at the Slasher on the front page. "How did *he* get hurt?"

Cassandra stacked pancakes on a plate.

"Slipped on a banana peel trying to escape."

Cassandra peeled a banana, sliced it, made a smiley face on the top pancake out of it. She poured her son a glass of milk.

"Jason!"

He bounded into the kitchen, sat at the table, and picked up his fork.

Cassandra's mother looked at Jason through the top part of her bifocals. "What, Grandma's like a piece of furniture around here?"

The boy climbed from his chair and went to her. She raspberried him on the neck and he giggled. She pointed at Cassandra on the front page.

"You see who that is?"

He looked at the paper.

"Who is that, Jason?"

"Mommy."

"Who?"

"Mommy."

"That's right. Your mommy's famous. She stopped a bad guy. Now we don't have to worry about him no more."

Jason looked Cassandra in the eye and smiled. She smiled back.

Her mother patted him on the butt. "All right, Papito, sit down and eat."

Jason sat and ate one bannana slice at a time. First the eyes, then the nose, finally the smile. Always in that order.

Cassandra poured pancake batter. She included an extra one for her mother. She spied her child from the corner of her eye and felt the fullness of love.

CHAPTER 3

Politics

Cassandra checked herself in the mirror of a musty ladies' room at City Hall. She wasn't exactly nervous, but anxious about the press conference. She wanted to make sure she was ready for the cameras.

She removed lipstick from her teeth with a tissue and dotted the tiny mole over the left corner of her mouth with black eyeliner. In high school they called her Cindy Crawford.

She examined her profile. The chocolate suit and subtle pumps hit the right note. Her curly hair was blow-dried straight, silky, to its true length, halfway down her back. Her precious gold ring was on a strong new necklace, under the blouse.

Cassandra tugged the sleeves of her jacket to their length, shouldered the purse, stepped into the hallway. Her face stopped at Deputy Chief Acosta's decorated chest.

She looked up and saluted. "Sir."

Acosta stood straight in his uniform, the full six-foot-three, his stomach flat as ever. "It isn't a formal medal day, Detective, but why didn't you wear your uniform like you were told?"

"The dry cleaner misplaced it."

Acosta paused to let her know he knew she was lying. "You showed a lot of courage on this case."

"Thank you, sir."

"I knew when I pushed you, you were ideal."

Cassandra knew that he pushed her because he wanted to sleep with her, despite the fact that his wedding band was as polished as the stars on his shoulders.

"Some argued you couldn't handle it," he said.

Cassandra resisted the temptation to ask who.

"You made me look good, Detective. I won't forget it."

She did not like the sound of this. "Did you speak to the chief of detectives?"

"About?"

"My transfer to HI-PRO?"

Acosta's eyes did not flinch. "Not gonna happen, Detective."

Cassandra's heart dropped. "What? Why?"

"HI-PRO's an elite unit."

"So? I'm decorated."

"There's a long list of personnel with more experience."

Acid flooded Cassandra's stomach.

"Also there are problems developing with the Salazar file."

The Marathon Slasher had been identified as a Colombian national named Salazar. His lawyer had already filed an excessive-force complaint against Cassandra.

"Why'd you have to tune him up like that? Salazar claims you popped his rotator cuff on purpose."

"That's a lie."

"Keep your voice down."

"He tried to run after I cuffed him."

"Save it for the inquiry, Detective. This is still City Hall."

"Meaning?"

"The mayor cannot be seen rewarding a cop, even a hero cop, who is facing a civil rights complaint. The way this city's wired? You realize we're heading into a primary?"

Cassandra could not believe this. The reason she had accepted this crazy assignment was that she expected a transfer and a raise if she were the actual decoy to lure the Marathon Slasher into the net.

"Chief, this isn't fair. Politics already kept me out of Homicide."

"Cassandra, things take time."

"What about me making grade?" Cassandra had assumed she'd be getting a bump to second grade, a higher salary.

Acosta shook his head again.

The heat traveled up Cassandra's legs. "You gonna let me get mugged? I delivered public enemy number one."

"You are one helluva cop, Maldonado. But you're young. Barely ten years on the job. Quit trying to move faster than is natural."

Cassandra pictured the pile of bills on her kitchen table. She had counted on that bump in salary.

Acosta tried to soften it. "The mayor recognizes the public's affection for you right now."

"How big of him."

"That's not to be wasted. He wants to give you a commendation."

"Another ribbon?"

"For your actions in apprehending Salazar."

"What good will that do?"

"If it turns out you violated the prisoner's rights *after* capture, the mayor has an out. The recognition was for actions prior to the actual arrest. This keeps you from becoming a political liability."

"A liability?"

"Yes. You might become one. One, by the way, who'd be due a bigger pension if she threw her papers in after getting bumped up a grade."

"Throw my papers in? Who said anything about retirement?"

"It could be worse," said Acosta.

"How?"

"You'd be due nothing if you got fired."

Cassandra swallowed.

"That wasn't a threat, Detective. It's just—"

"The mayor needs his cover."

Acosta put his hand on her shoulder. "Mature of you to understand."

A mayoral aide appeared. "His Honor has arrived. Everybody into the Blue Room."

Acosta nodded. "We'll be right in." He turned to Cassandra. "Don't look so glum. This is still a big day for you. We'll take a picture with the mayor."

"Great. I'll send copies to my creditors."

Acosta did not react. They walked side by side toward the crowd that spilled into the hallway. Cassandra had just been robbed.

CHAPTER 4

Spin

By the time Cassandra entered the Blue Room, ten seconds later, she was fuming.

Light applause broke out. Cassandra nodded half absentmindedly and joined people behind the podium, beneath a portrait of Alexander Hamilton.

Politicians she had never met kissed Cassandra as if they were old friends. They shook her hand, slapped her back, maneuvered around one another to get into the photo op with her.

The mayor walked in, trailed by the police commissioner. Each waved, pointed, and gave audience members the thumbs-up.

The mayor took the podium. He acknowledged nearly every elected official in the room but left a couple conspicuously out. He smirked when he thanked the Bronx district attorney for coming, "all the way downtown."

The mayor gave an update of where the case against Salazar stood.

Finally, he mentioned Cassandra.

"One of New York's finest. A genuine Big Apple hero.

The reason we are here and why women of this city feel safe again."

The mayor invited Cassandra to stand next to him while he read the commendation. Cameras zoomed.

Acosta nudged her. "The mayor called you."

Cassandra made her way to the podium. The mayor kissed both her cheeks. He smelled of stale cigar smoke.

"Detective, for your heroic actions during the *capture*," he let the word linger, "of a dangerous individual, it is my privilege to bestow upon you this commendation."

The mayor read an official statement. Cassandra did not listen. He handed her the commendation.

A reporter asked Cassandra how it felt to receive the ribbon.

"I have a lot of these in a drawer at home."

Nervous laughter.

"Detective, tell us about yourself."

She looked around the room.

"Well, I'm a mother. Early thirties. Been in the department for a decade. I was raised in the projects, the Mitchel Houses, in the South Bronx. I own a house now. I won't say where."

"What was it like to come face to face with the alleged Marathon Slasher?"

Cassandra nodded. She flashed to her terror in the dark woods.

"They say the training kicks in. Frankly, this work is scary. Salazar tried to slice my face off."

One reporter jumped in. "What about the allegation *you* attacked *him* after he was under arrest? His lawyer says he was already cuffed."

"No comment."

"You feel like a hero, Detective?"

Cassandra was already tired of the word.

"This is a job. You do it selflessly. To serve and protect. In the end it's a way to pay the mortgage and feed my son."

Cassandra scanned the room.

Newspaper writers, radio reporters, TV talking heads, cameras, mics, tape recorders. She got an idea.

Cassandra glanced at Acosta. He seemed clueless.

She turned to the media. "I struggle like everybody. Like all of you at home. That is why—"

She glanced again at Acosta. Alarm finally registered on his face.

Cassandra decided to gamble.

"That is why I almost cried, minutes ago, when I was informed the mayor ordered the department to promote me to detective, second grade, which means a raise. Plus, he ordered me transfered to the HI-PRO Unit, effective immediately. This way I can best serve the public and take care of my son."

The cameras, microphones, tape recorders, and notebooks captured all of it.

The mayor looked suprised. The commissioner knotted his eyebrows. Acosta pressed his lips into a thin line.

Cassandra said that would be all and stepped away from the microphones. She returned to her spot next to Acosta.

He leaned over and whispered in her ear.

"You just threw the noose around your own neck, Maldonado. The commissioner will never stand for this."

Cassandra got in Acosta's ear. "If I don't get my grade money and transfer, I'll sue. I'll go straight to the media."

"With what?"

"I've been keeping a file about department discrimination since the Police Academy. Can you imagine how thick it is?"

It was a bluff, but Acosta swallowed. Cassandra turned toward the podium.

The mayor was asked about Cassandra's promotion. He stuttered, then said of course, the city was proud to reward her performance.

The press conference ended. Several reporters approached Cassandra for follow-ups. Commissioner Riley interrupted.

"Excuse me, Detective, a word?"

"May I finish these interviews?"

"In a minute. I need to speak to you privately. Some details about your promotion."

Cassandra excused herself. She followed Riley away from the Blue Room, outside of hearing range, to a small room. It was just big enough for the commissioner, the mayor, Chief Acosta, Cassandra, and an old coat rack.

Acosta shut the door. He stood behind Cassandra. She half-wondered whether she was in for an old-fashioned NYPD tune-up.

Riley got in Cassandra's lashes. "Maldonado, you got a real set of stones on you."

"Thank you, sir."

"That wasn't a compliment. Acosta notified you of our decision. No promotion, no transfer. That was insubordination."

Cassandra did not disagree.

"Think you're gonna get away with this?"

"I'd better."

The mayor wrinkled his forehead.

Cassandra said, "A lawsuit during the primary would be bad news all around."

The commissioner reddened. "I could have your shield for this."

"Where do you want it?"

The vein in Riley's neck popped.

The mayor spoke to his commissioner. "Can't do anything about it now, Malachy. Let's live with it."

Cassandra looked at the mayor. "Mature of you to understand, Your Honor."

Riley wouldn't unlock from her. They were nearly the same height.

The commissioner threw a sudden karate chop at the coat rack to her left, but it didn't snap. Cassandra was a veteran of street standoffs and had not flinched.

"You're gonna get what you bargained for with me, Maldonado. In spades."

Riley let the wildness in his eyes run loose for three seconds more. He pushed past Cassandra and faced Acosta.

"This is your cluster-fuck, slick. You sponsored her."

Acosta took the glare. Riley stomped out. The mayor followed.

Cassandra remained with Acosta. "Like you said, Chief, my public approval was not to be wasted."

Acosta kept his mouth flat. He shook his head once, then walked out.

CHAPTER 5

Black Diamond

Later that night in a flashier part of town, Sabio Guzmán the entertainment lawyer weaved through traffic.

His ride was an aqua-blue metallic Porsche convertible. He drove it with the top down. The tan leather seats were designed to feel like buttercream.

Yet the lawyer was not comfortable. He was too tense.

He parked and tossed the private club's valet the keys. Sabio was a member.

He flashed his card and breezed through reception, pushed the top button on the elevator. The sun had set but Sabio slipped into his shades.

The elevator door slid open onto a rooftop hot spot. A thumping hip-hop bassline rolled in then back out over the city like a swollen tide. Sabio waded into the crowd.

Blondes, long-haired Asians, Wall Street assholes, a finalist from a modeling show, a reality TV castoff, the latest indie movie princess, all acting as if they did not want to be noticed. Every drink arrived in a jewel-colored glass.

Sabio spotted his boss, FYSHBone the rapper, record producer, hip-hop icon, president and CEO of KUT-THROAT Records.

FYSHBone and his posse occupied prime real estate next to the turquoise swimming pool. The entire entourage wore KUTTHROAT's clothing line, identifiable by the emblem: a fish skeleton puffing a large marijuana joint.

It was so humid that Sabio fantasized jumping into the pool and staying under the cold water. He moved to the edge of the roof, next to a sign that read NO DIVING. A waiter recognized him and brought him a double shot of tequila plus a cold beer.

The DJ segued to an all-FYSHBone set. She dropped the opening beats to FYSHBone's first number-one single, "If the Blood Must Spill (Let It Flow)."

All eyes were trained on the rap superstar. FYSHBone did not look up from texting but raised his fist.

The crowd buzzed.

Sabio turned to absorb the hawkeye view of swanky Soho. Everything he had come to New York City to accomplish more than a decade ago was finally just within reach. He had every card on the table and he was all in.

Win big or flame out.

Or worse.

In either case the city still sparkled.

Sabio threw the double tequila down. He leaned over the edge of the roof.

A van pulled into a spot under a tree across the street. Sabio knew the passengers to be members of the NYPD's worst-kept secret: the so-called Hip-Hop Squad, a crew of cops assigned exclusively to spy on rappers and other members of the hip-hop world.

Sabio was about to make a phone call when he felt a tap on the shoulder. He turned.

It was Slow Mo, the six-foot-six-inch goon who worked bodyguard detail for FYSHBone.

"Bone says get over there."

Sabio flipped open his cellphone. "Just let me call my bookie. I see a certain Yankee infielder slumping over a half-empty bottle."

The bodyguard wrapped his giant hand around Sabio's. He sandwiched the phone shut. "Bone says get over there now."

Sabio yanked his hand free. He drained his beer bottle, placed it on a passing tray, and followed Slow Mo to the doghouse.

Lawyer and client did not shake hands. They had to nearly shout to be heard over the music.

"What's up, FYSH?"

"Ain't that what I pay *you* to do? To tell me what's up?"

"What's the matter?"

"I'm tripping."

"Nervous over the big merger?"

"It ain't you who got a whole dynasty on the line."

"FYSH, your entire enterprise is about to explode."

"That's what I'm afraid of. Will it still be mine?"

"A thousand percent."

"Can I still do my thing?"

"That's up to you."

FYSHBone looked at one of his boys. "See what I mean? Lawyers never guarantee shit. Except the fee." He turned to Sabio. "You trust them corporate scavengers at KAMIKAZE Vynil?"

"No need to rely on trust, FYSHBone."

"Not even with you, Sabio?"

"That's different."

"How?"

"Lawyers have an ethical duty to be straight with their clients."

"Could've fooled me."

"What I'm getting at is trust the contract. It's all in the writing."

"What about a hostile takeover?"

"Have you been playing on the Internet again? I told you that's just rumors. Remember the corporate structure?"

It was complicated, but Sabio reduced the basics of the merger to one spoken paragraph outlining limited liability companies, joint ventures, conglomerates, shares, financing, and rights. "You really need me to break it down again?"

"What if I do?"

The lawyer put his index finger to his mouth. In his mind, he saw his precious stake in the merger do circles in a giant toilet bowl. "FYSH, you're gonna mess around and blow this."

FYSHBone rubbed the oversized medallion that hung from a thick platinum chain on his neck, a white diamond replica of KUTTHROAT's weed-smoking fish skeleton trademark. The joint was rendered in amber. Its lit tip was a shiny red ruby.

"FYSHBone, you need this deal. You need the capital."

"So you say. Did you talk to Dulles?"

The chief of operations. "Yes, we spoke."

"And?"

For a moment Sabio considered telling the truth. He straightened his silk tie. "Certified. We're squared away."

"Do we have to worry about the Feds?"

One *always* has to worry about the Feds. "Leave the worrying to me, FYSH. Just keep being a musical genius."

FYSHBone let go of his medallion and leaned forward.

Sabio sat down next to him. "FYSH, KAMIKAZE Vynil came to us, remember?"

"So?"

"They're the ones with the big crush."

"You saying the money's right?"

"It's huge."

"That is not what I asked."

"You worried about valuation? The *Wall Street Journal*'s gonna write this like you're a genius. You will get a huge infusion of cash. You still get to make music, produce. It's perfect."

"What about videos?"

"Total control. As raunchy or as cinematic as you like."

FYSHBone pointed at his crotch. "I do what tickles these nuts?"

"Haven't you always? You're like Picasso after *Guernica*."

"Meaning?"

"After that he could have crapped in a coloring book and it would have been worth millions."

FYSHBone rubbed his medallion. He shook his shoulder-length micro braids. For Sabio the moment drew out like a thousand ticks on a cuckoo clock.

The posse shifted. FYSHBone eased slowly back into his chair.

Sabio smiled. "So? We agree? Tomorrow you sign, you get richer than you ever dreamed possible."

FYSHBone read a text on his cellphone. "Snap. It's Princesa."

FYSHBone's supermodel girlfriend.

"You know how she gets."

Sabio ground his molars.

FYSHBone texted frantically. He asked Sabio if it was too late to cancel the merger. The signing was two days away.

Sabio tilted his head to alleviate the sudden pounding. "They say free will is all that distinguishes us from the animals."

FYSHBone stopped texting. "Right. And my dog only goes in the garbage when she thinks I ain't looking. It's double talk like that that makes me feel I'm about to get sucker punched."

Sabio unwrapped a peppermint. "One last piece of advice, FYSH?"

FYSHBone put his finger up. He read his girlfriend's latest message. "Crazy." He nodded for the lawyer to speak.

Sabio looked around to make sure no one eavesdropped.

"This is a private club, FYSH, but tabloids got rats all over."

"All publicity is good publicity, right?"

"True. But every rule's got exceptions. KAMIKAZE is a publicly traded company."

"So?"

"In the stock market, bad publicity is lighter fluid and a match. Keep shouting your anxieties and pretty soon a spy—maybe this jerk slinging your drinks—as soon as he makes out you got issues he's on the line with the gossip columnists. They'll run it in their first editions."

"Saying what?"

"'Guess who's got cold feet over his merger with KAMIKAZE Vynil? Is there a dirty little secret Wall Street ought to know about KUTTHROAT Records?'"

FYSHBone trained his hazel eyes on Sabio.

"Now the whole deal's suspect. Even if it goes through, skittish investors will dump and the stock price will drop."

FYSHBone ran a weary hand down his dark chocolate face.

"That's what I'm telling you, FYSH. Pay the check. Go home. Get a good night's rest. Tomorrow take your boat to City Island. Get some seafood. Relax. Don't even read. Don't listen to nobody. Next day, we get up, we do this. Announce it at the press conference like we scheduled. We'll tell the whole world how in love you are with KAMIKAZE Vynil. Then we ride the stock market like it's our own golden chariot."

FYSHBone curled his lip. "If it's that easy why does it feel like I have to see around corners?"

"Because you are paranoid. Which reminds me." Sabio moved closer. "What do we do about Gator?"

"Gator? Why are you sweating him?"

"You know why. Any thoughts?"

FYSHBone pulled back. "Don't confuse your problems with mine."

"You understand we gotta deal with him, right?"

"Yo! Are you deaf? Act like a lawyer. Let me worry about gangsters, all right?"

Doing wrong by Gator. This ship was headed for trouble.

Sabio whistled for the waiter and ordered a double.

CHAPTER 6

Supernova

FYSHBone floated in his own dimension, in his private studio, alone at the controls. It was the middle of the night. He puffed a joint and cleaned crazy, ridiculous beats.

Music was usually his escape. This night it failed him.

The lawyer's words knocked around the steel drum of FYSHBone's mind like a ball-peen hammer. Sabio had made the KAMIKAZE deal sound like chocolate frosting on yellow cake.

But FYSHBone's mother had taught him that if something looks too easy to obtain it is worthless. Or an illusion.

FYSHBone crushed the blunt and dialed the lawyer. Straight to voicemail.

"Yo! I need to hear from you. Tonight. I need answers. This ain't how I operate."

FYSHBone flipped his cellphone shut. He looked at Pretty, his pampered little affenpinscher—a dog so ugly the Germans named it "monkeylike."

FYSHBone knew people laughed behind his back. A hardcore rapper who totes a hideous, prissy little black dog? What was his problem?

Those people had not been there when FYSHBone saw Pretty for the first time. How she pulled a baked chicken out of a grocery bag he put down for one second, dragged the whole thing under FYSHBone's Hummer, then swallowed it whole.

If anyone had seen that, and understood FYSHBone, that person would know why he lured the dog with more treats and made her his own.

He pinched her little mustache. "Gotta mail another letter to the president, baby?"

Pretty had a weak digestive system. She wagged her tail.

Guided by the reasoning that leaves seatbelts dangling on short trips to the corner store, FYSHBone left his bulletproof vest on the console. He tucked his custom .50-caliber handgun into his waistband and pocketed his cellphone, wallet, and keys.

He bent to the little fridge he kept in the studio and grabbed a chilled coconut. He ice-picked the eye open and slipped in a flexible straw.

Pretty whimpered and thumped her tail against the floor.

"Coconut gives you the runs."

The dog licked her chops but soon forgot. She headed for the elevator.

Master and mascot rode down in private.

The large building was an abandoned former piano factory in a desolate corner of the South Bronx. It had no other occupants. FYSHBone had bought it to convert to condos, but the only conversion was the top floor, which he hooked up with an illegal studio and megaloft for himself. There was a little zoning problem, and FYSHBone had not yet found the right public official to bribe.

The dog went out and sprang for the gutter. FYSHBone's Hummer with the custom glittery metallic-blue paint job and flytastic twenty-four-inch rims was still parked where he left it. He always half-expected it to be gone.

FYSHBone could not believe how hot it still was, even at that hour. He sipped cold coconut milk and beat-boxed an old-school tune.

He could not wait to get back to his music.

FYSH did not hear the footsteps approach.

He felt the icy tap on his shoulder.

FYSHBone spun with his hand reaching for his weapon.

"Hey." He eased. "It's only you. What are you doing out here?"

No response.

"Are you high or something? Listen, we gotta talk." FYSHBone paused. "How come your hand is behind your back like that?"

The gun came up and pressed against FYSHBone's forehead.

He felt the horror. "Why?"

The gun exploded like a supernova in his face. A big bullet pierced his forehead and tore through the back of his neck, but not before it had carved through his brain, severed its connection with his spinal cord, and shattered the back of his skull.

FYSHBone's body toppled.

The shooter stood over him and pumped ear-piercing rounds, looked around, removed the famous necklace, and fled.

Blood haloed. Water oozed from the coconut where it had cracked against the sidewalk. Over in the gutter, Pretty, the ugly little affenpinscher, howled.

CHAPTER 7

Police Line Do Not Cross

The call from Detective Operations caught Cassandra busy in her kitchen.

It was to be her first day at HI-PRO, a fact that had her more motivated to go to work than she had been in years. Unfortunately, instead of headquarters downtown in two and a half hours, she was ordered to a crime scene, a homicide, in fact, in the South Bronx, forthwith. That meant step on it.

To Cassandra's knowledge, HI-PRO did not generally investigate homicides. She wondered if the celebrity involved was the victim or a suspect.

Who could it be? Already it was exciting.

Cassandra turned to Jason. "Papito, we're doing cereal today. Mommy needs to hurry for work."

He stopped lining up toy cars and frowned.

Cassandra did not need an episode. "I'll tell you what. I'll get Grandma to make you oatmeal with raisins."

"Smiley face!"

"She knows. But you have to get busy right now while she makes it. Go to your room, get dressed, because Mommy has to go as soon as you finish eating."

He scowled.

"Go."

He moved, slowly.

"Thank you."

Cassandra stood at the top of the steps to the basement apartment and called down. She explained to her mother what she needed and ran to her bedroom.

Cassandra jumped into a suit, snapped her hair into a bun, grabbed her purse, cuffs, gun, shield, and a brand-new small spiral notebook.

When she checked on Jason, he was in his underwear lining up toy cars on the floor of his bedroom. She quickly dressed him and brought him to the kitchen, where her mother arranged raisins over a bowl of oatmeal.

Cassandra ran out and filled the tank of her minivan while Jason ate.

Gas had gone up again.

Twenty minutes since the call.

Cassandra hoped her mother would be on the front steps with Jason ready to roll, but no such luck. She was tempted to honk, but that usually only agitated him. She parked and went in.

Jason had hardly touched his oatmeal. He stirred it and sang.

Cassandra's mother shrugged. "That's all he wants to do."

A new tic. The teenager next door played loud music. Jason would hear the latest hits, memorize the hooks, and sing them over and over. He sounded fine, but his persistence was annoying.

Cassandra negotiated the bowl away from him. She ushered him to the car, strapped him in, and got on the road.

Straight into traffic. By the time she walked her son into the school it was more than an hour after the call. She headed back to the Bronx. It was the height of rush hour.

Cassandra finally made it an hour and forty-five minutes after being summoned.

She parked on Willow Avenue, around the corner from the crime scene, and took two minutes more for foundation, eyeliner, and maroon lipstick. She released her bun and combed it into an efficient ponytail.

She climbed out and clipped her gold shield to the lapel of her sober gray suit jacket, hung her gun and cuffs on her belt, and grabbed two pair of latex gloves from a previously unopened box.

She slipped the notepad into her back pocket and whispered a quick prayer.

Port Morris is an industrial area, with scarce traffic and rarely a pedestrian. The peaks of the massive Triboro Bridge, which was recently renamed the Robert F. Kennedy, could be seen in the distance.

An unlikely part of town for anything involving a celebrity. Cassandra could not wait to learn some details.

Around the corner she found the street clogged with randomly parked blue and whites and unmarked squad cars.

Turret lights turned without sirens. Members of the Crime Scene Unit unloaded equipment from vehicles parked on the sidewalk. An ambulance rested near the center of the traffic jam.

Uniformed officers stood at the perimeter to keep away civilians.

A reporter recognized Cassandra and hustled over with a cameraman. Other reporters followed.

They peppered her with questions.

"Detective, already detailed to HI-PRO?"

"Is HI-PRO assigned to this case, Detective?"

"Is that a celebrity under the sheet?"

"Who is it, Detective?"

"Can you tell us?"

Cassandra put her hand up. "No comment."

She badged her way past patrol officers.

Yellow police tape was strung in a parallelogram from light posts and traffic signs to mark the working boundaries of the primary crime scene, the area where most physical evidence was likely to be discovered.

Inside the tape, on the sidewalk, was a body covered by a sheet.

Nearby was a Hummer with a special blue paint job. Someone had taped a piece of paper over the license plate to conceal the identity of the owner from resourceful reporters who could call their contacts at Motor Vehicles.

Police Department policy requires protection of a victim's name until next of kin are notified.

Cassandra wanted to duck under the tape and see.

She spotted the green police standard and lantern in front of a warehouse across the street. That signaled a temporary headquarters, technically a secondary crime scene to serve as a command post for the administration of the start of the investigation.

Communications personnel would be inside setting up phone lines and computers so that relevant units and commands could be kept abreast. Cassandra needed to check in.

She nodded at a uniform and entered. It was a large space, evidently used for the loading of trucks. Taped boxes and sealed drums bore addresses in the Dominican Republic. The place seemed to trap heat.

Detectives, technicians, patrol officers, and white-shirted supervisors milled and caught up with one another. Cassandra recognized some, but none she knew well.

The ones who looked her way pretended not to recognize her, despite her recent press coverage. Some gave a faint, almost imperceptible nod. Cassandra's reputation as a boss fighter had preceded her. It was the cop form of leprosy.

She recorded her name, shield number, and time of arrival in the crime scene log. A Bronx assistant district attorney had already signed in. So had an assistant medical examiner.

Cassandra spotted the man she was to report to—a name gossiped about in whispers, throughout the department, Lieutenant Salvatore Moretti, Detective First Grade. Second whip of HI-PRO. A legend.

Cassandra knew what Moretti looked like because newspapers had run stills from his segment on *The View* about celebrity stalkers.

Lieutenant Moretti stood inside a circle of cops, technicians, and the ADA. He finished an unfunny joke.

Cassandra walked over. "Lieutenant Moretti?"

Moretti wore a baby-blue portly sport coat over navy slacks, a white oxford shirt, and solid black tie. His puffy face was flattened.

Cassandra extended her hand. "Good morning, Lou. I'm—"

"In over your head?" Moretti did not take her hand.

"Maldonado, sir. Transferred to HI-PRO."

"We got the memo. You take the scenic route?"

The circle around Moretti dispersed.

"My apologies, sir. I take my son to school in the mornings."

"Save it." Moretti wiped his forehead and the back of his neck with a handkerchief. He chewed a stick of gum into shape. "Promised my daughter I'd give up the cancer sticks. You Puerto Rican?"

Here we go, thought Cassandra. "Yes, sir. Heart and soul."

"No need to make a parade out of it." Moretti chewed with the side of his mouth. "I had a Puerto Rican goumada once. Know what that is?"

A whore? "A mistress, sir?"

"I collared her pickin' pockets in Parkchester."

"Let me guess. You figured out a quick bail arrangement."

"The second she moistened her lips." Moretti flashed what little remained of his dimples. "Listen, this is a tough assignment. I know normally when you get detailed to a unit there is some period of adjustment where you get to know all the fellas and get shown where the copier is and the coffeemaker and all that slow stuff. This here is real police work. We're gonna be in it up to our tits. Can you handle that?"

"I'm a quick study, sir."

"This'll be on-the-job training and problem-solving. Trial by fire."

"I'm ready."

"We'll see. So the skinny on this situation is HI-PRO is locked in a squatting contest with Borough Homicide over this body."

Cassandra was happy to get to business. "How come, Lou?"

"They don't wanna cede the case. The way the locals see it, Humpty Dumpty drops in their yard, it's their eggshells."

"That makes sense. They're used to snatching high-profile homicides, not losing them."

"Correct. And they initiated the investigation according to normal protocols."

Cassandra nodded.

"But if One Police Plaza wants HI-PRO on this case, on this case we'll be." Moretti gestured toward a tall, auburn-haired woman with broad shoulders. "Captain Vargas just read their whip the facts of life."

Cassandra glanced at Vargas, the commanding officer of HI-PRO, and one of the highest-ranking Latinas in the department. Cassandra had seen the captain at different events before her ascension to HI-PRO, but had never worked up the initiative to begin a conversation.

Vargas stood, arms crossed, captain's shield gleaming. She conferred with other bosses.

Cassandra turned to Moretti. "Who's the body?"

"No positive ID yet, but it looks like FYSHBone. The rapper."

Cassandra's eyes widened. She felt a sudden unexpected pang of sadness. FYSHBone had made hits for nearly a decade and a half. His music was everywhere. It had been part of the soundtrack of Cassandra's life ever since high school.

"What happened?"

"That's what we're here to determine."

Captain Vargas walked over.

Moretti straightened his back. "You read them the riot act, Captain?"

"They get it. They'll step aside."

Vargas put her hands on her hips. "ME just pronounced a homicide—death by gunshot—so we're officially a murder investigation. Local squad'll provide bodies and expertise. We oversee. Lieutenant, you're in charge on the ground. I'll make sure you get what you need from management and collect the Fives," Vargas said, referring to the Detective Division's ubiquitous DD-5 reports.

Moretti nodded.

Vargas turned toward Cassandra. "Maldonado?"

"Yes, Captain?"

"Finally decided to show?"

"I came as soon as—"

"Not interested in excuses."

Cassandra did not speak.

"HI-PRO does sensitive work, Detective."

"I understand."

"We have a veteran public information officer in our squad to handle press."

"Great."

"Maldonado, you are never, I mean never ever to speak to the media, on or off the record, without my prior approval. Understood?"

Cassandra hated being silenced. "Yes, Captain."

"No more press bombs like the one you dropped on the mayor."

"That was a mistake."

"You bet it was. Don't try it with me."

Moretti joined the pile-on. "That birdshit don't fly in this burg."

"I got it."

Vargas let off the pressure a little. "Listen, I understand. Women have to hustle twice as hard for half the juice. But this is an investigative unit, a place to work, not practice politics."

"Understood."

"I don't have a partner for you, so shadow the lieutenant."

Moretti bowed.

"Follow him, watch, and listen," said Vargas. "Don't make trouble." She looked at Moretti. "I'll be downtown."

"Aye, Skipper."

Vargas left.

Moretti pointed at Cassandra. "You're doing the paperwork."

Cassandra didn't mind. "I'm surprised we caught this case. Didn't think HI-PRO handled homicides."

"Didn't used to. New policy delivered on stone tablets from the fourteenth floor. Downtown's effort to consolidate high-profile cases. If the stiff's got any standing among the bon vivants it goes to us. Again, think you can handle it?"

"Like jelly on toast, Lou."

"Right, Shirley Temple. I saw your personnel jacket."

"What's that mean?"

"You never served in a homicide command. Not even a precinct squad. Round-robined as an undercover and in narcotics."

Cassandra bit her lip. "I removed hundreds of guns and millions of dollars' worth of drugs off these streets."

"And still the flood continues."

Annoying. "Your point?"

"Everybody else in this unit's got true grit."

"Meaning?"

"Borough Homicide, Precinct DTs, Intel, Hostage Negotiation, Major Case. You're the least qualified."

"My medal board goes past my shoulder."

"I'm not saying undercover narcotics is a tango through the tulips, kid. I'm saying it's the easiest way for some people to get a gold shield."

Cassandra knew it was true that minority cops were herded into playing drug addicts and dope dealers in undercover operations. And that this in turn was also a fast track to becoming a detective.

Still, she said, "That's department bullshit. White guys making excuses."

"Maybe. Either way it leaves a question mark."

Cassandra felt a slow boil. "This ain't even my first body."

"No?"

"I patrolled the Two-three when Spanish Harlem was still Kosovo. My first boss made me search every DOA in the projects."

"They say that builds character."

Cassandra dropped an indirect threat. "How much character you think *he* built when Internal Affairs uncovered his habit of going through the pockets before me?"

Moretti grinned. "I get your drift. But this is your first body as an investigator, isn't it?"

"It is."

"Well then. Gotta get your muffin buttered sometime. Let's take a look."

CHAPTER 8

The Blood Beneath

The body formerly known as FYSHBone was no longer under a sheet. His privacy was now protected by portable canvas partitions set up like a tent.

He had been documented from every angle by a female Crime Scene photographer. She turned slowly around the body in a tightening circle.

She snapped a picture of every detail. A member of the Bronx DA's Video Unit did the same with a video camera.

Cassandra looked at the body and resisted the urge to cover her mouth.

FYSHBone wore vintage Air Jordan basketball sneakers, toes pointed up. He was in a white tracksuit with red parallel striping along the leg and down the arm. His torso was riddled with bullet holes and soaked with a giant Rorschach stain of blood. A strange-looking gun, a large one, protruded from his waistband.

Cassandra noted the big bullet holes in the jacket and crotch area, which was also soaked. Her eyes traveled slowly up the body to the head.

She swallowed.

FYSHBone had been shot once in the forehead and once in each eyeball, which left dark pulpy ovals.

Moretti gave Cassandra an excuse to turn away by introducing her to Detective Goines, a middle-aged black male who dressed like a British banker, in a charcoal-gray three-piece complete with vest and pocketwatch chain.

Goines was working on a drawing. It showed the placement of the body on the sidewalk, noted its distance from the curb, the hydrant, the streetlamp, the building, and each casing on the ground.

Everything was numbered. He'd drawn a legend and a cross indicating true north.

Moretti patted Goines on the shoulder.

"Mr. Debonair's our detail man. Brains of the outfit. CSU'll sketch the scene using the grid method, but Chester here's an artist. His partner's out with a team recording the plate number on every car parked in this radius."

The CSU photographer took several close-ups of the gun butt in FYSHBone's sweatpants. She moved on to the shell casings under the seven numbered markers. She shot the casings from various angles and in relation to the body and the other casings.

She placed a short tape measure next to each casing to provide dimension in the close-ups. Each casing would later be individually marked on the inside wall of the shell, by the mouth, then examined for fingerprints and serology and vouchered.

Cassandra watched.

Since it is known that a percentage of all violent criminals return to the scenes of their crimes, and a much smaller percentage have a compulsion to do so when police are actually at the scene, the photographer snuck periodic shots in the direction of the civilian onlookers.

Cassandra asked and Moretti confirmed that the local precinct had undercovers working the crowd.

Goines finished his drawing. Moretti dispatched him to join the canvass.

Cassandra and her new supervisor were left with the corpse.

Moretti looked down on FYSHBone. "They really minced his meat. Think it was a crime of passion?"

"Could be a cool professional trying to make it look personal."

"Could be."

Cassandra noted again the shell casings grouped to her right on the sidewalk and in the gutter as she faced the body. One was a little behind her.

She thought out loud and acted out the shooting: "Shoot him once, he falls backward. Stand over him, empty your weapon."

Moretti popped gum. "Accounts for the placement of the casings. The one on the forehead is a tight contact wound."

"How do you know?"

Moretti bent at the waist and pointed with a pen. "No fouling, i.e., soot from the barrel deposited on the skin. No stippling or tattooing where the bits of gunpowder leave little burns. These things need space to travel short distances. They ain't there. All the other wounds—to the eyes, the torso, the crotch—as you can see, these all show soot and stippling. Those shots were at close range, no contact."

"How do you know the shot to the forehead wasn't from far away? Too far for the debris to travel but not the bullet?"

"An excellent question."

Moretti got down on one knee.

Cassandra breathed through her mouth and bent at the waist to look.

"Oh, no, sunshine. You're never gonna solve any homicides from way up there."

Cassandra steeled herself and got down closer. She looked where Moretti pointed.

"See how the wound looks almost star-shaped? That's typical with tight contact wounds over the skull, especially large-caliber weapons."

"How come?"

"Hot gases from the barrel inject so fast they bounce against the other side of your skull before the bullet even has a chance to open an exit wound. The gases blow back toward the entry wound with such intensity they get under the skin and rip it apart around the entrance. Happens in an instant."

Disgusting. Cassandra stood up.

"So FYSHBone allowed his killer to get close," she said. "They knew each other."

"Maybe. Maybe the shooter just got the drop on him."

They were joined by a Ballistics investigator, another old friend of Moretti's.

"You the lead on this, Sally?"

"A victim of my own success." Moretti asked about the man's wife, then got to business. "Tell me about the murder weapon."

"A big one."

Moretti looked at Cassandra like, *What did I tell you?*

Cassandra did not mention that this fact was obvious from the casings on the ground.

The Ballistics man used forceps to hold a casing under a magnifying glass. "Fifty caliber."

"Ouch. Helluva lot of stopping power." Moretti looked at Cassandra. "Recover many .50-caliber weapons while you were out mopping the streets, Nancy Drew?"

"Sometimes."

Moretti put on his glasses and looked through the magnifier. "During the crack wars every wannabe gangster had a .50 caliber."

The Ballistics man agreed. "Desert Eagle was the most popular. Israeli. Vicious firearm. Lousy for self-defense because of its weight and explosive report."

Moretti removed his glasses. "Perfect for sawing the competition in half, though."

"No question."

Cassandra looked through the magnifying glass. She did not know what to look for. "So the gun that ejected this casing was a Desert Eagle?"

"I don't think so. The firing pin, ejector, and extractor marks on the casing are slightly off. Must be some other make and model that closely resembles the Desert E. Or a custom weapon."

Cassandra clucked her tongue. "Special gun for a special target?"

Ballistics shrugged. Cassandra looked again at the gun butt in FYSHBone's waistband. Moretti read her mind.

"That's a big gun right there, isn't it, Maldonado. CSU already shot pictures of it. Put your gloves on."

Cassandra's nerves skipped. She removed a pair of gloves from her pocket, slipped them on, and squatted near the corpse.

The elastic waistband was sticky with drying blood. Cassandra peeled the pants from FYSHBone's trunk.

She pulled out the handgun. Blood thickened on the weapon.

She said, "It's gonna need a serological workup."

"That is indeed a unique weapon," said Moretti.

The gun was very large. It appeard to be gold-plated, with diamond-encrusted designs on the grips.

Cassandra recognized the weed-smoking fish skeleton.

The words KUTTHROAT AVENGER were etched on the slide.

"It's custom. KUTTHROAT's the victim's record label. These designs on the handle are his company logo. This gun was made specifically for FYSHBone."

Cassandra sniffed the barrel. "Hasn't been fired recently, so it's not some joke where the killer plants the murder weapon on the body."

Moretti scratched his chin. "So two weapons of the same rare caliber meet on the streets of the Bronx."

"Same maker?" said Cassandra.

"We'll run the number on this one and see where it leads," said Moretti. "Could be a coincidence. Could be the shooter and our victim were members of some .50-caliber gun club."

Cassandra noted the number in her pad, then handed Ballistics the gun for vouchering and later test-firing at the lab for operability and to verify that FYSHBone's gun was in fact not the murder weapon.

She noted the discussion about the gun and casings and wrote a reminder to herself to draft a letter of transmittal so that chain of custody for the weapon would not be compromised.

Cassandra wanted to seem at ease around the body. She adjusted her gloves and spoke to Moretti as she went through FYSHBone's pockets.

"Crime Scene dust the vehicle for fingerprints yet?"

"We called for a hook and it'll get the complete proctology at impound, but yeah, they're dusting."

Cassandra recovered a wallet, cellphone, and car keys from FYSHBone's pockets.

Moretti put on gloves and took them. "Clearly not a mugging." He looked through FYSHBone's wallet. "Ten crisp one-hundred-dollar bills. Driver's license. Credit cards. His birth name was LeRoi Edwards III."

Cassandra nodded.

It would all be in the ME's report, but she checked for algor mortis, the cooling of the body, by feeling the temperature on the side of the neck with the back of her hand.

She tried gently to turn the neck and felt resistance, which was duplicated when she tried gently to pull the mouth open. Cassandra pianoed the corpse's fingertips, as she had once seen Sidney Poitier do in a movie.

"Still warm. The onset of rigor makes me think three to eight hours since time of death."

Moretti whistled. "Are you trying to impress me?"

Cassandra asked about the first radio call and the radius of the canvass, in which detectives would go door to door looking for eyewitnesses. Moretti told her the local streets that formed the boundaries of that effort.

Cassandra was familiar with the area, having grown up less than a mile west. It seemed to her the grid could have been wider.

"Not too many residents around these parts right here," she said. "No traffic."

"Epecially at night," said Moretti. "Still, it's incredible if nobody heard that cannon go off."

"There's a hooker stroll three blocks that way," said Cassandra. "I worked it undercover to catch the Hunts Point Rapist."

"I'll put our friends from Vice Enforcement on the local talent."

Cassandra looked at FYSHBone's corpse. "Think that's what he was doing out here?"

Moretti scrunched his eyebrows. "You'd think a guy with dough would go for something classier, but you never know. The number on his crotch does make me think angry female."

"Women don't fantasize about shooting men in the *plátanos* as much as you imagine, Lou. This thing with the eyes isn't very feminine."

"Reminds me of them ancient plays my wife drags me to."

Cassandra thought about that. "Think it's a message?"

"For who?" said Moretti.

"That would be the question."

The detectives pulled brown paper bags over the corpse's hands to preserve evidence on the fingers or under the nails. They turned the stiffening body over. It felt like a rubber mannequin.

The blood beneath had darkened and turned to gelatin.

Moretti cocked an eyebrow. "Yeah, see?" He pointed at the wound at the base of FYSHBone's skull. "Nice-sized hole. See how it bevels out? That means a bullet exited that way, probably the forehead shot, which I'm guessing is the first. These other exits all show signs of shoring."

"What's that?"

"Like when you shoot someone who's up against a wall or in a chair or something. In this case, with his back against the pavement."

Cassandra said, "Aren't exit wounds usually bigger than entrance wounds?"

"Yeah, generally, because the bullet expands or tumbles through the body. But if the exit surface is shored, supported by something firm, the exit wounds get more circular. They look like long-distance entrance wounds. Neater. Rounder. Like these."

Moretti had Crime Scene take more photos. The DA's office shot more video.

They rolled FYSHBone onto his back again.

Cassandra bit her lip. "This is so sad."

She could not believe it had come to this. The rapper from Red Hook. The rolling stone who rocked a million microphones.

"Years ago my girlfriend and I were clubbing at the Copa and we saw FYSHBone in person, just chilling. Dancing. My friend was his biggest fan back then. She actually cried just to see him."

Cassandra noticed finally the shape of FYSHBone's mouth. The trademark half-snarl half-smile was down. It had been replaced by a permanent frown.

CHAPTER 9

Splash

FYSHBone had been murdered while he walked his dog.

They determined this within minutes of bagging the body because Cassandra noticed half-dried little turds in the gutter and looked and whistled until she found the animal shivering under her master's vehicle, her snout coated in blood.

CSU collected samples and checked the tags after Cassandra coaxed the terrified dog into her hands with baby talk.

Cassandra deduced from this that if FYSHBone walked his dog around there, as unlikely as it seemed, he probably lived or stayed nearby.

She tried FYSHbone's keys on the nearest door, an abandoned factory of some sort, and presto, within minutes they were inside riding an elevator to FYSHBone's studio and adjacent loft.

The place reeked of marijuana.

Moretti pointed at the blunt in the ashtray on the console. "Figures." He pointed at the bulletproof vest on the floor next to the console. "That was smart."

"Wouldn't have made a difference."

The studio had new-looking equipment and a sound booth with many colorful guitars lined up on guitar stands, a baby grand piano, and a drum kit.

Moretti leaned over the piano, played "Chopsticks," and smiled.

"A man of many talents," said Cassandra. "Why do you think HI-PRO is on this instead of the Hip-Hop Squad? They're also a special force unit."

"Yeah, but they're supposed to be a secret, since most of the people in hip-hop are still 'of color.' The mayor is afraid of being charged with racial profiling."

"I have a friend who works that detail," said Cassandra. "I'll reach out and see if they have a FYSHBone file."

She and Moretti checked the adjacent apartment.

It was painted all white, including the brick walls, the thick wooden pillars, the wood-beamed and wood-planked ceiling. The hardwood floor had been sanded, lightly stained, and varnished.

The space was sparsely furnished with a few simple pieces of minimalist furniture, all of it flat and square and low to the ground, which accentuated the room's unusual height.

The space had an echo.

It had a large dance studio mirror and ballet barre on one wall.

"Why do you think he might have that?" said Moretti.

"He was like the Alvin Ailey of rap, if you see some of his videos. This must double as a rehearsal space."

Moretti raised his eyebrows. "Seems kind of frilly for a gangster rapper to have a ballet barre in his home. Maybe he was light in the shorts."

Men. "Well, Lou, there is a movement in martial arts

called martial ballet or martial arts ballet that combines ballet training with things like kung fu. Lots of balance and discipline and the ability to throw kicks and jump. Capoeira is a Brazilian form of dance that is also based on martial arts—lots of kicking."

"Actually, now that you mention it, Maldonado, I think I read that Jackie Chan studied ballet as a child."

"Right. So maybe he was in here training to kick ass. Feel better, Lou?"

Moretti shrugged. "Either way, he wasn't gonna stop seven bullets."

The room's energy was centered on a large, striking blue sofa. There was also one glass-topped table and one very large, very thin flat-screen TV bolted to the wall.

There was a large, virtually empty armoire and a dresser drawer with few clothes. The new stainless-steel refrigerator held almost no food.

Moretti kept his hands in his pockets. "This place don't feel lived in."

The super-king-sized bed was designed to look almost as if it floated on air, suspended over its burnished steel base.

"His driver's license says his residence is in Brooklyn. Maybe this place is just a splash pad," said Cassandra, referring to the spare apartments some cops keep on the side or chip in for like roommates as a place to get away from their wives.

There were maybe a dozen paintings, simple ones, in different sizes, not hung, but leaning against one wall, stacked against one another as if stockpiled.

Moretti went through them. One was a colorful stick-figure rendition of two fish jumping out of their separate bowls to kiss in midair.

Moretti shrugged.

There was a large, red, heavy punching bag mounted to a wooden ceiling beam by a long chain. It hung in the corner. Wrist wraps and heavy bag gloves were on the floor next to the punching bag.

The word CLEMENTI was written in large capital letters in black marker on the surface of the bag at about face-punching level. The area where this word was written was scuffed. In fact, it was the only surface in the entire apartment that showed evidence of wear.

FYSHBone had apparently pounded the crap out of that word.

Cassandra punched it once herself. The bag hardly moved but the contact shocked her knuckles, which were still tender from her fight with the Marathon Slasher.

Cassandra asked Moretti if "Clementi" was an Italian word.

"I think it was the name of a pope."

Cassandra wrote it down.

Moretti called from the bathroom. "At least we know he has a girlfriend."

"You find a second toothbrush, Lou?"

"I wish."

The toilet flushed. Moretti came out with his nose crinkled.

"There was a used tampon floating in the water."

"Really, Lou? Why didn't you voucher it?"

Moretti looked at Cassandra like, *Are you friggin' serious?*

"Let's go notify the next of kin."

CHAPTER 10

Assignments

FYSHBone's body got shipped to the morgue. Animal Care and Control picked up the dog.

The dog wore a diamond-studded dog collar that had to be vouchered as property. Cassandra removed the diamond collar and vouchered it, but before she handed it over she tried it around her wrist.

Beautiful.

Moretti assigned two members of his team to stay with Crime Scene at the studio/loft inside the abandoned factory and also to check out the rest of the building to see what they could find.

He assigned Detective Goines and his partner to the address on FYSHBone's license. It was barely past midmorning.

FYSHBone's mother's number was in his cellphone under Momma. Her address page was empty. Moretti quickly contacted a friend at FYSHBone's cellular carrier and within minutes and off the record had Tamora Edwards's name and address in the Red Hook Housing Projects.

They rode in Moretti's champagne-colored Cadillac

Escalade. He wore aviator sunglasses and kept his eyes on the road.

"I hate this part."

Cassandra nodded.

"The best policy is just come out and say it. 'I'm sorry, your son is dead.'"

"Direct," said Cassandra.

"Get her to sit. Make sure there's nothing sharp within reach. With the older ones, be ready to call an ambulance."

"I imagine the important part is to show compassion."

"Right, but get to business. We're there to collect facts. Let her know we need someone to go to the morgue to identify the body. We have her son's driver's license, we know it's him, so don't let her go into a whole denial trip."

"Safe Horizon runs a program for victims' families."

"Great, get her the number. But remember, we're there to learn about her son. Who he had beef with. His love life. What's up with his money."

"Motive," said Cassandra.

"Precisely."

They rode the FDR Drive southbound along the edge of Manhattan and passed the United Nations building. The East River flowed on their left along the curves in the road. Skyscrapers rose to their right. A man jogged with his dog.

Cassandra said, "Let's remember to ask who should get FYSHBone's mutt."

"Somebody better. That thing is so ugly nobody will adopt it. You know what that means."

Moretti made the sound of a trumpet playing the first

three notes of "Taps" like at a military funeral. If nobody claimed the dog within a given period it would be put to sleep.

At another moment Cassandra might have found that funny. At that moment she was nervous and sad about telling FYSHBone's mother the news about her son.

Moretti called HI-PRO's public information officer and told him to prepare a press release. He would call back to verify when it should go out, which would be after they notified the mother.

"Then we'll stop in FYSHBone's place of business, the record label. See what we kick up there."

Cassandra made a mental checklist of what little they had learned so far: that the victim kept a recording studio and apartment in an isolated area of the Bronx; that he had an apartment in a high-rent area in Brooklyn; that he apparently had not been robbed, but shot while he walked his dog at a late hour; that he was shot at close range with a large weapon of rare caliber, possibly by somebody he knew; that he was in possession of a customized gun of the same caliber as the murder weapon.

Maybe they would know more after the autopsy. Perhaps the mother could provide some leads.

Already it was a puzzle.

CHAPTER 11

The Pain

FYSHBone's mother lived in Brooklyn's massive Red Hook Housing Projects. Sunlight came in powerfully at a high angle from the east, but it did not blanch away the unfortunate fact that those thirty red brick buildings, home to the very poor, once known as the "crack capital of America," still had a long way to go.

The area was isolated even though it was the only neighborhood on the planet with a full frontal view of the Statue of Liberty. Cassandra had worked many undercover assignments in the area.

"I'll warn you, Lou. The buzzers never work in these buildings. Neither do the elevators."

"Sunshine, you think I've never been to the projects?"

The detectives waited for someone to exit, then slipped in. The elevator was indeed broken. They climbed the stairs.

"Nothing like project hallways during a heat wave," said Moretti, trying not to overbreathe.

The hallways reeked of urine, weed, and stale beer, mixed, even at that early hour, with the aroma of rice, beans, fried chicken, and collard greens.

Something, apparently a human being, had taken a large dump on the concrete steps.

"Shangri-Fucking-La," said Moretti.

On one landing three young men stood with no apparent purpose, although they very likely sold tiny plastic bags filled with drugs.

The three got quiet when they heard the detectives' footsteps.

Cassandra squeezed past and tried not to show that she was winded. Moretti was directly behind. His nostrils whistled.

Cassandra cleared her throat. She spoke up without stopping. "Anybody whose name does not appear on a lease for an apartment in this building who is still on these steps when I come back down goes under for trespass."

Moretti did not say a word.

When the partners were two flights up, one of the punks shouted, "Fuck you, bitch!" up the stairwell.

Their laughter echoed off the cinder-block walls, but so did the sound of their footsteps racing down.

Moretti chuckled.

The detectives caught their breaths and wiped sweat off their brows in front of FYSHBone's mother's door.

Moretti put away his handkerchief. "I don't get it. With FYSHBone's money, how could he let his mother live like this?"

Cassandra knew that as crappy as project life is, New York City apartments are impossible to get. People don't part with them. The average public housing tenant stays for twenty years.

She knocked.

Feet shuffled and stopped on the other side of the door. The light in the little peephole changed. They were being inspected.

A timid voice asked who it was.

The detectives held their shields up. Cassandra said their names and that they were looking for Tamora Edwards.

After a pause the bolt slid, locks tumbled, and the door opened a crack. The chain was still on. A dark-skinned woman in a bathrobe and head scarf examined them.

Cassandra tried to keep an even tone. "Mrs. Edwards?"

"Why are you up here?"

"I'm sorry, ma'am, we need to speak to you."

"You got a warrant?"

"We're not here to arrest anybody or search for anything."

"You gonna look under my bed?"

"No, ma'am. This is about your son."

"LeRoi?"

"Is he the rapper known as FYSHBone?"

"That's what he calls himself."

"May we come in?"

Cassandra thought she saw some understanding of what was actually happening register in the woman's face.

She closed the door, took the chain off, opened, and pulled Cassandra in by the forearm.

"People will think I'm snitching."

FYSHBone's mother locked them in, then led them to her living room. The space was tight and crowded by cheap-looking mismatched furniture, all of it covered in plastic.

There were books everywhere, in all sizes and colors. It seemed to Cassandra that every potentially empty space—the floors, the dining table, the coffee table, the windowsills, the top of the TV, the corners—had been stacked with chaotic piles of books.

The only open book was a thin one on the coffee table that was marked and highlighted, titled *The Prince*.

The only place without books was the dusty faux-wood bookshelf, which was crowded with pictures in plastic frames, bronzed baby shoes, and other tchochkes.

Tamora Edwards sat in an easy chair. She indicated the couch.

Cassandra and Moretti sat. From the couch they could enjoy the apartment's saving grace: an up-high view toward lower Manhattan.

The window had the familiar New York City Housing Authority window guard screwed into the window frame to prevent children from falling out. Cassandra could not help but liken these to prison bars or a cage at the zoo. This ready association always bothered her.

An oscillating fan pivoted back and forth and did its best to spread cool air. They were past midmorning. The temperature was still rising.

Mrs. Edwards remained silent for ten seconds, then looked Cassandra in the eye. Cassandra wanted to melt into the plastic on that couch, become a part of it, anything to not have to continue.

The woman reached for two knitting needles, a ball of yarn, and a small gray blanket. She pointed the needles at the pictures on the faux-wood shelving unit.

"There goes my son right there."

Pictures of FYSHBone through the years—in school

photos and as an eighties teenager break-dancing. A little older with a thick gold rope chain and a dollar-sign medallion. With a nineties flattop. Next to celebrities and politicians as his career took off.

Mrs. Edwards began to knit. "Why don't you say what you came to say?"

Cassandra glanced at Moretti. He nodded. There was no point in delay.

"I'm afraid we have terrible news."

Silence.

"Your son is gone." Cassandra's emphasis on the last word left no doubt what she meant.

FYSHBone's mother stopped knitting. Her face twitched. "No. No no no, don't say that."

"I'm sorry."

"Don't even speak it."

Tamora Edwards's hands trembled. She held the needles tight.

Cassandra remembered Moretti's warning about sharp objects and kept an eye on Tamora's hands.

Suddenly the needles dropped to the floor. The ball of yarn rolled away.

Tamora wept. She began to hyperventilate.

Cassandra had seen the asthma pump. She handed it to her.

Tamora took a hit and slowly came down from her runaway grief. She wiped her nose.

"Was there an accident?"

Cassandra paused. "No, ma'am."

Moretti leaned forward. "Your son was murdered."

Tamora covered her mouth.

"Somebody shot him."

Her lip quivered. "What? Who? Who did it?"

"We don't know."

"That's what we're trying to determine," said Moretti. "Any ideas?"

Tamora looked at a spot on the floor and went private. Tears flowed but she remained composed.

Cassandra squeezed her knee. "Are you okay?"

No answer. They sat in silence for a long time.

After a while Moretti cleared his throat. "We understand it's a difficult moment. The worst in life. The last thing you wanna do is talk, especially to cops. But homicide investigations happen really quick or not at all. This young lady here, this is her first day with this unit and she hasn't even been to the squad yet to see her new desk. That's because our best chance to capture the animal who did this occurs in the first forty-eight hours. After that the trail gets cold."

Tamora sniffled. "What do you want to know?"

Cassandra took out her notebook and pen.

Moretti aimed for a more conversational tone. "Did your son have any problems with anyone?"

"Everybody loved him."

"An angry girlfriend? An ex?"

"He's always had women all over."

"Anybody special?"

"LeRoi never found anybody good enough to bring home."

Moretti glanced at Cassandra with a raised eyebrow. FYSHBone looked young for his age, but he was technically a middle-aged man.

"You saying he never married?"

"No."

"Children?"

"Several. But none that I got to know."

"He take care of his kids? Financially?"

"As far as I know."

"Any family feuds? A jealous relative maybe? Someone who felt FYSHBone wasn't—"

"LeRoi. My son's name was LeRoi."

"Someone who felt LeRoi wasn't spreading the wealth?"

The woman shook her head. "My son treats his sisters good. He was the only boy. Also the youngest. They spoiled him. His friends are no good."

"You mean his posse?"

She nodded.

"Any of them in particular?"

"All of them. Vultures. They live off my son's money and fame."

"Any names?"

Tamora shook her head. "Only one that's been with him since the beginning is Slow Mo. A big dummy. He grew up across the hall."

Cassandra said, "What about his father?"

Disgust showed on Tamora's face. "LeRoi's father was not around."

"Even after your son became rich?"

Cassandra noticed that Tamora hesitated. "LeRoi's daddy died when he was just a child."

"Oh."

Moretti said, "Your son had a very high-caliber handgun on him when he died. Custom made. Know anything about it?"

"No."

"Ever seen him with a gun?"

"Only in the movies."

"Know anybody else who might own a special gun? Very large? Special designs?"

Tamora looked down at the knitting needles. She picked them up off the floor. "This here's my only tools. I wouldn't know one gun from any other."

"Know anything about your son's business affairs?"

"No."

"Problems at the office?"

She shook her head.

Moretti nodded. He looked around the apartment. "Forgive me for asking, but... was your son involved with criminal activity? Drugs?"

"He grew up in these projects."

"I understand. Anybody around here we should talk to?"

"Detective, I'm just another old woman in the ghetto afraid to leave her apartment."

If Tamora knew who was trouble around Red Hook, she did not want to go into it. The fan turned back and forth constantly and still lost its battle with the heat.

Cassandra said, "Does the word 'Clementi' mean anything to you?"

Tamora blinked several times. She waited long enough for any thoughts on the word to travel a long distance. "No."

Cassandra waited to see if there was more. There wasn't. It looked like the DD-5 for this interview was going to be marked NR for Negative Results.

"Do you know if your son wanted somebody to have his dog?"

Tamora said, "She's got a weak digestive system. Needs

to be walked every two hours. I can't be going up and down them stairs twelve times a day. Not in this heat."

"Understood."

They sat in silence.

"Do you really want to know about my son?"

Cassandra closed her notepad. "Please tell us."

Tamora blinked and did not really look at them.

"LeRoi was special. You know right away when a child is that gifted. LeRoi did everything early. Walk, talk, read. He made eye contact the day he was born."

Cassandra felt an unexpected twinge of jealousy.

"Nobody taught my son anything. He just knew. Used to sit in front of that window and stare at the city and dream. Talked all the time about the things he would do. The trips he would take. All the things he would buy."

Moretti scratched his head. "On that topic. I was wondering. Seeing as how your son was so successful, why do you still live in these projects?"

Tamora looked as if she might say, *Where else would I live?* Instead she said, "Money wasn't at the root of our relationship."

"Of course not."

Tamora stood. She paced for a moment, knotted and reknotted her robe as if trying to decide which way to go. She went to the bookshelf and lifted a picture frame to eye level.

FYSHBone in a school pic, circa age ten. Huge smile. Hair messed up.

"Third grade my son plays hooky for three days. Ducked under the turnstiles for the train. Wandered Manhattan. You know the library with the lions?"

Cassandra nodded.

"Security catches him stealing a book. I get this boy home. Before I put the belt to him he says 'I was bored, Momma. I was bored.'"

Tamora bit her fist. She held the picture of FYSHBone, the boy, for them to see. Behind her was the window to the shining city.

"Detective Maldonado, are you a mother?"

"I am."

"Have you ever lost a child?"

Cassandra had suffered two miscarriages. It was no comparison.

"No, ma'am. Nothing like this."

"The pain. It's unbearable."

CHAPTER 12

White Collar Blues

FYSHBone's lawyer, Sabio Guzmán, took the freight elevator up to the corporate offices to avoid the media gathered out front. It was still morning. His boss's murder was all over the news.

The radio stations were in full homage. They played old FYSHBone interview clips, took bereavement calls, ran down the greatest hits.

Sabio could not believe this had really happened. Even with all the times that he had gone over this scenario in his mind, he had never imagined what the emotions would be.

FYSHBone no longer ruled him. He was surprisingly sad. Nervous. Afraid. Excited about the possibilities.

Sabio exited on the floor leased by KUTTHROAT Records. The air conditioner was on high.

The receptionist's eyes were bloodshot. She saw Sabio and her eyes began to well. "Did you—"

"They just reported it on the radio driving in. I'm in shock. Have we heard from the police?"

"No." She wiped her nose and pointed at the ringing phone. "It won't stop."

"Get someone from public relations up here to help. Tell the press no comment. We'll release a statement later."

Sabio asked for the chief of operations. "Seen Dulles?"

"He ran off when I told him."

"Call his cell. Tell him to wait for me in my office. Hold all my calls."

The receptionist wiped away tears. "I don't know how I'll go on."

"Me neither," said Sabio. It was the first of many lies he would tell that day.

Sabio passed his own office and went to the one in the corner. He looked around, then slipped in.

For all of his renegade style, FYSHBone's office could have housed any insurance exec or sales manager, albeit a fairly successful one. The cabinets, desk, and minibar were all mahogany with Corinthian details. There was an original Tiffany lamp in one corner and an original Frank Lloyd Wright in another. The beige suede couch was big enough for four professional basketball players. There were several platinum records and People's Choice awards, a picture of FYSHBone in the batter's box at Shea Stadium holding an invisible baseball bat, and a still photo of the famous time he wept about "the plight of the sea otters" on *The Oprah Winfrey Show*.

Over the couch was a Warhol-style multicolored four-paneled portrait of Pretty, FYSHBone's beloved dog. The white carpet was plush.

Sabio sat at the desk and turned on the computer. While it booted he looked out the window down at the morning bustle in Times Square. Yellow cabs darted like schools of yellow fish.

A jagged thought cracked the surface of Sabio's mind, like the sudden appearance and disappearance of a shark fin in the water: *What have we done?*

He quickly pushed the thought down, buried it at the bottom of some deep, turbulent sea.

The computer asked for a password.

Sabio tried FYSHBONE, KUTTHROAT, HIP-HOP, MONEY. All invalid.

He cursed. He tried the names of some of FYSHBone's children, plus half his babies' mothers. These were also wrong. He looked at the eighteenth-century grandfather clock in the corner.

The chief of operations was sure to be anxious and would not wait long. He would need to be reined in.

Sabio closed his eyes and uttered an old Buddhist chant he had learned from a yoga instructor. He opened his eyes and they fell on the ridiculous portrait of FYSH-Bone's dog.

He typed PRETTY. The computer's hourglass began to spill.

So obvious I could kick myself.

Sabio opened files but found nothing. He did a desktop search. Nothing. He scanned all the icons.

Where is it? I know you have it.

The grandfather clock chimed.

Damn.

Sabio wondered whether FYSHBone might have printed the document and deleted the file. Some forensic computer asshole from the police department would take five minutes to discover that.

Sabio clicked the recycle bin and found it empty.

He got up and went through every drawer and file cabinet in the room but did not see it. He looked in the closet, under the couch, behind the couch, and still nothing. He checked for a secret safe behind the dog's portrait but there was none.

It occurred to Sabio that a hard copy of the document might be at FYSHBone's DUMBO penthouse or at the recording studio/loft in the Bronx. If so, that meant the police would have the information by afternoon.

A bubble of acid rolled up Sabio's esophagus.

He sat on the couch to think things through and noticed that the cushion did not give. He looked under the cushion and—*lucky break!*—found a laptop. Now it just needed to be the one that he was looking for.

Tell me you left it here.

Sabio opened the machine, started it, typed in the dog's name, and got in. He began to open files.

Nothing.

The battery on the laptop was low. The plug was nowhere to be seen. Sabio was confident this machine contained what he was worried about.

He began to log off.

A nasal voice interrupted: "What are you doing?"

Sabio jumped.

It was Dulles. He shut the door. "What's going on?"

Sabio shut the laptop. "Nothing. Taking care of, um, FYSHBone's—"

"What?"

"Private matters."

"Private?"

"FYSH made certain legal arrangements."

"In case of his untimely demise?"

Sabio almost winced. "Maybe we should think of a different way to put it."

He picked up the laptop.

Dulles squinted. He was short. Slender. He wore black, thick-framed glasses that could have been issued by the U.S. Army during Vietnam. They connected with the ring of hair that ran from ear to ear along the back of Dulles's otherwise bald head.

Dulles adjusted his glasses. "The police are likely to come here."

"Of course."

"FBI. Treasury agents."

"This is a homicide. It'll be NYPD."

"What'll we do?"

Sabio did his best to look unworried. "About what?"

"What if they suspect racketeering?"

Sabio almost repeated the word. "Why would they?"

Dulles's eyes went to the laptop. "We could be in a lot of trouble."

"Stop talking."

"You, me, the—"

"Shut up."

"I told you—"

"Cut it out." Sabio mouthed the words, "*This office could be bugged!*" He put his index finger to his lips. At full volume he said: "You're post-traumatic. We all are. We've lost our leader. Stop talking nonsense."

Dulles looked up at the ceiling.

"Go home, Dulles. You're not gonna get much work done today."

"What about—"

"Seriously."

Sabio walked to the door. "I'll call when I figure out what the next steps are. In terms of corporate."

Sabio held the door open with his back. Dulles went tentatively past. Sabio grabbed his forearm and whispered.

"Not a word to the police, Dulles. You hear me? They question you, refer them to me. I'm general counsel."

Dulles's mouth drooped.

Sabio squeezed his fluffy arm. "*Omerta*, Dulles."

"*Omerta?*"

"If you don't know what it means, look it up."

CHAPTER 13

The Rich Are Different

Sabio was startled to find bodies in his office. Leland Bishop, the British head of KAMIKAZE Vynil, sat in Sabio's chair, talked on Sabio's phone, hung his feet on Sabio's desk.

When Sabio walked in, Bishop signaled for him to hold a sec while he wrapped.

"Yes, yes, brilliant. You are the best. Never a loose end."

Bishop listened and laughed. "Of course, old sport, of course. Payment in the usual sum. Zurich. I still have the number."

Bishop stood as if to welcome Sabio into his own office. He had a weak handshake.

"Mr. Guzmán!"

Sabio hated Bishop's accent.

"Please accept the condolences of the entire KAMI-KAZE family."

Sabio did his best to appear grim. "We're all in disbelief."

Bishop gestured at the phone. "Please do not think me presumptuous. The Continent. Wireless would not do. You remember my associate, Hegel."

Sabio nodded at the tall blond German who stood guard with a briefcase. Hegel had a face like parchment with a swimmer's build.

Hegel always wore a black, form-fitting short-sleeved shirt and a large silver diving watch. His eyes were trained on the laptop.

Bishop dimpled his chin toward the computer as well. "Computing, are we?"

Sabio held it up. "You know how it is. Work never ends. I carry this everywhere."

"Without a special bag?"

"Yeah, well, um, I was, you know, using it out there, so ... Do you mind?"

Bishop moved to one of the chairs in front of Sabio's desk and sat. Sabio went around to his place behind the desk. He put the laptop underneath, out of view.

Bishop's face had that plastic-surgery shine. "Our little business deal appears to have lost its wheels."

Sabio wanted to appear confident. "A minor setback."

"No, I'd say it's quite clearly a major one."

Sabio put his hands on the desk. As a lawyer with a decade of experience he was not in a hurry to speak.

Bishop didn't mind. "You realize I have money in play, of course."

"We all do."

"I doubt you and I mean the same thing, Mr. Guzmán."

Bishop came from English land barons. Besides milking pop acts, he was a famous adventure seeker.

Sabio shared the fragment of a smile. "I saw your reality show on cable."

"Wonderful, which episode?"

"You wrestled a crocodile."

"Ah yes. These cufflinks used to be his teeth."

"Bishop, is there a reason you came to my office?"

The tycoon's eyes creased. He said something in German. The blond opened his briefcase.

Bishop removed the top file and slid it to Sabio.

Sabio did not pick up. "What's this?"

"The deal must go on."

"FYSHBone's body isn't even cold. It isn't even time for brunch yet, and you are already here with paperwork?"

"Yes, well the living need to eat, and the invisible hand of economics plucks our strings."

Sabio was curious to look inside the file. He waited.

"Bishop, we're still working out succession."

Bishop nodded at the file. "You will succeed with this. A memorandum of understanding and a new version of the contract for Tamora Edwards."

"Who?"

"FYSHBone's mother."

That made no sense to Sabio. "What does she have to do with this?"

"FYSHBone recently executed a will."

Bishop's assistant opened the briefcase and handed him another file.

"FYSHBone named his beloved mother the sole heir to his estate. This includes his interest in this entity. She now controls KUTTHROAT Records."

Blood drained from Sabio's head.

Bishop spoke more slowly. "Guzmán, I need you to secure this woman's signature on the MOU. After the will is probated you secure her signature on the contract."

Sabio was confused. He hadn't thought about wills since the bar exam. The second file contained a copy of a will dated three days ago. Signed by FYSHBone, it named Tamora Edwards, his mother, as his sole heir. The signature appeared genuine.

Sabio breathed. How could he not know this? What did it all mean? And how was Bishop in possession of the will?

He picked up the first file.

"Let's see what we have."

Sabio knew every contour of the original contract. He flipped to the section that mattered, read the numbers three times. His hand almost shook. He lobbed the contract onto the desk.

"Is there a problem, Guzmán?"

"Stop parachuting off skyscrapers, Bishop. The vibrations got your brains scrambled."

"Excuse me?"

"Five cents on the dollar from the original offer?"

"An adjusted assessment of value."

"Based on what?"

"FYSHBone is dead. He *was* this company."

Boy, these people sure move fast. The news had barely broken and already they had drastically amended documents at the ready.

Sabio made counterarguments, as he would in any negotiation. "Death improves an artist's stock. The work becomes limited. Scarcity drives up value." Sabio had learned that at state school.

Bishop dusted his lapel. "My family has collected since Rembrandt."

"And?"

"Rap music is not fine art."

Sabio flipped to his sales persona.

"Bishop, you still want this. You want it more than ever. FYSHBone produced a huge catalogue. Tons of hits hardwired into the minds of a young generation."

"Ephemeral."

"Really? What's Elvis still earn? Next twenty, thirty, fifty years, every time technology changes, FYSHBone's entire catalogue needs to be repackaged, remastered, resold. How many cassettes, CDs, and MP3 downloads have Hendrix, Jim Morrison, and the Beatles sold since death? Look at Michael Jackson."

"Do your homework," said Bishop. "FYSHBone's mother still lives in public housing."

"What's that matter?"

"Five million dollars will make her eyeballs fall from her head and roll down the stairs after you, as if in a cartoon. Convince her."

Sabio was careful to smother his emotions before he spoke.

"I didn't see anything in here about my compensation."

Sabio had laced the original deal with goodies, including stock options and a job as a VP in the newly formed joint venture.

The German pulled another file.

Bishop did not slide this one over. "Guzmán, you must be the one who advises FYSHBone's mother to sign. If I send my solicitors she may later sue for unfair bargaining."

"Really, Bishop, your lawyers must snort cocaine all night just to keep up with you."

Bishop read from the file. "Guzmán, your finances are a wreck. Credit cards, a Porsche, even your phone, always late, always the minimum."

Sabio tilted his head. *What the—?*

"You love to bounce checks. Three years ago you bought your mother a tiny house in Puerto Rico."

Bishop flashed a recent photo of Sabio's mother on her patio, watering plants, unaware she was being photographed.

"Quaint. Except the house is on the verge of foreclosure."

Sabio tensed. "You spied on my mother?"

"You have borrowed every penny's worth of equity generated by your condo. Your savings account would cover dinner and a movie if you went alone."

Sabio balled his fists.

"I shall warn you now, Guzmán, if you do not know from my show, I am a third-degree black belt. And Hegel here would break both your wrists before you left that chair."

Sabio looked from one European to the other.

Bishop continued. "Guzmán, you earn a decent salary. What is your problem? We captured a urine sample. You could smoke Bob Marley to sleep, but that is not expensive. You do have one true vice."

Don't tell me.

"You are a degenerate gambler."

Sabio felt embarrassed. Violated. The fact that they could discover these things scared him.

"How is any of this any of your business?"

"You are in debt to a Brooklyn loan shark named Antwoine 'Gator' Moses."

"I don't know anything about him."

"Do you know you owe him over one hundred thousand dollars? Tidy. At four and a half points that's around five thousand dollars cash, per week."

Sabio knew the numbers.

"Six weeks ago you defaulted. The debt gets fatter. We who enjoy the privilege of money especially love the principle of compound interest. How long do you think this dance between you and Gator will continue if you fail to deliver?"

Sabio had counted on the merger to turn everything around.

"Guzmán, did you know Gator did four years as a juvenile? Castrated a lad over a pair of tennis shoes."

"Where is this going?"

Bishop closed the file. "Close this deal, Guzmán. Get FYSHBone's mother to sign the MOU, then the contract. Once it is all executed and I am in control, I will wipe clean your slate with Gator Moses."

Sabio let that sit. It was a start. "Okay, what else?"

"What else? I'm offering you a chance to save your life."

"Bishop, you're putting a gun to my head."

"You put that there yourself, Counselor."

Sabio could not think.

"I will let Moses know you and I are working toward a solution. This way you don't turn up bloated in the Gowanus Canal before we're finished."

Sabio thought about that. "Do not under any circumstance tell Gator Moses what it is precisely that you want me to do, Bishop."

"Why not?"

"You're the one with all the research. But trust me, you don't want to find out."

Bishop took that in. He studied Sabio's face. "As you wish."

Sabio had a million questions—well, in reality, he had just one.

"So when I get FYSHBone's mother to sign these documents, what happens next? For me?"

"You tender your resignation. Human resources will send you off with a sharp letter of recommendation. Clearing your debt with Moses shall be your severance in full."

Bishop handed the "Sabio" file back to Hegel without showing the contents to Sabio.

This was not what Sabio had imagined. After all his calculations and sacrifice. After the things he had done. His imaginary millions were evaporating.

His secretary buzzed.

Sabio almost put his finger through the button. "Didn't I tell you I wanted to be left alone?"

"I'm sorry, it's just the police are here. Two detectives. Should I send them to Dulles?"

"No! Uh, ask them, actually send them into the conference room."

Bishop stood and buttoned his suit jacket.

"Guzmán, we have a deal?"

"Bishop, this is extortion. When the press hears about this—"

"The press, old sport? We own the press."

The tycoon slipped his sunglasses on. "Guzmán, did you watch the entire episode where I wrestle the croc?"

"I did."

"Remember how it ends?"

"Yes. You broke its neck."

CHAPTER 14

Sparks

Cassandra and Moretti saw Leland Bishop and the middle-aged blond male assistant from the reality show in the hallway at KUTTHROAT Records.

The tycoon's eyes were hidden by sunglasses, so Cassandra was not sure it was him. He excused himself in the familiar British accent as he passed. The assistant stared coldly forward.

The detectives went to the floor-to-ceiling windows in the conference room high above the sunny mosaic of Times Square. The sun, headed for the center of the sky, brought out the teeming kaleidoscope of colors.

Moretti sounded wistful. "I started as a patrol officer down there, at the Crossroads of the World."

"From up here," said Cassandra, "the cars look like my son's toys."

"Back then it was pimps, punks, pushers, and prostitutes. Real *Taxi Driver* days. I got cut like five times. That was before all the corporate welfare turned it into giant fast-food joint."

"It'll never be like it was," said Cassandra.

"No, never."

The lawyer walked in.

Cassandra turned. She disguised her surprise. Sabio Guzmán was striking.

"Detectives."

Everyone introduced themselves.

"Sorry for the wait."

Guzmán's handshake was clammy. He seemed distracted. But he gave Cassandra a long, deep look.

The detectives expressed their condolences. They sat at a long table. Cassandra resisted the urge to stare.

"Was that Leland Bishop?" said Moretti. "I love his show."

The lawyer seemed annoyed to hear that. "He came to offer support."

"That's personal service."

The lawyer got right to business. "The radio said FYSH was shot?"

Moretti put away his sunglasses. "Yes. Multiple times."

"Any witnesses?"

"We were hoping you could help."

Cassandra took out her notepad.

Moretti stroked his chin. "Usually somebody gets shot, it's shocking. But the identity of the killer is rarely a surprise."

The lawyer shifted.

"You follow?"

"I guess."

The lawyer's broad shoulders filled the corners of his dark navy suit. He smelled good.

"Counselor, did your boss have enemies?"

"Not to my knowledge."

"Business competitors?"

"Detective, I know the record business has a reputation, but—"

"KUTTHROAT, right?"

"Yes, but that's mostly an image."

"You mean 'Either your brains or your signature will be on that contract' is made up?"

The lawyer blinked.

"Don't rap stars usually have rivals? East Coast/West Coast?"

"That's old news. Nobody beefs like that anymore."

"What about litigation? A company like this, high-profile? You must get sued all the time."

"We do."

"Anything someone might take personal?"

"FYSH got sued by his exes a lot. The mothers of his children. Child support, palimony suits. They usually named the label."

"Why?"

"To 'pierce the corporate veil.' Assert the company was just a front to protect FYSHBone's assets. It never worked."

Cassandra scribbled. "You have those lawsuits on a spreadsheet?"

"I'll have my assistant get you a copy."

"Other than that," said Moretti, "no trouble from his business?"

Guzmán had a clean-shaven, pretty bald head. Cassandra imagined him with a neatly trimmed goatee.

"No."

Cassandra had the feeling of having seen Sabio before, that rare and powerful sense that someone you just met,

you have already met, or have known or have always
known or were destined to know.

Guzmán was five or six years older than Cassandra.
She could so deal with that.

She asked if FYSHBone had a girlfriend.

"He dated a lot."

"Anybody in particular?"

"No." The lawyer's eyes conveyed a different answer.

Moretti tapped his coat pocket. "We have his cell."

"I think he was seeing Princesa De los Santos."

"The model?"

Cassandra was not aware that FYSHBone had been
dating fashion's current top model.

"Is that public knowledge?"

"It hasn't been long. Lately FYSH kept his sex life out
of the limelight."

Moretti winked. "How was their relationship?"

"He complained she was in his grille a lot."

"In English?"

"She didn't give him space. But FYSH said that about
every female. Hot one minute, sparks, then sick of her the
next."

"Was he cooling on the supermodel?"

"Like clockwork."

"How'd she take it?"

"I don't know. Ask her."

Cassandra tapped her notepad. "What about drugs?"

"He smoked a lot of weed."

"Anything harsher?"

Moretti tilted his head. "We're going to see his blood
work."

"What difference would it make?"

"Could be he was meeting his dealer and things got ugly."

The lawyer shook his head. "Doubtful."

"When was the last time you saw FYSHBone?"

Guzmán seemed to measure his words. "Last night after sundown."

"Eight forty-five, nine o'clock?" said Moretti.

"Round about."

"Where?"

Sabio gave the name of the private club.

"Anybody else join you?"

Guzmán ticked off the nicknames of FYSHBone's posse.

"Who's this Slow Mo we keep hearing about?"

"A bodyguard. More like a gofer. He grew up across the hall from FYSHBone."

"Bodyguard? He didn't do a very good job."

"FYSHBone liked to be left alone. Especially late at night. Called it his witching hour. That's when he felt most creative."

"That common knowledge?"

"I don't know."

"Was he at the loft often? Did he live at the studio?"

"Sometimes."

"How'd you know he was there last night?"

Again the lawyer seemed to measure his words. "The radio said his body was found in the Bronx."

Moretti nodded. "What was the relationship like between FYSHBone and Slow Mo?"

"I'm not telling tales out of school. This is not privileged."

"Speak."

"FYSHBone was a handful. Difficult to work for. But nobody took crap from him like Slow Mo. Humiliated him constantly."

"The bodyguard? Is he big?"

"Huge. Tall and very fat."

"He let himself get pushed around? FYSHBone looks to be about a featherweight."

"Slow Mo threw his tantrums in private, behind FYSH-Bone's back."

"Like?"

"I don't wanna give the wrong impression."

"So give the right one."

"FYSH gave Slow Mo a boa constrictor for his birthday."

Snakes weirded Cassandra out. She drew one on her notepad.

Moretti squeezed his hands together. "That's the breed that crushes your bones. FYSHBone gave somebody that as a gift?"

"Plus he threw Slow Mo a roller-skating party at the Roxy."

"Sounds like a good friend. Weird but generous."

"Depends how you see it. Slow Mo brought along a female, which is rare for him. Soon as she met FYSH-Bone they were off in a corner."

"How did Slow Mo take that?"

"He carried the glass box with the snake outside. I followed to try to calm him. He smashed the glass and grabbed the snake by the tail and whaled it against a brick wall until it broke into a bloody mess."

"Anybody else witness that?"

"No."

"What'd he tell FYSHBone?"

"Somebody stole the snake."

Moretti jutted his chin.

"Detectives, do you have a theory yet as to what happened?"

Moretti kept a finger against his chin for a long, solid moment. He openly studied the lawyer.

"We can tell you whoever did it was motivated. Coolly stood there and handled a wild weapon like mowing the lawn."

The lawyer bobbed his Adam's apple but remained silent.

"Shot your boss's eyes out. Any idea why somebody would do that?"

Guzmán stared at a spot on the table. "Madness? How do you know it wasn't random?"

"Did we say that?"

"You said the shooter was motivated and cool. This implies premeditation. Maybe a professional. Maybe personal. But how do you know it wasn't just a mugging?"

"We found his wallet in his pockets and a golden gun in his waistband. Know anything about that?"

"FYSHBone was licensed to carry. Celebrity exemption."

"I'm asking about the weapon. It looks custom."

"KUTTHROAT AVENGER. A prototype. German manufacturer. They made a line FYSHBone was going to endorse."

Cassandra looked up from her notes. "You're kidding."

"FYSH endorsed all kinds of products. For example, he had his own condoms, tobacco, sheets, and hot sauce. He learned a lot when KISS endorsed a line of coffins. Anything can be harnessed to generate income."

Moretti shook his head.

"The manufacturer made FYSH's personal AVENGER out of gold. But FYSH burned the Germans and pulled from the deal after the shipment arrived. It's in litigation. FYSH gave away most guns as gifts and calling cards."

Moretti crooked his nose. "You have an invoice for those?"

"My assistant will get that to you."

"Did FYSHBone give *you* one of those snazzy .50-caliber guns, Counselor?"

"He did."

"Where is it?"

"In a box in the back of my closet."

"The call history on your client's cell says 'Shyster' around three something in the morning."

"I noticed when I got up. We didn't talk."

"Too busy?"

"I was sleeping."

"Somebody with you?"

Cassandra looked up from her notepad.

"No."

"Did FYSHBone leave a message?"

"Yes."

"What was it?"

"That's privileged."

Moretti looked at Cassandra. "Like pulling teeth, this guy."

Guzmán wore a dark navy suit cut to his body. Light blue shirt. Silk baby-blue tie. No wedding band.

"You never mentioned the chain," he said.

"What chain?"

"FYSHBone's necklace. You recover it?"

"We did not."

"It's worth half a mill."

Moretti whistled. Sabio described it in detail.

"Counselor, how do you know it isn't in a safe somewhere?"

"He never took it off."

"Never?"

"It was his talisman. Find that necklace, you'll find your shooter."

Cassandra knew the necklace from FYSHBone's videos and had already drawn it in her pad, but she asked Guzmán if the label had a picture available.

"It's in publicity photos on our website."

"Counselor—"

"Call me Sabio."

In other circumstances Cassandra would have smiled at that. "Does the word 'Clementi' mean anything to you?"

"The ball player?"

"With an I at the end."

"I don't know. Italian or Latin for 'clemency' maybe?"

Moretti squinted. "Is that a lawyer's word?"

"Sure. Mercy. An 'act of clemency.' Like when a governor lets somebody out of the electric chair."

"Right."

Cassandra jotted. "Any special meaning for FYSH-Bone?"

"None that I know."

Cassandra asked whether Sabio knew who might want FYSHBone's dog.

The lawyer made a face. "That dog is a handful. Plus she never liked me."

Sabio apologized that he needed to meet with staff. All stood and shook hands.

Moretti asked for the lawyer's card.

"I'm out, but I'll take yours." He looked at Cassandra. "Great pictures of you on the front page of the papers."

In her running shorts. Great. Cassandra hoped she wasn't blushing.

"All in a day's work," she said.

"Detective, do *you* have a card?"

The lawyer played it cool, but his face looked capable of great expression. Cassandra found a card with the NYPD logo, scratched out "Missing Persons" and the old number, printed "HI-PRO Unit," and added her cell.

CHAPTER 15

Badlands

Moretti had a hunch that the lawyer was hiding something. "Shady people get antsy after encountering police," he said.

Sabio's assistant brought the documents he had promised. Moretti double-talked the young woman to discover where Guzmán parked his car, as well as the make, model, and color.

They followed the lawyer from the moment he exited the lot.

Cassandra still smelled Guzmán's cologne. "You really think he had something to do with the murder, Lou?"

"Kid, I suspect everybody until I eliminate them. Slick lawyer move, avoiding giving me a fingerprint with the old 'out of cards' routine. Are you hoping to clear his name?"

"Just asking."

"You're not seriously interested in that guy, are you?"

"Not meeting in this circumstance, but otherwise why not? He's nice looking and he has a job."

"Is that all it takes?"

"There's more?"

Moretti told her about a radio call he had taken when he was still in uniform. A husband blackened his wife's eye. She was still pretty, so when the judge sent the husband home Moretti was waiting.

He beat the man woozy, knocked three teeth out, and warned him that if he returned, Moretti's throwaway .38 would find a hole in his heart.

"That worked?"

"He went to live with his mother."

"And the wife?"

"She was mine for a while. It was hard to get rid of her. This is what I'm telling you. It's not good to get involved."

Cassandra said she understood.

Guzmán's shiny blue car was easy to follow in traffic.

Cassandra put on her sunglasses. "Where do you think he's going?"

"I don't know, but I bet it's trouble."

They crossed the Brooklyn Bridge again. It was high noon.

Moretti turned the music down. "Maldonado, your personnel file says you won a Combat Cross out here in the Badlands."

"I wish I hadn't."

The Combat Cross is awarded to members of the force who survive a battle to the death with an armed assailant.

"How'd it happen?"

"Lucky shot, Lou."

"No such thing."

Cassandra did not want to relive it.

Moretti waited. They passed beneath the bridge's Gothic arch.

"Six months out of the academy my partner, Stetson, and I answer a DV call. We're thinking we'll get there, the woman'll change her mind like usual."

"That's part of the abuse pattern," said Moretti. "The victim protects the tyrant."

"Whatever. Stetson knocks. The door opens a crack. Before we know what's happening, poor Stetson catches a shotgun blast in the neck. His arteries sprayed the ceiling."

"The neck is the worst."

"I pull my Glock but I wanted to run. Stetson slid to the floor, already gone. I heard the pump-action behind the door and kicked it open from the side. The shotgun went off into the opposite wall. Before he could pump again I dove across the open doorway and plugged him once in the center of his forehead."

"Bravo."

"It wasn't pretty, Lou. And it ain't something I'm proud of."

"Maldonado, you didn't choose that."

"I found his wife's body on the corner of their bed, half her face blown off."

Guzmán parked his expensive car in Carroll Gardens on the cleaned-up, high-rent side of the Gowanus Expressway, a couple of blocks from the Red Hook Projects. He slung a laptop bag over his shoulder.

Cassandra got out and followed him under the expressway. She saw him check addresses and go into FYSH-Bone's mother's building. The midday sun felt strong enough to peel paint.

Cassandra came back and reported.

"Lou, why do you think he's visiting FYSHBone's mom?"

"It ain't to dry her tears. Let's toss his car."

Moretti found a small case in the back of his vehicle. Inside was a slim-jim he used to open the Porsche's door lock. He began an illegal search.

Cassandra noticed the stick shift. The car's interior smelled of Sabio's cologne.

Moretti felt between the seats, under the seats, inside the pockets, under the mats.

"No gun, no necklace."

"Lou, Guzmán wouldn't send us after the necklace if it was in his possession."

"People are strange." Moretti popped the trunk, which was in the front of the car. "Check in there."

Cassandra looked.

"Nothing, not even a spare tire," she said. "A can of sealant and a small air compressor."

"Nothing in the glovebox either. No change or fast-food wrappers or old newspapers or mail. Nothing in the ashtray. No dust on the dashboard. This guy cleans up after himself."

Moretti popped the hood, which was in the rear.

"Maldonado, check the engine."

"For?"

"I once found a brick of heroin taped to the bottom of a car battery. Go look and keep an eye out while I dust for prints."

Cassandra looked at the shiny engine, but again saw nothing.

Moretti unscrewed a small tin of fine black fingerprint

powder and used a fine, soft brush to quickly and carefully dust several surfaces. He used fingerprint tape to lift prints, which he attached to separate index cards. Then he added detergent to a small bottle of water and wet a cloth to wipe away the dust. He wetted another cloth with clean water to rinse the surfaces and used a third cloth to dry.

"Maldonado, the speedometer says it goes to 225. Think your new boyfriend can get it up that fast?"

Cassandra was anxious. "Lou, we better hurry."

Moretti shut his case. "I'm tempted to hotwire it and check his GPS. See where he's been."

"What if it was just a quick stop? We shouldn't let him catch us in his car."

Moretti left the car as he had found it and locked the door.

They climbed back into Moretti's vehicle.

Cassandra asked what would happen if they got a hit on the prints. The search was not legal and evidence recovered would not be usable.

Moretti put his shades back on.

"We'll cross that lagoon when we come to it, sunshine. Let's go see what this Slow Mo character is all about."

CHAPTER 16

Flip the Script

At that very moment Sabio sat on FYSHBone's mother's plastic-covered couch. Drawn curtains made the place dark in the middle of a sunny day.

Tamora Edwards wore a simple black dress. Her natural gray hair was full and beautifully micro locked past her shoulders. She had a broad, strong nose and piercing dark brown eyes.

For some reason Sabio felt like the guy who turns to stone in *Clash of the Titans*.

"Again I'm sorry. Is there anything the label can do to help?"

"Are you a man of faith, Mr. Guzmán?"

"I was an altar boy."

"You believe in the Resurrection?"

Sabio was not sure. "I want to believe there's hope for human redemption."

"You came to say something."

Sabio had prepared his pitch about the will, her pending ownership of the company, and KAMIKAZE's offer.

He planned to leave out the part about it being pennies on the dollar. His mind could not find the Play button.

"Mrs. Edwards, I don't want you to think I'm heartless."

"I know exactly where your heart is." She picked up a pair of knitting needles and began to knit.

"I hate to discuss business at a time like this. You are in such awful pain."

"Say what you need to."

"Your son—"

"Please don't call him FYSHBone."

"LeRoi was in negotiations with a company, KAMI-KAZE Vynil—"

"I know, they was gonna put two companies together and make a new company."

"Something like that."

"Exactly like that. Go on."

Sabio glimpsed where FYSHBone got his strong will. "The fact that LeRoi passed does not mean the deal collapses. KAMIKAZE is still interested."

"Of course. Wanna see their idol?"

FYSHBone's mother reached into her dress, inside her bra, and fished out a roll of tens and twenties. Sabio guessed it was maybe $100 to $150.

"There goes the One *they* trust." She buried the roll.

Her anguish was clear. Sabio felt embarrassed to be there, ashamed of his role.

How had he painted himself into this position?

"Did you know my son well?"

"We worked together for several years."

"What did you think of him?"

Thorny. They say you should never speak ill of the dead.

"I knew him in a professional capacity."

Her eyes were glassy.

Sabio was moved to say something comforting.

"FYSHBone was brilliant. His appetite for knowledge was endless. Seeing all of these books in your home, I realize he got that from you."

Sabio wondered whether she had really read *Origin of Species.*

"FYSHBone was a workaholic. Ambitious. His music was larger than life."

"His music was a curse," she said.

Sabio had once heard FYSHBone describe it as such but got blown off for asking. This time he didn't bother.

"I saw the good things. The way people reacted to him. Your son took me to Japan for two months while he trained for his part in the Tarantino movie. Everybody on the street and in the countryside knew him and posed for pictures. He juggled peaches in the street for children. On a whim we scheduled a concert at Budokan and it sold out in an hour. Fifteen thousand screaming Japanese knew all the hooks to all his songs and drowned him out."

It really had been one of the highlights of Sabio's life.

"The sound had to be re-engineered for *Boogie Down at Budokan*, the live album. FYSH turned around and donated the money from the album and the show to rebuild a hospital destroyed in an earthquake."

Sabio left out the part of the Japanese odyssey where FYSHBone's entourage spent the entire time living in a geisha house FYSH rented out for them. Or the fact that FYSHBone set up a very scary major drug deal with some nine-fingered Japanese gangsters known as Yakuza to "stay sharp" and get into character for the movie shoot.

Tamora Edwards turned up her nose. "My son always picked up strays."

"He was a patron for good."

A mother's tears formed. "Why did this happen to my son?"

Sabio could have told her why. He didn't.

"I don't know, ma'am. It hurts. We can only hope that he is at peace in the bosom of the Lord."

Sabio waited. There was nothing left but to get to business.

"LeRoi signed a will the other day naming you as his sole heir. I know it probably means nothing to you in light of the circumstances, but you control his estate. At least you will when a judge declares the will official."

"Probate."

"Correct. After that you control the label. You're free to sell your interest and let somebody else worry about the headaches."

Mrs. Edwards remained in her chair. Sabio thought the moment was right to show her Bishop's memorandum of understanding. She stopped him.

"Mr. Guzmán, is your mother proud of you?"

"Excuse me?"

"All the sacrifices she must've made. Is this what she wanted you to do? To use your good looks, your slickness and school learning to take advantage of a poor bereaved mother? From the projects, no less?"

Sabio had not expected that turn in the conversation. All of his confidence from the moment earlier faded.

"What do you have in the bag?" she said.

Sabio panicked, afraid that she knew what was in the laptop.

She went on: "A memorandum of understanding and a contract of sale, perhaps?"

Okay, she didn't know what was in the computer, and that was a relief, but how the hell did she know the exact documents?

She seemed to read his mind.

"It's only logical. This is what you're going to do. Go back to your new puppetmaster, Bishop. Tell him if he wants to see my name on a contract he better come correct. I don't care what you all talked about with LeRoi. He always ate with his eyes."

Sabio was beyond surprised. "I'm sorry?"

"You work for me now, don't you?"

"Well, uh, technically—"

"Your marching orders are to renegotiate with the Europeans. Whatever the deal was when my son was alive and wasting his talent, I want 50 percent more. You feel me? I don't want no *before* deal. I want me an *after* deal."

"Mrs. Edwards—"

"Things are different now. I lost my child. So you go back and you tell them I want 75, 80, 90 percent more than LeRoi wanted. Shock them. Make them cover their jewels. Then you jibber-jabber your way down in drips and drabs. Act like they're squeezing the lime juice out of you. When you get them to fifty points above, I'll sign. Make it happen or I'll fire you."

Sabio felt backhanded.

"I have a book around here on negotiation. You want it?"

"I'm okay."

"No. You are not."

Tamora Edwards stood as if to let Sabio know the meeting was over.

"And one more thing. I know full well the terms of my son's deal. Do not try any double-cross."

Sabio's presumptions, prejudices, instincts, and biases, the intelligence he had thought he had gathered were all off.

The MOU never saw the inside of Tamora Edwards's apartment. Normally Sabio would reason, argue, educate, and inform his client that there was no chance to strike the deal she wanted. But she had made it clear his words would cut no ice.

The gap between the parties now stood at 150 to 5. If Sabio floated KAMIKAZE's proposal now, Tamora Edwards might run him out of there with a butcher knife.

He stood. "Very well then, ma'am. I'll communicate your counteroffer."

"Communicate. And stick your nose in them housing regulations."

"Why?"

"This apartment is low-income and I need to figure out how to keep it now that I am a lady of means."

CHAPTER 17

Gotham City Shakedown

Out on the street, Sabio wondered what the hell had just happened.

He had entered ashamed yet prepared to take advantage of FYSHBone's mother. He exited pushed into the middle of a great divide.

The sun beat down. It was almost one in the afternoon. Sabio would not solve his problems in Red Hook.

He had parked on the gentrified side of the highway because he did not want anybody to break into his Porsche. That meant he had to walk through the rough part. The suit drew looks and the occasional compliment.

A silver Mercedes with tinted windows passed going in the opposite direction. Sabio tracked it from behind the pink lenses of his sunglasses. The sedan did a slow, deliberate U-turn and cruised back in his direction.

Here comes the wolf pack.

Sabio's car was within sight, but breaking for it made no sense. He would never make it, especially with the laptop. Even if he did, if he was faster that day, made it to the car, got it open, started it, peeled out, and left his hunters in tire smoke, Gator and his mercenaries would just haul up to him at some later point and multiply the sting by a thousand.

Sabio decided to walk and pretend he didn't see.

The Mercedes pulled even and rolled alongside. Sabio kept face forward. The automatic window powered down. He braced himself.

"Brotha man! No respect?"

Sabio stopped and turned toward the car. He slid his shades to the tip of his nose.

"Gator! Fancy running into you."

"Nothing fancy about it."

Gator Moses had a Barry White baritone, which even in low volume had a percussive force. He was sixty but he had ebony skin that did not wrinkle. He had perfect teeth. He was a former professional bodybuilder who still spent four to five hours a day pumping iron.

The kingpin of Red Hook unfolded from the backseat. He bulged his enormous neck muscles to make his loud, form-fitting yellow short-sleeved shirt hang just right. Gator's size-thirteen green alligator shoes seemed like live reptiles.

"You've been ignoring my calls, Sabio."

"Don't take it personal. What with the merger, now the murder, I've had a lot to deal with."

Gator wore his hair relaxed and parted to the side. "You look all broken up about it. Let's take a walk and talk."

Gator never conducted business in the car, which could easily be bugged.

He removed the laptop bag from Sabio's shoulder. "Let me help you with that."

"It's just a computer."

"I know what it is."

Gator tossed the bag through the open window of his Mercedes, which immediately powered up.

"Move."

They walked side by side on the sidewalk. The Mercedes followed.

"A shame about our friend," said Sabio.

Gator's massive pectorals twitched under the yellow shirt's slippery material. "You talk to the cops?"

"About what?"

"Drop the games, Sabio."

Sabio cleared his throat. "They tried the good cop/bad cop routine. I didn't bite."

"What about when they pull the plunger-up-the-ass routine?"

"I got nothing to say."

"They ask you about your whereabouts?"

"Why would they?"

Gator laughed, but the thick neck vein throbbed.

Sabio went at him. "You worried they'll peg FYSH-Bone's body on you, Gator?"

Gator's laughter tripped. That was just the type of comment that played on his fear of being recorded.

"Somebody oughta sew your mouth shut."

"My ex-wife would give you a footrub for suggesting it."

Gator's face iced over.

"I guess this is your first homicide since—"

"Hey! To your knowledge, Sabio, I ain't never been involved in no homicides, right? Say it."

"That you have been implicated is a matter of public record, Gator."

"Anybody suspect me of being in the Bronx last night? No, right?"

"Isn't that what you wanted to talk about?"

Gator stopped and the Mercedes stopped and so did Sabio.

"You gonna take care of your obligations, lawyer?"

"I have something in the works."

"The British dude says he gave you a project. What is it?"

"That's privileged."

"This ain't no courtroom."

"Yeah, well you don't want me telling your business and neither does he. Let me do my job."

"I'm gonna need that money from you soon, Sabio."

"I'll need time."

Gator looked at him like, *Motherfucker, you ain't* got *no time*.

"At least a couple days," said Sabio.

Gator didn't answer. He folded himself into the sedan, threw the door, powered the window down. Sabio leaned in.

Two muscleheads sat up front.

In the back was Gator's woman Oxana, a beautiful blonde Russian. She finished a chocolate bar. Sabio watched her drop the empty wrapper through her open window and slide her entire middle finger in her mouth to suck the chocolate off.

The sharp nail on Gator's own middle finger flicked Sabio in the ear like a bee sting.

"Ouch."

Gator handed over the laptop. "Next time have that for me."

Sabio covered his ear. The lobe felt hot. "You trying to coerce me, Gator?"

The kingpin kept purposefully quiet. He snapped his fingers. The Mercedes rolled off.

CHAPTER 18

We Own These Streets

Cassandra and Moretti had decided to hold off on FYSH-Bone's bodyguard and follow Sabio a bit longer, which paid off. As a result, they saw when the Mercedes pulled up and the big bodybuilder exited.

"Oh-oh," said Cassandra. "What do you think this is about?"

Moretti pulled a pair of binoculars from his glove compartment. He focused.

"Unbelievable. That's Gator Moses."

"The gangster?"

Cassandra had known Moses by reputation when she worked undercover as a Brooklyn drug dealer. She never saw him in person.

"Old-school pimp," said Moretti. "Loan shark, pusher. Competed for the Mr. Olympia thirty-odd years ago. Said to be the biggest steroid dealer in the city outside of Staten Island."

"Didn't he beat a case a couple years back?"

"One of his hookers told the Feds he was laundering money through real estate. Buying buildings, turning them into brothels, letting each individual franchise pay its own mortgage, then not declaring the profits."

"Sounds clever for a bully type."

If Cassandra remembered the news accounts correctly, the night before jury selection the main witness had jumped from the high window of a hotel where the Feds had stashed her. The case fell apart.

Moretti said, "What do you think he's talking to your boyfriend the lawyer about?"

Cassandra wondered. She asked for the binoculars. Moretti was parked in a lousy spot.

"I can't see anybody's lips well enough to read."

"Maldonado, you lip-read?"

"A little."

Cassandra kept her eyes glued to the binoculars. Sabio did not look intimidated.

Oh, my God! "Lou, I think Guzmán just said 'first homicide.'"

"What'd I tell you?"

"He said 'implicated.' Blah blah blah. Oh, my God. Okay, the pimp just said 'in the Bronx last night.'"

"See?"

"'Obligations . . . courtroom.'"

"This is juicy," said Moretti. "Sounds like a shake-down. Gator knows something."

They watched the rest of the exchange.

The back window on the driver side powered down. A woman's hand dropped what looked like a candy wrapper out the window. She sucked her middle finger, then held it up.

The gesture felt deliberate. The woman turned her face in Cassandra's direction and made eye contact with the binoculars.

The Mercedes sped off.

Moretti put his car in Drive.

"We'll leave the lawyer for now. Let's stay with Gator."

They followed the sedan.

"How'd you learn to read lips, Maldonado? FBI seminar?"

"I got sick as a kid. Bad fever. Woke up temporarily deaf. I spent a month at the hospital in a world of silence and developed this skill. A month later I woke up and my ability to hear had returned."

"Crazy. Then again, they say every superheroine needs a special power, right?"

The experience had left Cassandra with a lifelong fear that deafness would return. She wrote down the license plate, what they had discussed about Gator, and the words she thought the men had spoken.

Moretti leaned over. "I think it's time for some traffic enforcement."

He hit the siren and pulled Gator's car over.

The four passengers were searched and lined up on their knees facing a brick wall with their fingers laced behind the backs of their heads.

Each knew the routine. Cassandra guarded them while Moretti searched the vehicle.

The three men looked as if they drank steroids for breakfast, the way their muscles rippled. Gator wore a tight, bright short-sleeved yellow shirt with a neckline to the sternum that showed big hard biceps with thick, engorged, visible veins. The other males were styled similarly, in lime green.

The blonde woman had a small head, long neck, short torso, and white tennis shorts that revealed long, lean legs. Cassandra noticed her short, flat feet with visibly high arches shaping the white ballerina flats.

Gator sported a thick gold bracelet and a necklace with a medallion in the shape of a round, old-fashioned dumbbell.

Gator had intense green eyes. He spoke over his shoulder.

"We were just on our way to lunch. What is this harassment? You ain't got no legal reason to stop us."

That was true.

"No turn signal," said Moretti. "I'm searching the car because you acted nervous."

"Why would I be nervous?"

Moretti pressed the button to unlock the trunk. He went back and rummaged. Cassandra and the four detainees could not see.

"Aha!" Moretti came from behind the car twirling a snub-nosed .38 around his index finger.

Gator shook his head. "Naw, man, don't even try it. That gun is yours."

"Your car, isn't it, Gator? Your car, your gun."

"That's not my weapon! Send it to the lab. No fingerprints, no DNA, nothing."

"Really?" Moretti stepped to him. He pressed the side of the weapon against the side of Gator's sweaty face. Not rough, just to make him feel it. He dragged the barrel against Gator's sweaty temple.

"You really don't think we'll find your DNA, Gator?"

Gator's eyes widened.

Moretti pulled the gun away. He tapped his gold shield with the barrel. "We own these streets!"

"No doubt."

"I make whatever case I want."

"Yes, sir."

"Is this your crew?"

"No, man, these two Dominican brothas are my training partners and protégés. I'm gonna manage them when they go pro. Show him what you can do, fellas."

While still on their knees, the two muscleheads began to flex and strike strained poses, such as the double biceps and the javelin throw.

Moretti said, "Enough, you morons! Turn your faces to the wall!"

They did.

He pointed at the blonde. "Is that your girlfriend?"

The woman turned her cool blue eyes toward them. The blueness of her eyes reminded Cassandra of a Siberian husky that lived in the projects when she was growing up.

"She hardly speaks English. She's a Russian Jew. Israeli, too. An ex-ballerina."

Gator spoke with the pride one hears from someone who describes a prized show horse. His tone annoyed Cassandra.

"How do you and your Russian girlfriend communicate, Gator?"

"The international language."

"Oh, right, you think you're a pimp. How'd you two meet?"

"Poker game with some Russian mobsters. She came with their leader but left with me."

Gator left the detectives to imagine the circumstances of that maneuver.

The woman turned her gaze back to the wall.

Moretti sniffed. "What were you talking to the lawyer about?"

"What lawyer? I know so many."

"Guzmán. Just now on the street."

"Oh, that? We know each other from the party scene."

"He a customer of yours?"

"Listen, I own a health-food store, and a vegetarian takeout joint, and some property on the right side of the tracks. That's how I make my money. The lawyer don't patronize any of those."

"What do you know about FYSHBone?"

Gator spat on the sidewalk. "Apparently somebody was fed up."

"With?"

"His racket."

"You know him personally, Gator?"

"He grew up around here."

"When was the last time you saw him?"

"We don't see him much anymore. He's always busy bringing mosquito nets to Africa."

"You knew him well enough to sound jealous."

Gator rolled his green eyes. "Everybody around here talks like he's the favorite son."

"Yeah, I know. You might have been as big as Schwarzenegger had your footage from *Pumping Iron* not wound up on the cutting-room floor. You're still sick about it."

Gator faked a laugh. "Man, I'm too busy eating pussy and counting money to dwell on the negative."

Cassandra cut in. "You know FYSHBone's family?"

"His mother was one of the biggest hoes of her generation. Until she got religion."

"His father?"

"His father was a Christmas card with no money inside. Killed himself on the little man's seventh birthday."

Cassandra remembered the restless boy in FYSHBone's school photo. His father was a suicide. On his birthday, no less. She felt sad.

"FYSHBone's reputation has always been that he got started dealing drugs," she said. "Supposedly that's how he got the money for the label."

"Those are just rumors, Mami."

"I'm not your daughter and you're not my man so don't call me Mami."

Gator's jaw tensed. The big vein in his neck throbbed.

"FYSHBone never denied those rumors in any interviews."

"That's Hollywood hype. I was out there at Venice and Muscle Beach. Publicists make stuff up. Like that thing of it always being sunny in California? Not true."

"So what's the true story about FYSHBone and drug dealing?"

"That boy was always under his mother's watch. She was strict. He didn't do anything without her say. She had him locked up in that apartment reading all the time. Piano lessons, book reports."

Moretti was not buying that. "FYSHBone never dabbled in the streets?"

"I'm sure he messed around with a nickel bag or two. It's a rite of passage around here. But he never dealt weight like the rumors say. He was just a runner. A nobody. He was never gonna reach the top. It don't take much to start a record label."

"You got a real condescending tone," said Moretti.

"I never liked him. Normally I don't mind giving a kid a cookie, but that boy always had an air of entitlement. Like everything belonged to him."

"Can you account for your whereabouts last night, Gator?"

"Aw, brotha, don't even try it."

"FYSHBone ever give you one of his special guns?"

"Why would I need a gun? I'm in the health-food vegeterian takeout real-estate business."

"Ever see his necklace?"

"That gaudy piece of shit? Money don't buy class, do it?"

"You don't think those sparkly diamonds would make a great consolation prize for never winning the Mr. O?"

Gator pounded himself in the chest once to pop his dumbbell medallion. "Yo, I got my own jewelry! You dig?"

Moretti stayed on him. "Tell the truth, Gator. That witness in the money-laundering case. You threw her out the window, didn't you?"

"I had an ironclad alibi. I was eating steak with a senator."

Moretti grabbed one of the kneeling bodybuilders by the ear. The 225 pounder squealed.

"Maybe you had one of your flexing protégés toss her out the window for you?"

"Whatever they do with their extracurricular activities is their business."

Moretti let the ear go.

Cassandra asked something slightly off topic. "How does it feel to make a living exploiting women?"

Gator took a beat or two. "You know any man can be

a pimp, Detective. Pimping is the easiest, most natural hustle in the world."

"Is that right?"

"All's it takes is getting a woman to need you. To feel like Daddy finally showed up. We both know how easy that is, don't we?"

Cassandra did not bite or give any reaction.

"You wanna know the hard part?" said Gator. "For most men? The reason pimps are a special breed?"

"School me."

"A pimp can look at that woman that is so hooked on him. So special and so sweet. She can do everything for him. Call him Papi when they're in bed. Wash and iron his socks. Trim his hedges. But if his neighbor says, 'Your girl got a pretty mouth,' a true pimp sees the fifty dollars. No jealousy. A pimp is a lover but a pimp don't care."

Cassandra shook her head. "That's sad."

"What's really sad is it don't even matter. A woman could be old, fat, skinny, toothless, and you still make money because the world is full of desperate men and every woman qualifies."

Cassandra had had enough of this a-hole.

Moretti had obviously been faking about charging them with his planted throwaway. They let them go.

Cassandra said, "Gator, one last thing. What does 'Clementi' mean?"

Gator stopped at his door and thought.

"Isn't that like bad weather or something? I don't know. Look it up."

CHAPTER 19

Borough of Brooklyn (County of Kings)

Cassandra and Moretti sat in the air-conditioned comfort of his ride. He had the satellite radio tuned to the seventies station.

They watched Slow Mo's apartment building, a low rowhouse in the middle of a block of run-down rowhouses in Crown Heights. A flock of pigeons circled. They had spent over an hour on the stakeout.

"Crime Heights." Moretti looked up through his windshield and squinted. "Supposedly this is getting cleaned up."

"This block still looks like a dump."

"You got pockets of Lubavitcher Jews, but 90 percent of this area is still African-American or West Indian. Blacks from the Caribbean."

That kind of intro signaled uncomfortable topics for Cassandra. "What's that supposed to mean, Lou?"

"I'm saying where you have few whites, the government lets things decay. You disagree?"

She didn't.

It was past two in the afternoon. The birds flew in some kind of unison. Cassandra was nervous about bringing up her schedule.

"Lou, I'll need to take my meal in a couple of hours. That's when I pick up my son."

Cassandra explained her routine at Missing Persons, and that she understood this was a homicide investigation, which meant long hours. She would be back after driving her son home.

"Are you serious? This is why they worried about letting females on the job. You don't have help?"

"My mom takes care of him. She don't drive."

"Where's his father?"

"His father is a mistake I made. He's still in the projects in Mott Haven. Probably enjoying his ten thousandth day in a row of no work. He lives off what his mother collects from the government."

"That's not your ex-husband who was on the job though?"

"No. That one's in Florida renting jet skis to tourists."

Moretti changed stations. "I heard he was a good cop. Solid Irish stock like his old man. What happened?"

Cassandra had been down the long dark road that leads to divorce. She was just seeing light again. She did not feel like talking about it. The flying pigeons cast dizzying shadows on the asphalt.

Moretti got the hint. He called his wife and the other teams of detectives and updated Captain Vargas.

Moretti checked FYSHBone's cell while they waited and read Cassandra a text.

"Maldonado, listen to this: 'You think you're gettin away? You're gonna pay!'"

"Who sent that?"

"Princesa. The girlfriend."

"Can you see his response?"

"No."

"Are there other messages from her?"

"Tons. At one point she was sending one every two minutes for an hour and a half."

"What else do they say?"

"You used me . . . I'm not some dirty rag . . . We belong together I love you . . . You're a monster I hate you . . . I'm good for you . . . I'm the best thing that ever happened to you . . . How could you not want me? . . . Where are you? . . . Is anybody with you? . . . I swear to God I don't know what I'll do."

"The lawyer did say she was in his grille. Obviously we have to check her out."

"Why don't you call her? I have a feeling from these messages she will be more off-balance with a woman than with a man."

Cassandra wasn't so sure, but left Princesa a voicemail. She then called her mother to touch base and let her know it would be a long day, and to ask if she could please take care of Jason for the night.

Moretti scored hot Jamaican beef patties at the bodega on the corner. They ate in the car and pushed them down with cold coconut sodas.

"So, Maldonado, I hear you were the queen of the gun collars."

"The streets are full of them."

"False modesty. You carried every precinct. Made your felony quota on the first or second of every month, then spent the rest of each month letting every slacker in the precinct take credit for your extra collars. How come?"

"Nobody likes a showoff, right?"

"How'd you get so good?"

"Watching closely."

"C'mon."

"I'm serious. Concealing a gun on your body changes your center of gravity. The weapon tugs in the direction you're carrying. Left side, right side, shoulder holster, ankle holster, belt. The weight of the gun affects your posture, how you walk, the alignment and wear of your clothes. It's subtle. I started by watching other cops."

"Female undercovers have it easy," said Moretti. "They can just walk up and feel. Especially if they look like you."

Moretti was right that a fair percentage of Cassandra's gun collars were men who had just let her sidle up.

"No substitute for good police work," she said.

"How'd you start making the charges stick?"

Veteran cops learn most recoveries of weapons and drugs occur in unconstitutional circumstances. Cases get thrown out and young cops learn to lie.

"Justice finds a way. Look! That must be Slow Mo."

A tall, fat, mocha-skinned African-American wobbled up the block. He wore an oversized T-shirt with the KUT-THROAT smoking fish emblem. He shone with sweat and carried more plastic grocery bags at once than Cassandra had ever seen done.

"A mountain," said Moretti. "Let me handle him."

Cassandra had not had enough chance to observe for a concealed weapon. The man was so large it was difficult to tell, but she thought she noticed a slight shuffle.

"Lou, he might have a gun tucked in his pants in the

front, on his left hip, so he can reach across with his right."

The detectives climbed from the SUV. Cassandra followed Moretti across the street to intercept Slow Mo as he got to the front of his building. She unclipped her holster.

Slow Mo spotted Moretti as he slid between parked cars.

The big man took off. His grocery bags flew.

Moretti reacted. "You gotta be shitting me—*Stop!*"

By the time Moretti said that, Slow Mo was inside the building. When the detectives ran in he was at the top of the first flight fumbling for keys. Slow Mo's nickname had nothing to do with the way he moved.

"Halt!"

Slow Mo spun and—PAH! PAH! PAH!—let off an unexpected triple of incredibly loud, wild shots.

The cops dropped. Plaster rained onto their backs.

They looked up with their guns drawn. Slow Mo was out of sight. They heard him run upstairs.

"He's headed for the roof!"

Rowhouses connect to one another in rows. You can access any building in a row once you access the roof of any other building within that row. Access a rowhouse roof and you can quickly disappear.

Slow Mo shouted down the stairwell. "I don't know nothin'!"

He fired off another pair of incredibly loud shots that splintered wood railings and pulverized plaster. Cassandra felt the vibrations in her clothes.

Cassandra and Moretti hustled with their backs to the walls.

"Throw your gun down, Slow Mo! We only wanna talk!"

BAM! BAM!

"That's seven!" said Cassandra.

Unless Slow Mo had a replacement clip, he was out of ammo.

They heard him exit onto the roof.

Moretti radioed a "shots fired" alarm and gave the address.

They ran up. Cassandra controlled her breathing. The stairwell was lit by a dusty old skylight.

Moretti kicked the door to the roof open but held back to avoid another blast. None came. He moved forward in a combat position. Cassandra followed.

Slow Mo was nowhere to be seen. The rooftops of all the rowhouses on that side of the street connected for the distance of the entire block. The guy moved so surprisingly fast he could be inside any building. He might already have reached the street.

They crept to the edge and peered over.

Where'd he go?

The pigeon flock circled above them like a squadron ready to bomb. Moretti pointed at a pigeon coop and put his finger to his lips. They crept with their guns pointed down but ready to aim and fire.

The sun's rays bounced off the black-tarred roof in hazy waves. The pigeons cooed inside their coop. Their wretched waste smelled something awful.

Moretti threw open the door to the pigeon coop.

Nothing.

He peered inside, gun first, and got hammered in the hand with Slow Mo's gun. Moretti dropped his weapon but quickly karate-chopped Slow Mo's wrist, knocking the big gun loose.

The men grabbed each other and spun. Cassandra jumped on Slow Mo's back and tried to choke him into submission. They banged into the coop's walls, freaking out pigeons and sending them colliding. Their loud flapping wings kicked up hundreds of loose feathers.

The three wrestlers tumbled out, and Slow Mo literally spun Moretti by the necktie. He flung Moretti with such force the 220-pound veteran simply rolled.

Cassandra applied pressure with the headlock, the gun still in her right hand. She rode Slow Mo.

"I don't know nothin'!"

"Stop resisting!"

Slow Mo's arms were such hamhocks, he could not reach around and knock Cassandra off.

He staggered toward the edge of the roof. One more misstep and Cassandra and Slow Mo were over the side and falling three stories to their death.

No!

Cassandra yanked and the large man tottered drunkenly backward toward the door. She leaped off.

Slow Mo tripped, stumbled, then—

"Watch out!"

He crashed through the skylight with a magnificent clatter of breaking glass.

Cassandra and Moretti ran.

Oh, thank God! Thank you, Lord, thank you!

Slow Mo had not rocketed three flights down to make contact between the floor and his skull. Instead, because of his momentum, he had cleared the well, broken the railing across the way, and landed on the top flight on his back, in a shower of glass.

He was alive and finished fighting.

Pigeon feathers stuck to his sweaty forehead. He craned his neck to look at Cassandra.

"Who *are* you?"

Moretti was out of breath. "We're the two who should come down and stomp you. Don't move. You're under arrest."

Slow Mo let his head drop.

Sirens finally approached.

The detectives took the stairs.

CHAPTER 20

Big Business

Moretti got in Slow Mo's face. He held Slow Mo's KUT-THROAT AVENGER up with a pen through the trigger guard.

"The last skell who took a shot at me ain't been heard from. You out of your mind, shooting at police?"

Slow Mo's lower back was so wide they had to link both sets of cuffs to make it across the expanse. They had him on his ass, on shattered glass, and leaned against the wall. The halls were crawling with local cops and bright with sunlight.

Slow Mo rocked his head at Cassandra. "I didn't see her. I only saw you."

"That make it okay to shoot?"

"Look at you, I thought you was Mafia."

The rumors Cassandra had heard about Moretti involved his being too close to La Cosa Nostra.

"Watch what you say, punk."

Slow Mo looked away and stayed silent.

Cassandra leaned toward Slow Mo's field of vision. "Why would gangsters come after you?"

He turned toward her. "Look what happened to FYSH."

"That got something to do with organized crime?"

"I don't know."

"Where were you last night, Slow Mo? Aren't you supposed to be FYSHBone's bodyguard?"

"FYSH liked to be left alone. Especially at night, so he can do his thing."

"His thing?" said Moretti. "His thing involve banging somebody else's girl?"

Slow Mo glared. "I know the lawyer put y'all on to me."

"You got an alibi for last night, Slow Mo?"

"I was home alone."

"Oh, did you just invite us into your home? Don't mind if we do. Get up!"

Slow Mo's apartment was a disaster. Dirty clothes all over the floor and on the furniture. Empty food containers and garbage. Flies. Cassandra was glad the local precinct was there to search.

Moretti deposited Slow Mo in a chair. He put the big gun out of reach. Cassandra had the casings.

Moretti looked around. He kicked garbage out of his way. "Living the high life, huh, Slow Mo? Must be time for your afternoon snack of three thousand calories. Where's the necklace?"

"What necklace?"

"You know the one."

Slow Mo looked at Moretti and waited.

"We know you had a motive to kill FYSHBone. And

you got zero alibi, Slow Mo. Face reality. You're automatically at the top of the list."

"The lawyer told you that."

"Anybody can see. You grew up across the hall from FYSHBone in a hellhole. He makes it big and look at you. FYSHBone's errand boy living in a pig sty. Then he takes your girl?"

"That lawyer's got you so far off the scent."

Cassandra asked how.

"He was the one who wanted to make this crazy deal."

"A drug deal?"

"No. With the British dude from TV. The one who's always climbing things and scuba diving. He owns KAMIKAZE Vynil."

"Leland Bishop? What kind of deal was he doing with FYSHBone?"

"Some shit where they make a new company that owns all of FYSHBone's music. That was supposed to happen today."

Sabio had said Bishop was at the office to offer support. "What makes you bring that up? What's it got to do with the murder?"

"FYSH said he wouldn't know until the last minute if he was gonna sign."

"And?"

"He wasn't dealing with shorties selling nickel bags, lady. Big business will hire a contract killer to get rid of you like bad merchandise."

Slow Mo looked at Moretti. "That's why I thought you was a hitman."

"Why would anybody pay good money to have *you* whacked?"

"They killed FYSHBone. They might wanna bury his secrets, too."

"Yeah? Which ones?"

Slow Mo kept his mouth shut.

Cassandra said, "Why did you keep saying that you don't know anything?"

The big man remained silent.

"What about Princesa? FYSH was breaking up with her, right?"

"FYSH was always attracted to the wrong ones."

"What was so wrong about Princesa?"

"Go talk to her, you'll see."

"Was she angry FYSHBone was leaving her?"

"She's hot-blooded and she talks crazy. One time she threw an ashtray through a TV because they showed a commercial about hungry kids with cleft palates and FYSH didn't change the channel fast enough."

"What was going on between the lawyer and FYSH-Bone?"

"That lawyer was a nobody trying to make his name and fortune off FYSH. He ain't even from New York. He grew up in Chicago."

"How does he gain from FYSHBone's death?"

"Watch what he does now. I bet he tries to get his paintings back."

"Paintings?"

"He kept losing them to FYSHBone behind bad bets. It wounded his pride. FYSHBone didn't even like the paintings. He just likes to win."

Cassandra said, "That ain't worth shooting someone over, is it?"

"Pride? Pride is the only thing that doesn't have a price."

"Like *you* know," said Moretti. "Why would the lawyer be talking to Gator Moses?"

"You saw Gator? When? You didn't mention me, did you? Did you tell him you were coming to see me? You know what—I got nothing else to say."

"Why are you afraid of Gator?"

"Ain't you afraid of the dark arts?"

Moretti stepped back.

Cassandra did not like that comment either and decided to ignore it. "You grew up across the hall from FYSHBone. What was his family like?"

"I don't remember FYSHBone's father."

"What about his mother?"

"The head of the family. Made FYSH play piano for hours."

"Didn't he like it?"

"FYSH wanted to quit piano after his father died. His mother didn't allow it."

Cassandra said, "Wasn't FYSH only seven when his father died?"

"He had been playing for years by then. He always played. We could hear him practice from our apartment. Hours every night."

"Nobody complained?"

"He played beautifully. I can't believe he's gone."

Slow Mo pressed his lips together. His eyes watered.

Cassandra said, "You loved him, didn't you?"

Moretti glanced at her as if it were a senseless question.

Slow Mo's voice had the timbre of genuine grief.

"I could never make friends growing up. FYSH was always good at sports and he was always a captain and he always made sure to pick me and let me play. Gave me a chance to touch the ball. Like a big brother. You know what that is? When all the men in a community got the system on their backs?"

Moretti said, "Too bad I forgot my violin. But again, what about the fact FYSHBone had to take all the girls?"

"That's just the way it was."

Moretti looked incredulous.

"Man, if I didn't get any papaya I would be in a rage. I wouldn't care if it was Jack Kennedy standing in the way."

Slow Mo did not respond.

Moretti raised his voice.

"Guys, take this sack out of here. I've had enough."

The local precinct would process Slow Mo for firing at an officer. Moretti would swear out a complaint.

As Slow Mo was led away, Cassandra took a shot and asked if he knew "Clementi."

"Is that an Italian restaurant?"

Moretti pointed at the gun. "You better pray this ain't the murder weapon, Slow Mo."

"Man, I'm not saying another word. I want a lawyer. And it better not be that backstabber Guzmán!"

CHAPTER 21

Star-Crossed Lovers
(Soul Sonic Force)

After his encounter with Gator, Sabio went to his reefer spot in Bushwick.

He then stopped at a strip joint in Long Island City on the Queens side of the Queensboro Bridge to place a big bet with one of the few bookies in town who still took Sabio's action.

He passed on a free lapdance.

Once behind the wheel again, he puffed and inched across the bridge. It was past two in the afternoon.

Good thing Sabio had removed the documents from the laptop bag and stuffed them in his pants before he left FYSHBone's mother's building. Otherwise, when Gator had his woman go through the bag, they would have learned what Sabio was up to. Something told Sabio that would not have been good.

The pimp's woman, Oxana, had left a chocolate fingerprint on the laptop, but the machine had no power, so she wouldn't have been able to see anything.

Sabio was glad to be past that encounter. He smoked

weed in stop-and-go traffic over the East River. The high
bridge fed into Midtown Manhattan at Fifty-ninth Street.
A red-and-white air tram like a large enclosed ski lift
glided and dangled high above the water to his right.

Sabio agreed with the guy from *The Great Gatsby*: To
see Manhattan from this particular bridge is always to see
New York City for the first time. He did not mind that the
traffic moved slowly.

The river beneath shattered sunlight. A big boat
floated. Sabio reflected on the night he had met FYSH-
Bone, a wild night when his life took a very rough turn,
many years ago.

It was a West Side story at the old Copacabana on West
Fifty-seventh Street in Manhattan, where Sabio, the Chicago transplant, had been a regular since law school.

Salsa had been his father's music, but Sabio's first night
at the Copa he became a fanatic. The wall behind the
stage was decorated with a display made of thousands of
tiny lights in the shape of fireworks exploding over the
New York City skyline. La India sang with such power
the hairs on Sabio's arms stood on end.

Sabio had met FYSHBone in the early days of his practice. The lawyer's "office" then was actually his studio
apartment off the Grand Concourse, the back of his sput-
tering car, the courthouse steps, wherever he could open a
briefcase and work a cell.

Sometimes Sabio would hang where gangsters flaunted,
like Jimmy's Bronx Café. He would plant business cards
on everyone and brag that they should hire him while they
could still afford to.

This rarely yielded business, but sometimes it put him in circles where champagne corks flew and somebody else settled the bill.

The night he met FYSHBone, Sabio was in the disco room at the Copa, where DJs mixed hip-hop, freestyle, and house. He danced with a gorgeous twenty-two-year-old single mother from Mott Haven. They made lots of eye contact and jammed in unison to the crazy beat in the Jungle Brothers' "I'll House You."

Sabio shouted over the music, "Ever meet someone and feel it was destiny?"

The fine female did not roll her eyes, but she did not bat her lashes either.

Someone bumped Sabio from behind. He swung around and saw Slow Mo for the first time.

Dressed all green in Jets gear, hat tilted to the side, the fat young man swept people out of the way. He was followed by a posse of other black men all dressed in the same green gear.

FYSHBone the rap phenomenon rode in the pocket created by his linemen. The entourage pressed toward the long bar in the back, and suddenly all of the energy in the crowded room focused on them.

People stopped dancing to crane their necks and point and smile about FYSHBone.

The single mother from Mott Haven slapped her thigh. "I gotta tell my girl in the salsa room. She's FYSHBone's biggest fan. We'll meet again later."

She split.

Sabio never got her name. *Damn.*

He moved to the bar. The bartenders collected at FYSHBone's end.

The DJ spun into a string of songs for break-dancing. A crew of young B-Boys had collected near FYSHBone's crew.

The B-Boys began to battle.

They competed to outbreak one another, but also for FYSHBone's attention. He clapped with the rest of the crowd.

That is until "Planet Rock" came on.

The music got into FYSHBone. He jumped into the circle and went straight for the most skillful dancer.

FYSHBone top-rocked, Bronx-rocked, Brooklyn-rocked, Latin-rocked, and pop-locked. He did a variety of drops, including the coin drop, knee drop, sweep drop, and corkscrew. He flared and did windmills, then spun up into the classic arms-crossed freeze.

The young B-Boy hopped on his hands with legs straight in the air. He went down into a hand glide where he balanced his entire body on one extended forearm and propelled himself in circles with the other hand. He did power moves, like the Boomerang, the Gorilla, and the Buddha.

Sabio was impressed. The single mother from Mott Haven and her butch homegirl returned and pushed their way to the front of the circle. They clapped and cheered FYSHBone on.

FYSHBone jacked the competition with freezes and a back flip. He clobbered the B-Boy with crisp centipedes and halos.

By the time the song rocketed to its climax, the two were locked in a battle of head spins, legs in the air. They literally spun on the tops of their heads like old-fashioned tops, watching to see who would quit first.

The chorus pushed them to rock it and not stop it, over and over.

The entourage shouted the chorus.

The head spins continued.

Finally the kid toppled. FYSHBone rode out the song and leaped up, victorious. The crowd roared.

Sabio's twenty wilted in his hand. No bartender looked away from the dance battle.

"Yo! Long Island Iced Tea!"

All three bartenders ignored Sabio to watch FYSH-Bone light a giant victory cigar.

Sabio recalled something his mother had said: Every man who needs a big cigar is a *comemierda* and a back-stabber. Sabio leaned toward the bartender with the implants.

"Can I order?"

She gave Sabio the "wait a minute" with the index finger. That was enough. Sabio tapped one of FYSHBone's bodyguards.

"No autographs."

"I look like I need his signature? I wanted to comp everybody's drinks, but I guess not."

The bodyguard said, "My bad," and stepped aside.

Sabio threw his arms wide. "FYSHBone!"

FYSHBone looked annoyed to have his cigar puffing interrupted.

Sabio put an arm around his shoulder. "Sorry to cut in, I know you're a big star, but I need those silicone snow cones behind the bar to mix me a drink."

FYSHBone's hazel eye seemed to spin. "That it?"

"That's it, brother."

FYSHBone glared at the bodyguard who let Sabio into the circle. He turned to the bartender.

"Why you making him wait?"

The bartender got busy.

Sabio's instinct for self-promotion kicked in. He pulled the silver business card case that his ex had given him when he graduated from law school. Her final gift.

"By the way, I'm a lawyer. Put my card in your wallet. I'm sure you have counsel, but I'm a hustler."

FYSHBone handed the card to one of his bodyguards. Sabio's drink arrived without a smile.

"What makes you such a hungry lawyer?"

Sabio took a sip, really tasted it. "I grew up in Chicago. Skinny fish get eaten in that town."

FYSHBone hopped in place. "Never heard a shyster talk like that. You know my music?"

"I like 'Dead Niggaz (Tell No Tales).' Really paints a picture of how cutthroat the business is."

"No doubt."

Sabio dismissed himself. "Anyway, you find yourself in a jam, superstar, give me a call."

The lawyer threw the weary twenty on the bar and turned to go.

FYSHBone grabbed his elbow. "Hold up, G. What are you doing after this?"

The next thing Sabio knew he was puffing a giant spliff on a big, fast boat named the *Pequod*, navigated by one of FYSHBone's henchmen.

It was the same boat used in the video for FYSHBone's recent smash, except now there were no bikini-clad females, just Sabio, FYSHBone, and his men.

The sea air was fresh and cool. The clouds were sparse. There were many stars.

Sabio felt part of the clique. Like a Jet with his first cigarette. Like when he almost joined his cousin Eddie's street gang growing up in Chicago.

Heavy metal blasted from a giant boombox.

The June moon was big, bright, and silver, high in the night sky. It electrified the sea.

FYSHBone took the joint from Sabio. They were headed for a club in the Hamptons, a retreat for New York's wealthy.

"Women out here got class," said FYSHBone. "You can make it with two or three of them at once and not worry about disease."

Sabio held in reefer smoke and nodded even though he did not know that to be true. He had really felt for the single mother from Mott Haven and wished he hadn't lost track of her.

Slow Mo opened magnums of champagne and everyone smoked ganja.

FYSHBone had dumbbells on the boat and did curls in between puffs and sips of the bubbly. He was very strong for his size. His muscles were well-defined.

When they were really high, FYSHBone gave Sabio a tour of the boat. He let Sabio handle the wheel.

"Feels like another form of drunkenness," said Sabio.

FYSHBone said, "Like the sea itself is your own magic carpet."

In the stateroom, FYSHBone had a nautical chart spread on a table. He gave a short lecture on how the chart revealed depths of water and the topography of the seabed.

FYSHBone showed Sabio a gold divider. It was a measuring compass like an upside-down V, with two spiked ends that could be opened against a ruler and then used with one spike on point A and another on point B to measure distance on the chart. It was open, with the spikes about an inch apart.

The rapper then opened a fancy wooden box and removed a sextant. He explained that it was an instrument for measuring distance and was used in navigation. Made of metal, it was characterized by an arc with numbers indexed on it like a curved ruler, and about a foot long. Attached was a little telescope.

It had a strap. FYSHBone put his head through the loop and held the instrument gingerly.

"Gotta handle this beauty with care. Sturdy, but very sensitive. Any change to the calibrations and you're lost at sea. But so long as this is right? And the stars are out? You'll never lose your way."

Sabio admired the sextant.

"We have satellite," said FYSHBone, "but I keep this around in case the power fails. Can't always count on modern technology to get the job done."

Slow Mo came into the compartment. "Boss, they're here."

The pilot cut the engine. Sabio heard the hum of another boat.

FYSHBone put the sextant back in its box but did not close it. He slapped his hands together.

"Sabio, I forgot to mention we're making a quick stop on our way to the Hamptons. A little rendezvous. Do you mind?"

Another boat bringing the bikini babes? thought Sabio.

"Naw, FYSH, I don't mind."

"Sweet. Let's go up on deck."

*   *   *

The boat that pulled up was the same size as FYSHBone's. It was named the *Pretoria Princess*. The pilot shut off the engine and the boats were tied together with ropes side by side by FYSHBone's men.

The three men from the second boat boarded the *Pequod*.

Two were blonds. Platinums. Each had an Uzi submachine gun in his hands with a strap attached and looped over his head.

Suddenly, Sabio felt nervous.

The ringleader had a receding hairline and a red face. He held a briefcase in his left hand.

He shook hands with FYSHBone.

"Mr. Edwards."

"De Beers."

The man glanced around at FYSHBone's henchmen. He stopped at Sabio.

"Who is this?"

The man spoke English, but had a curious accent.

FYSHBone thumbed his nose. "That's my new lawyer, don't worry about him. He's just here to finally keep you South Africans honest."

Normally, Sabio would have been excited to hear someone like FYSHBone describe him as his lawyer. But they had not discussed representation. They had not come to terms on fees. And Sabio had no idea what was happening.

He fixated on the Uzis and decided it was not the right moment to pull FYSHBone aside for a conference.

De Beers lingered on Sabio's face. "You do not appear like an attorney."

That annoyed Sabio.

"Feel free to give me a test. If you can afford me."

FYSHBone put a firm hand on Sabio's shoulder and spoke to De Beers. "Let's go inside and do this."

They went back to the table with the nautical charts and the spiked divider and the sextant in its open case. The South African stood on one side with his two bodyguards behind. The Uzis dangled from their necks.

FYSHBone's men were scattered throughout. Slow Mo stood behind his boss. FYSHBone maneuvered Sabio to stand next to him. It was tight.

De Beers put the briefcase on the table.

"You have the money, Mr. Edwards?"

FYSHBone pursed his lips at the briefcase. "Let me see the merchandise."

De Beers paused. He opened the briefcase, turned it, and slid it across the table.

Diamonds sparkled. Lots of them.

FYSHBone rubbed his fingertips together. "Ice ice baby."

He took out a jeweler's loupe, the kind you put in your eye socket to get a good look at what is happening inside a gemstone. He picked random stones and eyeballed them.

"What clarity! Sabio, you have to see this."

FYSHBone made Sabio look through the loupe. The lawyer was clueless what to look for.

But the diamond *was* very bright. Like looking directly into the heart of the North Star. Sabio put it that way as a bit of BS and FYSHBone giggled and slapped him on the back.

He put the loupe away, replaced the diamond in the case, and shut the case.

"I'm gonna make a necklace and a pendant shaped like my KUTTHROAT Records trademark. You know, the toking fish skeleton?"

"That's hot," said Sabio, even though he did not think so.

"I'm gonna make jewelry for my momma and my sisters with the rest."

"Copacetic."

De Beers cleared his throat. "The money, Mr. Edwards?"

FYSHBone paused for a second. He smiled as if embarrassed. "About that."

De Beers stiffened. His face reddened.

"I had a little problem on my way to the bank."

"Mr. Edwards—"

"You said you wanted a million U.S. but you wanted it in Krugerrands, correct?"

"That's correct."

"I got all confused."

"You brought it in U.S. currency instead?"

"Well, actually . . ."

De Beers's eyes slanted. His face was the color of a live lobster.

"Mr. Edwards, this better be some stupid Afro-American joke."

"Or?"

De Beers was locked eye-to-eye with FYSHBone.

Sabio did not like this.

One of the South African bodyguards sniffed. *"Bleddie fokken kaffir."*

FYSHBone cocked his head. "Say what?"

De Beers slapped the table. "Pass my diamonds. We are leaving."

"Hold up," said FYSHBone. "What did your man just call me?"

"That is not relevant."

"Your man just called me a bloody fuckin' nigger. You think I don't speak Afrikaans?"

Slow Mo took a step forward. So did the others in FYSHBone's posse.

Sabio wished he'd stayed with the single mother from Mott Haven back at the Copa.

De Beers shifted.

FYSHBone stayed on him. "Know what *kaffir* actually means, De Beers? It's Arabic. It means infidel. Unfaithful to God. I ain't no nigger. And I ain't no infidel."

De Beers shook his head. "You do not deal in good faith. I told you one million U.S. in Krugerrands at last Monday's exchange rate. And you—"

FYSHBone reached under the table.

The bodyguards tensed.

FYSHBone moved slowly but deliberately and pulled up a briefcase. He dropped it on the table.

"There's your blood money, De Beers. In Krugerrands like you asked. Enough to shove up your ass. How many miners had to lose an arm for it?"

De Beers eyed the new briefcase greedily.

"I was joking about not having the money. I ain't joking *now*," said FYSHBone. "What are you gonna do about his insult?"

The boat rose and fell.

De Beers appeared unmoved.

"De Beers, I practice nonviolence, but I have my limits. Are you gonna punish your man, or am I?"

The boat pitched like a big bell.

"I'm not gonna ask again."

The mouthy bodyguard huffed. *"Jou ma se hond se poes, kaffir."*

"My mother's smelly what?!"

After that it happened so fast, Sabio did not blink.

FYSHBone leaped around the table, picked up the spiked golden divider on the way, spiked the offending bodyguard through his pale cheek. The result was a snake bite that lands two fangs.

"Yahh!"

The man winced, wide-eyed, and checked for blood. The injury would have left a scar, but would not have been life-threatening had he accepted FYSHBone's punishment.

But before blood or saliva even leaked, De Beers slammed the table and screamed, *"Vermoor halles!"*

The two guards reached for their Uzis.

They never got their hands on them.

FYSHBone's men must have drilled for this type of a maneuver, because they immediately pounced on the two guards. One of FYSHBone's soldiers yanked the strap that connected the offending bodyguard to his machine gun into a garrote and strangled him. Another of FYSH-Bone's men did the same to the other guard.

Meanwhile, FYSHBone spiked the divider through De Beers's hand, pinning him to the table. He went to town on De Beers's hairline with the arc of the solid metal sextant. He chopped at the skull.

The rest of FYSHBone's men produced long knives, and went on a sharklike feeding frenzy. Manic stab wounds one after the other to the backs, necks, and torsos of De Beers and his men, through their livers, spleens, kidneys, hearts, and lungs.

Sabio heard every wet puncture and every cracked rib despite the fact that the diamond dealers flailed their arms and screamed in their native tongues.

FYSHBone and his men kept at it. It was tribal. Like what the senators did to Caesar on the floor of the Senate. Sabio was terrified, frozen.

The three bloodied bodies finally dropped.

Silence rushed into the boat in the wake of the men's final screams.

FYSHBone and his bloody men breathed heavily.

Sabio held his breath.

Slow Mo's voice boomed. "FYSH! The lawyer's a witness."

Everyone turned their attention away from the corpses to look at Sabio.

The boat bobbed and Sabio felt the weight of FYSH-Bone and his men distribute away from him, then back again in a wave. Every eye was trained on him.

Sabio put his hand up. "Wait a minute."

FYSHBone moved toward Sabio.

"This was self-defense! I'm a lawyer. I can help!"

FYSHBone's chest heaved. The sextant was in his right hand.

Sabio backed away. He talked fast. "Don't do this, FYSH. Be smart."

He backed out onto the deck. FYSHBone stayed with him. The blood-splattered, knife-wielding posse followed their leader, all bug-eyed on Sabio, ready to finish their work.

Sabio kept the bloody sextant and FYSHBone's men and their long knives in the corners of his eyes, but he looked directly into FYSHBone's pupils.

"People at the Copa saw us, FYSH. They know me. Plus, look, watch. I'm gonna show you. Real slow. You'll appreciate this."

Sabio reached slowly into his pocket. He brought up his cell.

"See?"

He threw it into the ocean.

"Now you don't know who I told I was with you. I come up missing, you will be the first suspect. Let me help."

FYSHBone held his place.

Slow Mo held his forehead. "Ice that muthafucka!"

"No, listen! Put the weapon down. Lawyers can't testify against their clients."

"He don't work for you!"

"Even if you ain't my client, you brought me out here to discuss business, FYSH. You told De Beers I was your lawyer. Whatever I learn is private. Right now I can't hurt you. You kill me, that's murder one. Death penalty."

FYSHBone stood in place.

Sabio searched for more. He lobbed a *Hail Mary*. "Dude, I'm a father."

Finally something cracked in FYSHone's madness. Tears began to stream. The sextant rested against his thigh.

"You're bigger than this, FYSH. Please."

FYSHBone and Sabio were face-to-face. Sabio reached slowly for the instrument.

FYSHBone released. He wept.

Sabio threw the sextant into the ocean. After that there was only the sound of the wind and the waves and the sobbing man.

Eventually, FYSHBone stopped crying.

"Slow Mo, get some bedsheets from below."

FYSHBone ordered his posse to wrap each body in a sheet along with some of the heavy dumbbells he had worked out with earlier. They used ropes to tie them tightly with nautical knots.

FYSHBone ordered the *Pequod* untied from the *Pretoria Princess* and sent some of his men aboard to follow in the South Africans' boat.

He ordered his pilot to take them farther out to sea.

The water foamed and the sea breeze that had so refreshed Sabio earlier now filled his sinuses with salt. The world grew dark. Thick clouds extinguished the once silvery moon.

Once FYSHBone felt they were far enough out, they flipped the bodies overboard. He took the golden divider that he had used for stabbing and tossed it into the ocean.

FYSHBone then took the two Uzis, one in each hand. He balanced on the bow of his boat and fired both at once into the air, arms upraised as if in praise. Muzzle flashes sparked the night like fireworks or private lightning. Their loud, explosive, disturbing strafing echoed across the solemn surface of the ocean. The rapid kickbacks vibrated FYSHBone's arms and body as if by electric current.

When the Uzis were empty, FYSHBone looked at Sabio.

"Been a while since I fired one of those."

He tossed the empty weapons into the water after their owners.

"Been a long time, too, since I hurt anyone like that. I hate to do it. But he really shouldn't have said anything about my momma. And when he did, he should have taken his punishment like a man."

Sabio was not so sure about the morals on that one, but at the moment he did not care to register any objections.

Under FYSHBone's orders, they moved the two boats from that location even farther out to sea. FYSHBone's men then ransacked the *Pretoria Princess*. They found nothing of value. One asked whether FYSHBone wanted to pilfer the South African's sextant, now that his was lost.

"Never rely on somebody else's compass," said FYSH-Bone, without looking at anyone.

His men drained the *Pretoria*'s fuel into canisters, then poured all of that throughout the boat.

They evacuated.

The *Pequod* moved away a safe distance.

FYSHBone balanced on the bow of his boat again.

In his hand was a flare gun. He extended his arms as if on a cross, his head turned toward the gasoline-soaked boat, the flare gun pointed. Sabio smelled the fumes.

FYSHBone said, "I commit thee to the sea," and pulled the trigger.

The flare rocketed to its target. There was a five-second pause, then *whoosh!* Loud flames engulfed the *Pretoria Princess*. Slowly, an unforgettable fire ate the body of the boat.

FYSHBone and his men watched the entire sacrifice, entranced. The firelight bounced off their blood-smeared faces and danced in their eyes.

The sea finally swallowed the boat, fire and all.

The *Pequod* sped off. They churned back toward Manhattan.

Sabio stood at the bow of FYSHBone's boat and prayed. He did not know yet whether his head was out of the noose. Certainly the rest of the crew did not look convinced. He hoped none knew the law on attorney-client privilege.

They passed beneath the massive blue-gray Verrazano Bridge, the tragic one from *Saturday Night Fever*. It was still dark, but on the edge of the purple that heralds the day's first light. They cruised toward the Twin Towers.

Sabio looked up at the Statue of Liberty's face. She looked unhappy.

Someone approached from behind.

Sabio reasoned it made less sense to kill him in city waters, but braced himself.

FYSHBone stood right behind him and spoke to Sabio's back.

"Violence is not a way to resolve our differences, Sabio. But they were going to kill us all. You saw that."

Sabio did not turn all the way but spoke over his shoulder.

"I understand," he said, even though he did not.

"Sabio, I need to know that you are not a rat."

"I'll take it to the grave."

There followed a long silence. "Good."

FYSHBone stepped next to Sabio and put an arm around him.

"You think on your feet. Plus you're street. You're my type of lawyer."

FYSHBone stuffed a fat envelope into Sabio's jacket pocket.

"Twenty thousand in hundreds. Not a bribe. A retainer. Bill me at your usual rate. We're gonna burn through it quick. You work for me now."

He handed Sabio a cellphone. "That's your glass slipper. When I need you, I'll call. Make sure you answer."

*   *   *

That was many years ago. Since then Sabio had become
FYSHBone's full-time lawyer. Over the years he had done
some fine work. The deal with KAMIKAZE Vynil was
set to be his biggest move yet.

As to why Sabio did not run from those thugs at first
light, an army of Upper West Side psychiatrists could not
properly answer.

What was certain now was that FYSHBone was dead
and Sabio's ass was in a vise. Slow Mo had never wanted
to let Sabio live. The fact that FYSHBone was no longer
around to protect Sabio meant *that* insurance policy was
canceled.

Now the pissing contest between Leland Bishop and
FYSHBone's mother threatened to push Sabio into Gator's
clutches.

Everything Sabio had worked for all these years had
turned to dust.

He needed to know what FYSHBone had kept on the
laptop, so he needed a replacement charger. He needed
to figure out how to close the $145 million gap between
Bishop and his new client, FYSHBone's mother. And he
needed some fast cash to get Gator Moses temporarily off
his back.

That meant Sabio needed to win his bet on his home
team, the Chicago Cubs, to win super big on the road.
Always a long shot. Maybe this time his ship would
come in.

CHAPTER 22

Strange Bird

After the detectives left Slow Mo's apartment, Moretti drove Cassandra back to the Bronx so she could get her minivan and pick up Jason.

By the time she climbed into her van, she had an hour before the end of Jason's school day, five o'clock. Cassandra put on soft music and drove, relaxed, enjoying a few minutes of alone time.

Her phone interrupted with a callback from Princesa De los Santos's assistant. Princesa was in the middle of a shopping spree and would be available for interview on a Madison Avenue street corner during a coffee stop in fifteen minutes.

The supermodel would only grant a five-minute interview.

Cassandra made a face. "Does your boss understand this is a murder investigation? Her boyfriend was killed."

"She's considering hopping a jet to Rio. Move now or you may not see her again until Fashion Week."

Cassandra checked the time. The rendezvous was on the way to Jason's school. She'd be cutting it close.

"Tell her to be on time."

Of course the model was not there when Cassandra arrived. Cassandra called and got voicemail.

She called Jason's school and warned them she might be late.

The teacher responded, in an annoyed tone, "Please hurry."

The problem was not common courtesy or that the teacher would abandon Cassandra's son. The problem was Jason's dependence on routine. The longer he waited, the more agitated he became. That made him a lot harder to care for. If Cassandra dragged on long enough he could be out of sorts for the rest of the evening. She didn't want that for him or for anybody involved in taking care of him.

The model's assistant called when they were fifteen minutes late to say that she was fifteen minutes away.

"You tell Ms. De los Santos that if she's not here in *five* minutes I'm leaving and I will call INS, so that she is not allowed to leave the country until we're finished with our investigation."

"Actually, Ms. De los Santos just consulted an attorney and knows that you cannot do that."

Cassandra was caught off-guard.

Princesa De los Santos was talking to a lawyer about fleeing? Why?

"She will be there in fifteen minutes, Detective. I'll warn you now, though, no pictures, no autographs, so don't ask."

*   *   *

A long pink limousine finally arrived. It was led by a black SUV with black-tinted windows and followed by another, similar SUV.

All three vehicles double parked in a row. Bodyguards in sunglasses and dark suits jumped out of every vehicle, checked up and down the sidewalks, and redirected pedestrians from the zone.

One of the guards wore a suit and a bowler hat that reminded Cassandra of the assassin in *Goldfinger.*

He opened the limo door. An anxious-looking, freckle-faced, college-aged woman got out. She hauled a huge shoulder bag, worked a cellphone, and held an enormous, clawing white cat. Cassandra made her for the assistant.

Everyone waited. Two or three minutes later a long, thin, tan leg in a pointy-toed stiletto emerged. It was followed by another.

Both legs stretched to a white miniskirt without hips, to a yellow blouse over a flat chest, to a triangular face with a pointy chin framed by big white circular sunglasses. The woman wore a garland of long black silken hair.

Cassandra approached. The bodyguards moved toward her, but she flashed her shield.

The model addressed her assistant. "Is this the person who requested an interview?"

The assistant clicked to end her phone call but was not fast enough. Princesa slapped the cell out of her hands. It cracked on the sidewalk.

"I spoke to you."

The assistant picked up the pieces. The white cat squirmed and hissed.

"Yes, Princesa, it's about FYSHBone."

"What does she want to know?"

Cassandra interjected: "Ms. De los Santos, do you mind? Address me directly."

Princesa De los Santos looked down at Cassandra. With her natural height and in the stilettos the model appeared to be a full head and a half taller.

"I have a funeral and nothing to wear. Nobody expects a 'black' event in midsummer. Let's make this quick."

The assistant wrestled the clawing cat into the shoulder bag, zippered it to the neck, then hustled into the café.

"You were dating FYSHBone?"

"He was in love with me."

"Was it exclusive?"

"I was expecting diamonds."

"How long were you dating?"

"A few weeks."

The woman moved fast. "Still in the honeymoon phase, huh? How was your relationship?"

"He couldn't stop thinking about me."

Cassandra wondered whether this was an attempt to throw her off the scent, or maybe a coping mechanism. Denial of some sort.

"Any idea who did this to him?"

"No. Is this going to make the news?"

"What?"

"The fact that I'm cooperating?"

"I'll be discreet."

"No, I mean it would be great if you could plant the story. I have someone negotiating with *People*. 'Public figure. Private pain,' that kind of thing. I figure I can pose for the cover next to a window looking sad with my big white pussycat. FYSHBone gave her to me."

Princesa removed her shades. Her eyes were enormous and supernatural, gray, innocent, and striking. She struck the sad pose she used to make millions. The one she intended for the magazine profiling her "grief." She held that sad pose with a slight pout that could make anyone wonder.

The model replaced her shades.

"I'll have to drug the cat, because she's not a professional and won't hold still."

"FYSHBone ever complain about his colleagues or other rappers?"

"No."

"He ever mention gangsters? Criminals, people from the past?"

"We hardly speak."

Sounds like true love. "Know a jerk named Gator?"

"Like an alligator purse? No."

"What did you think of Slow Mo?"

"Honestly? I don't like fat people."

Cassandra was starting to think she had wasted her time and needlessly put her son, his teacher, herself, and possibly even her mom through a prolonged frustration.

"Was FYSHBone the jealous type?"

"Aren't they all?"

"Are you?"

Princesa looked down her long, thin, pointy nose. "Why would a supermodel be jealous of anything?"

She must be on drugs. "You contacted FYSHBone quite a bit by cell. All the time. In fact FYSHBone would describe the contact as obsessive."

"Men crave attention."

Princesa tilted her head as if spotting something from afar. "FYSH did complain about the lawyer a lot."

Cassandra arched an eyebrow. "Sabio Guzmán?"

"FYSHBone didn't trust him."

"Over what?"

"He often said the lawyer was a liar, a backstabber, not that smart. He was letting him go once the deal got signed."

Really? "You know about the deal?"

"Puto was obsessed."

"Who?"

"FYSHBone."

"I thought you guys hardly talked."

"A man doesn't need to speak much for you to know his obsessions."

Cassandra felt annoyed to be lectured on anything, especially on the subject of men, and especially by a cracked pearl like Princesa De los Santos.

"So in all of his silent obsession about the deal, did you get the sense that FYSHBone had cause for concern?"

"My man liked to say that all of life was a life-or-death situation."

"What do you think about this static with the lawyer? Was it serious?"

"Macho stuff. Roosters. FYSHBone wanted to poison me against Sabio."

"Because?"

"I was with him first."

"Come again?"

"The lawyer. I met him at an event. We dated, but every time, FYSHBone would show, invite himself to our table, take over. One time I had to escape paparazzi through a back door. My limo was in front. Puto was smart enough to park his Hummer near the rear. I left with him."

"How did Sabio take getting cut off?"

"We never spoke again. FYSHBone kept him dismissed."

Cassandra did not know why it mattered, but asked anyway. "How did you feel? Dumping a guy for his boss?"

"The lawyer has no money. He's not even famous. It wasn't serious."

Cassandra said nothing.

"Don't get me wrong, Detective. I know there's more to life. And Puto was good at those. A strong hand. A good listener. He was funny. He baked me a cookie in the shape of a heart once. I tell you, he was in love."

Cassandra went hard. "So, how did it feel to know FYSHBone was leaving you?"

Princesa's mouth got very small, as if she had sucked a super-sour lemon. "Don't believe everything you read on the Internet."

"How about your texting to FYSH that you weren't going to let him get away? That he used you? That you didn't know what you might do?"

"Those texts are taken out of context. You never said anything crazy to a man?"

Keep me out of it. "Where were you last night, Princesa?"

It was impossible to see the model's eyes behind the big, white, round sunglasses. "I spent the afternoon stripping out of string bikinis."

"What does that have to do with where you were after midnight?"

"Hello? Bikini work is grueling. It always means I

spend the rest of the evening with my feet in ice and a migraine, with the lights off, alone."

Cassandra thought, *You can't make this up.* "You know about Clementi?"

"Is that that new designer out of Milan? They'll need to contact my agency."

Cassandra clicked off her pen.

The assistant emerged from the coffee shop on a different cell from the one that got cracked. She carried a massive cup of coffee topped with foam.

Princesa took it and sipped. She looked at the assistant.

Princesa raised the cup as if she might throw the hot drink in the assistant's freckled face.

Cassandra almost grabbed her arm.

Princesa poured the coffee to the ground. "Go tell those fat women 'skim.' And more foam." She tossed the empty cup.

"Right away."

The young woman picked up the empty coffee cup, turned, and rushed into the shop.

Cassandra looked at Princesa. Ordinarily a girlfriend would be a perfect person to ask to care for a dead man's dog. In this case, the mutt might be better off with a lethal injection.

Princesa licked foam off her top lip. "Can I go?"

"Please do."

"Good. My personal shopper'll eat his fingers until I show."

CHAPTER 23

Labios Compartidos (La Locura Automática)

By the time Cassandra got to Jason it was past five. He was spinning in angry circles.

He repeated, "Caca!" which was how he described anything unpleasant.

Spinach with his chicken?

"Caca!"

Changing the TV from cartoons to news?

"Caca!"

Shower time?

"Caca!"

Last boy picked up again?

"Caca! Caca! Caca!"

He had been stuck on the word for two years.

Cassandra got down to his level and took him in a bear hug, as she had read that it was his extraordinary need for sensory input that made him run around like that. The enveloping hug soothed that need. She hugged and apologized.

"Caca!"

"I know. Mommy needs to be here. I hear you."

"Caca!"

"Okay, Papito."

Cassandra hugged him and rubbed his back.

"Caca."

"Can we just take it down a notch?"

He said it again.

"Jason, please?"

He took it down. "Caca."

Nice and soft. Cassandra relished it when he responded.

"Can we go to the car now?"

Jason did not look at her, but she was certain that he thought about it.

"Let's go, Papi."

She took him by the hand and he followed.

Traffic was bumper-to-bumper at rush hour, but the boy was fine with his toy cars in the backseat and his water-fall-sounds CD turned loud.

A school administrator had been good enough to hand Cassandra a bill on the way out. Jason was in private school because no public school was equipped to handle him. Altogether what Cassandra spent on his education annually equalled one full year's salary at detective third grade, if she worked tons of overtime, plus a little more.

Cassandra managed, because under the law the city was obligated to pay for her son's tuition. The problem was every year she was required to pay first, then hire a lawyer. And even though she worked for the city, she had to sue the city for reimbursement and prove once again to the city that city schools were not equipped to handle Jason.

Cassandra had gotten the seed to juggle this enterprise by taking out a terrifying home equity loan. The whole thing was Kafkaesque and a house of cards that never evened out, since every year Cassandra put out more than she recovered, not to mention her time and stress, which were completely uncompensated.

It was worth it.

Jason's school emphasized traditional, cutting-edge, and rational techniques with proper structure and socialization and a one-to-one student-teacher ratio that left Cassandra feeling that her son was in the right hands.

Jason had not gotten the early intervention that might have meant a difference, because Cassandra had not understood the depth of his condition or the bureaucracy involved.

Her guilt over that was unfixable.

But her son had improved during his time at the school, and she was grateful to God for the means.

The ringtone on her cellphone was Ivy Queen, *"Que Lloren."*

It was Moretti.

"Yeah, Lou?"

"Got a text saying the preliminary autopsy is complete. How far away are you from Bellevue Morgue?"

Cassandra grimaced. "Still headed uptown, Lou."

"You mean you ain't even made it to the Bronx yet?"

Cassandra reported that the interview with Princesa had pushed her back a half hour.

"It's gonna take you at least another half hour to get your kid home and get back down, Maldonado."

"At least."

"I don't know about this. Is this going to be every day?"

"Only weekdays."

"That supposed to be a joke? Anyway, after the ME we got a meeting with Captain Vargas and the rest of the squad. We gotta see what everyone's been up to. Figure out which way we're going with this. Don't take no more than a half hour, Maldonado. I don't wanna go into that morgue alone."

Cassandra picked up speed and changed lanes to make progress. Jason sensed her shift in focus and began to kick the back of her seat.

Cassandra expected an outburst. She tensed.

This was when she began to resent things—in those unexpected moments when the stress persisted, when every effort to calm the storm provided only moments of relief, when suddenly she got hit with another minor crisis, another threat, another intrusion into the fleeting quiet that never really came.

This was not how she had imagined things would be.

Cassandra had married Michael to have a partner, to have a lover, to build a life with him. She had married Michael so she would never have to face the tough moments alone.

Today she had none of that.

The marriage got hard and life got hard, the facts got hard, and Michael went soft. Michael ran away. Michael decided he could wipe the slate clean and start all over, go all the way back to adolescence. He did that, and Cassandra was left to play the grownup.

Not that Michael was Jason's father. He wasn't.

Jason's father was a young thug from the building where Cassandra grew up. She had messed with him because it angered her father, and it ended the way that story always does.

Jason's father never worked or provided a cent or came around, which was just as well. Getting knocked up by a punk was the script where Cassandra grew up. Even though she had avoided all the pitfalls and graduated from high school with honors, second in her class, by the time she entered her twenties Cassandra was ready for rebellion. Big mistake, and it completed the work of alienating her from her father.

But she gained her son, and *he* gave every hardship purpose.

Michael, on the other hand, was an unexpected turn.

Cassandra had met her ex-husband at a racket, which is cop slang for a cop party, a scene dipped in liquor, testosterone, tough talk, and guns. Cassandra was a rookie but went with girls from the precinct.

The sandy-blond ESU officer came straight toward her, still in uniform.

"What up, *bonita*?"

"Impressed with your own Spanish?"

The white man grinned. He had nice teeth. Lots of them.

"Getting a taste on duty, Officer?"

"What, this?" He held up the plastic cup full of suds. "Strictly nonalcoholic."

A nice thick head of hair. His name was Michael Patrick Finnegan.

"How unique," she said. "An Irish cop."

"Fourth generation. You on the job?"

"Would I be here if I wasn't?"

"You could be a cop groupie."

"You wish."

"You're right, *bonita*. I do."

Just like that they were a couple. Michael was fun and respectful, he opened doors, he paid, and he even gave her baby-sitter money for her one-and-a-half-year-old.

He told Cassandra not to worry.

"One day I'll teach your mother how to make Irish stew. She'll love me for it."

For their first Valentine's Michael did the dinner, flowers, and chocolates, but what got Cassandra was that he brought a teddy bear for Jason.

He told her he wanted a house full of kids.

"What if one of them is the older stepbrother?"

"Any kid who lives in my house, *bonita*, is mine. Heart, body, and soul."

That was before Jason was diagnosed or Cassandra even understood that there could be something seriously wrong with him.

They sometimes brought Jason along, and Michael would hold and hug and even kiss the boy. One time he said Jason could pass for his son. It was not true, but the fact that he said it made Cassandra want to cry.

Cassandra lived with her mother and son in the projects. She did not want her son to grow up the way she had. That was why she became a cop, to provide a steady income and to get somewhere better by the time her child was ready for school.

Michael said, "Let's get married, *bonita*. We'll get our own place and make a family. Growing children need space. A basketball hoop in the driveway. Maybe even a yard."

Cassandra had always wanted a protector. Someone to make her feel like a princess. Her father never made her feel special.

She said yes, and Michael agreed to do it at St. Jerome's on Alexander Avenue across the street from where she grew up, cater-corner from the Forty-Fourth Precinct.

Within a month at their first apartment, Michael began to insist that they should buy a house. He promised to fix all that needed fixing, throw out the garbage, cap the toothpaste, and put the seat back down when he flushed.

They held their breath and with both of their incomes plus all of her savings and his parents' cosignatures, they bought the house in Castle Hill. Michael did most of what he said he would do, and they worked a lot, but she felt successful and happily married.

The problems started with Jason's diagnosis.

Cassandra's mother was the first to express concern that Jason was slow to speak and did not make eye contact. Michael said the boy did not want to connect.

When they got the results, Cassandra was scared and very sad and did not fully understand.

She was careful not to ask God why.

Michael made it sound okay by saying things that anyone might say—that things happen for a reason and that they would get through this as a family. He said God would provide and that it made him love Jason more.

Michael could feel so strong sometimes. She crawled into him.

Then it happened: "Mazel tov, Detective, you're pregnant."

Cassandra told her husband.

Michael stopped his rant. "Don't play with me, Cassie. You know how much I want this."

Cassandra smiled and rocked from side to side. She would never forget the way Michael jumped and lifted her with his powerful arms, spun her, kissed her stomach.

"This is it, baby. This is us! You and me. We'll live our dreams!"

The first six months were not a serenade.

There was the weight gain, the skin problems, the constant discomfort of pregnancy. Smells bothered her. Against her will the job dropped her from an undercover investigation into sweatshops and assigned her to a desk.

But she and Michael decorated the baby's room. They made love like they had that first spring. Michael slowed his drinking.

One morning at the start of the sixth month, Cassandra felt a solid, invisible punch. She dropped to her knees.

They lost the girl Michael wanted to name after a song.

"Not uncommon. There's nothing to say you can't try again."

Over months they went through it: sadness, anger, denial. Lovemaking became anxiety. Michael took his whiskey with less water. He said that he felt okay and that he knew God would send a child when they were ready.

His confidence inspired her.

Cassandra returned to undercover work. One morning

she awoke as the purple light seeped under their curtain. She barreled for the toilet. When she returned, Michael rolled over and put his arm over her.

"We're ready," he whispered. "Don't be afraid."

Cassandra sobbed into his chest. She wanted it to be so.

It happened again. The blood.

Michael's face came apart. "But why?"

He pulled away from her and into the bottle. One time he slurred, "Get pregnant again, Detective, take a leave of absence, why don't you?"

Cassandra pretended not to hear.

Sex became less passion, more a test of fate and faith, and she worried constantly that Michael would leave for someone more fertile. She checked his voicemails and emails and even tailed him from the station.

They would fight about it, and that would lead to screaming, shoving, hair pulling, and crying, but in the end Michael would wrap his strong arms around her and pull her in and tell her that it was her that he was in love with, that she was the one that he wanted. Cassandra. Cass. *Bonita*. Not some baby. Not some unseen, unborn person. Not some other woman. *Her*. His beauty, his love. His woman in flesh and blood. *She* was what he wanted. What he needed. *Her*. Nobody else.

When Michael talked like that and persisted and breathed on her and made faces, Cassandra wanted to tear her panties off.

But after that second miscarriage, she was through hoping. Cassandra was not quite ready to get her tubes tied, but she was finished just taking that risk.

*   *   *

Over time the marriage lost its bolts. Michael and Cassandra were on separate ice floes.

She became more serious about her career.

He became a more committed alcoholic.

They tried to get away and relight it all during one last glorious weekend in Boquerón in the southwest corner of Puerto Rico. A room with a balcony and a view of the smooth, clear, blue-green Caribbean. Michael booked it and she took this as a sign that he wanted things to work.

The sun drew close. They drank and laughed and floated in the salt water with their eyes to the sky. They kissed between waves and searched for seashells. Big boats docked in front of private condos and Michael fantasized.

"When I get mine I'll name it *Finnegan's Wake*. I'll take your old man fishing. That'll break his ice. Jason'll love it."

At night they barhopped, danced, and drank too much. In the street they people-watched. They ate shark shish kebabs and empanadillas spiked with Tabasco and filled with conch. They made out while Maná blasted from inside a bar.

They argued once on a side street. Michael caressed the nape of her neck and told her to forget it.

Cassandra beat her husband at billiards for the ten thousandth time, then let him win the last one. She sang karaoke, Shakira's *"La Tortura,"* and La Secta's *"La Locura Automática,"* the melancholy of which almost made her choke.

Michael led the ovation.

That night they made love with the lights off. The air conditioner ran very cold. Michael still tasted like the sea.

He mounted, and Cassandra was so ready, she arched and came within a minute. When it was his turn he pulled out and spilled himself on her back.

"Don't you like it inside?" she said.

"The condom broke."

The hallucination that they were a family evaporated like a drop of passion fruit nectar under the full Caribbean sun.

Back home, Cassandra returned from a tour of duty to find a letter taped to the bathroom mirror.

Oh, baby, please don't.

She ran around in a panic. Half of Michael's things were gone.

I gotta call. I gotta call.

Straight to voicemail.

"Papi, please, come back. We can talk about it." *Oh, God!* "I can change, Papi. Don't do this. Don't break up our family. I need you. Jason needs you. You're the only father he's ever known. Don't do this."

Why couldn't it be me, God? Why couldn't I make him love me?

"Michael, please."

The message timed out.

It wasn't fair. God, Michael was so good!

Cassandra could not give him what he needed and that was why this happened. The world was cruel! It was awful!

Cassandra looked at the new empty spaces on the shelves. The missing pieces of her life.

Their wedding portrait triggered a flood.

How she wanted him back!

But then she saw what Michael had left behind.

You bastard.

A picture of Michael with Jason. In it Cassandra's son looked so beautiful. He made direct eye contact with the camera and smiled like any other child. Cassandra had taken that picture and framed it as a gift for Michael for Father's Day.

And there it was like an empty wrapper.

Another knife in her gut. She really did feel like discarded waste.

She would never beg a man for anything again.

Without reading Michael's letter, Cassandra went to the stove, set the paper on fire, tossed it into the sink, and threw herself on their bed to mourn.

In the days, weeks, and months that followed, whenever Michael came around and tried to crawl into her bed, she just pictured her son's eyes in that picture and pushed the man away.

That was almost three years ago. The divorce was long since final. Since then, Cassandra had been all about carrying the mortgage and taking care of her son.

She dated a couple of men a couple of times and one man several times over several months. It was okay. Nothing that she had to do, and she really did not have the time. She was on hiatus.

The truth was that it still stung. The rejection. The failure.

How she had struggled to complete that picture that comes with the frame. To make Michael want her. To make him behave. To make him stay.

It did not work.

Many men wanted to sleep with her. The one she wanted went away.

What had Michael been thinking? Were any of the things he had said to her true?

Cassandra was afraid that she was not good enough. That her love and her body and her mind would never be enough. That she represented only a quick good time or a burden to a man. She felt a kind of shame about her failures as a woman and a mother, even though she knew better.

In any case, she was at a point these days where her body needed something. She was still a young woman. All that running in the park trying to lure the Marathon Slasher had her stoked.

She pulled into her driveway after the long drive. It never had gotten that basketball hoop Michael promised.

Most heads of households, at this time of day, they get to take a load off, sit down with their family to a decent dinner. Find out how everybody's day was.

Not Cassandra. It was back to the steel mill. Her mother took Jason inside. Cassandra was off.

Murder was to be investigated in Manhattan. Money needed to be made. Moretti waited at the morgue.

CHAPTER 24

Sonata in B♭ Minor

Moretti and Cassandra walked down a hallway inside the Bellevue Morgue. A young man wheeled a covered body.

Moretti popped a stick of gum. "You know Bellevue is French for 'beautiful view'?"

"Makes sense."

"Been to the morgue before?"

"When I was in the academy."

"Oh, right. The old 'shock and awe.' Let you watch an autopsy to thicken the stomach lining before you hit the streets."

"Worked on me," said Cassandra.

"Did you lose your lunch?"

She had, but she was not about to cop to that. "Cassie's always been a big girl, Lieutenant."

"Really? When the ME uses that saw to open the skull? Then he scoops the brain whole and puts it on a scale?"

They walked past the blue rubber tarp that hung over the entrance to the examining room. It was cool in there and didn't stink as one imagined it would.

The pathologist was listening to the *Moonlight Sonata*. He turned it down.

FYSHBone's nude body lay on an examining table. A sheet covered him from the waist down. His eye sockets were empty and purple and his face still had the waxen expression of shock that had frozen onto it at the moment of death.

Cassandra knew from her morgue trip with the academy that the pathologist used a scalpel to make a Y-shaped incision that curved under FYSHBone's pectorals and met at the breastbone to travel down to the pubic bone.

The blade was used to peel back the skin, fat, and muscle. The chest flap was pulled over FYSHBone's face to expose the ribcage and guts so his organs could be removed, weighed, and sampled. The Y-shaped incision was then sewn up.

Cassandra flashed to what the Marathon Slasher had tried to do to *her* face. She felt a chill.

"Good thing we got this outta the way before dinner," said Moretti.

The pathologist informed them that the victim's mother had just identified FYSHBone.

Moretti crossed his arms and nodded. "No great suprises, right, Doc? Death by gunshot?"

"Correct. Bullets entered the body at various points, including the head, torso, and groin. We recovered plenty of shrapnel, although there are various exit wounds. Proximate cause of death, for my money, is the bullet that entered his forehead."

The ME flicked the switch that lit an X-ray of the victim's skull. It looked like a closeup of the silvery moon.

The pathologist traced a dark streak with a pen. "This

one here sliced downward through the brain thusly, then severed the spinal cord at the cervical region on its way out of the body here."

"I'm betting that was the first shot," said Moretti.

"First and final where the patient was concerned. Pretty sure when that happened death was instantaneous, so the rest was just window dressing."

Cassandra said, "At least he didn't suffer." She went back to the body and pointed at a tattoo on FYSHBone's breastbone, right under the axis of the Y-shaped incision. "What was that?"

"A Sacred Heart tattoo. You can see he has tattoos all over. The rest are all music-related."

The pathologist handed over a file of pictures of all the tattoos, taken before surgery.

The images took work to figure out because of FYSH-Bone's dark brown skin, but he had several iconic ones. Bob Marley with guitar in lap and a large joint. Big Pun with a large Puerto Rican flag. Tupac from *All Eyez on Me*. Notorious B.I.G.

"Check this one out, Lou. Your *paisan*."

FYSHBone's biggest tattoo covered most of his back. It was a mug shot of a young Frank Sinatra.

The last two tattoos were on the inside of FYSH-Bone's wrists: musical notation and a Rolling Stones lips logo.

Cassandra asked the pathologist whether he had found a tattoo of the word "Clementi."

"The composer?"

Could that be it? A musical reference? Of course. "Who was Clementi?"

"He composed sonatas and sonatinas."

Moretti asked what those were.

"Classical music for piano. I took lessons as a boy and had to play them."

Interesting, thought Cassandra. "You read sheet music, Doc?"

"I'm rusty."

Cassandra pointed to the musical notes tattooed on FYSHBone's forearm. "What is that melody?"

The pathologist sounded it out: "Da-da, da-da da-da-da."

"Mean anything?"

"Not to me."

"Could it be from one of Clementi's pieces?"

"I don't recognize it, but that does not mean much. I started out thinking I would be a concert pianist but didn't have the fingers for it. Didn't have hands for surgery on live humans either, so I became a pathologist."

Moretti sniffed. "What about drugs?"

"Too soon for the lab work, but no needle marks for heroin or deviated septum for coke. He still has all his teeth. His lungs look pretty smoked out. He'd been drinking rum earlier and ate a ribeye steak somewhere within a few hours of death."

"Venereal disease?"

"No visible signs, but again we'll know after the lab work. He did have a vasectomy."

"Really?" Cassandra felt it went against type. "Any idea when?"

"At least a few years back, judging from the scarring."

Moretti said, "Anything else we should know?"

"Nope. Except the shots the killer supposedly took at the genitals actually entered the groin."

"Oh, when you said 'groin' earlier I thought you were using polite language."

"No, I meant the literal groin, the creases where the torso meets the legs."

Cassandra appreciated that the sheet covered this area. She did not need to see.

The pathologist said, "I mention it because everybody at the crime scene saw the bloody crotch and assumed he'd been shot in the privates. Angry lover or something."

Moretti asked the significance of shooting him in the literal groin.

"Not sure. Ordinarily I would say the shooter meant to guarantee death by hitting the femorals, which are major arteries that run up the thigh and lose massive blood when ruptured. In this case, as I said, the extent of the trauma from that first shot was certain to produce instant death. Those later shots were unnecessary."

Moretti looked at Cassandra. "We're back to the shooter making some kind of statement."

To her it was interesting that the shooter had not gone all the way to castration.

Moretti leaned close to the cadaver's ear. "FYSHBone! Tell us what happened!"

The sightless corpse said nothing.

Cassandra had more information, but felt no closer to the truth. They left the pathologist alone with his scalpel and sonatas.

CHAPTER 25

Clout

Cassandra drove down to One Police Plaza and walked in with Moretti. At that time of day any traffic was headed uptown, not down. They got to the Civic Center exit in a few minutes.

Moretti waited for Cassandra to park and walked with her toward headquarters.

"Maldonado, what's the supermodel girlfriend say?"

"Jumped off the bus at Crazytown."

"Nuts?"

"Mixed nuts."

"Psycho-killer nuts? Or Van Gogh 'I'd cut my own ear off' nuts?"

"I wouldn't say she's harmless, but I don't like her for the murder."

"Why not?"

"She gets worn out wearing string bikinis. She doesn't have the stomach for this."

"Does she have an alibi?"

"No. And she *is* hot-tempered and sadistic."

Cassandra recounted the cellphone breaking and acted out the coffee incident.

"The woman is too self-involved for the premeditation required for something like this."

"Interesting theory, Detective. What does it mean?"

"She lacks the focus. The passion, I guess."

"Do we know there was lots of planning here? This woman could have just been with the victim. He says the wrong thing, and BAM! She snaps."

"Possible."

"A person can form murderous intent in the blink of an eye."

Cassandra knew that to be true.

"I've seen men whimper after you notify them of their wife's demise to where the snot hangs from their nose," said Moretti. "Come to find out they got a mistress, secret bank accounts, tickets to Amsterdam, and if it wasn't for an errant hair fiber or a girlfriend with a big mouth they would've got away. Underestimate no one."

"I don't," said Cassandra. "I just don't know if Princesa has the disposition. And what does she gain by killing FYSHBone?"

"Well, if she's as bonkers as you say she is, her motive won't be rational. The classic 'spurned crazy woman goes off' fits just fine."

Cassandra answered her own question. "She does gain in that now her relationship with FYSHBone will be made public. She intends to capitalize on the publicity. She told me so."

"Why not? FYSHBone would. The supermodel sounds crazy as a fox."

Moretti took a phone call as they were about to enter the building. He hung up.

"About face. We've been summoned."

"By who?"

"City Hall."

City Hall is across the street from One Police Plaza. By the time the detectives had climbed the curved staircase inside the rotunda, Cassandra's nerves were twitching.

It had only been a day since her showdown with the mayor and the police commissioner following the Marathon Slasher press conference. While she had come away victorious, she wasn't interested in another round.

They badged their way past security, and the mayor's secretary showed them into his office. They walked in and found the police commissioner standing next to the mayor, who was dwarfed by the large chair behind his large desk.

A chair in front of the mayor's desk was occupied. The man in it looked straight at Cassandra.

"Butterfingers."

Cassandra felt her insides drop.

FBI Agent Erasmus Bollinger. A deputy director of the FBI office in New York and a major-league asshole.

Cassandra immediately flashed back to her awful experience with Bollinger. Years before, she had worked with him when she was assigned to score a quarter million dollars' worth of Ecstasy during a joint NYPD/FBI investigation.

The dealer would only meet Cassandra in the middle of the Williamsburg Bridge. Either end would be covered by FBI and NYPD backups. Train tracks pass down the middle. They figured the dealer had nowhere to run.

But nobody had imagined the dealer would walk a few feet from the exchange, shove the buy money into a black backpack, then tear up a protective fence to balance on a girder over the train tracks. Nobody knew he would be crazy or agile enough to jump down onto that moving stainless-steel train. Or that he would wave good-bye to Cassandra after he did that, like the French guy getting away in *The French Connection*.

Cassandra had signed for the prerecorded buy money. That made her responsible for it.

The dealer climbed down between cars and went inside as the train fed into the dark subway tunnel. Nobody from either enforcement agency had thought to cover this contingency. The quarter million was in the subway and easily within a minute of a million yellow taxicabs—the perfect New York City camouflage.

Cassandra got blamed. Bollinger, who had put the thing together in the first place, called her Butterfingers. The nickname stuck.

Cassandra had not seen Bollinger in years. Now suddenly here he was in the mayor's office on her first day with the HI-PRO Unit.

A terrible omen.

Moretti knew the FBI man as well. "Bollinger."

"Moretti."

Moretti spoke to the commissioner. "Sir, I thought you called us in for a sitdown on the FYSHBone file?"

The mayor blinked. "FBI asked for this meeting."

"What do the Feds have to do with our homicide?"

Bollinger put down his teacup. "You and Butterfingers stopped Gator Moses earlier today."

Moretti put his hands out. "And? He failed to signal."

"It was an illegal stop. You tried to plant a gun."

"You're out of your mind, Bollinger."

"The real problem is you unwittingly stumbled across an ongoing federal investigation. Lay off Gator Moses. Do not try to connect him to the rapper."

Moretti knotted his eyebrows. "What? Why not?"

"The less said the better. You don't exactly have a reputation as a locked safe."

Moretti breathed noisily. His neck reddened.

Cassandra knew what Bollinger was implying. Everybody knew.

Throughout Moretti's entire career there had been whispers. That he was too close to wiseguys. That he was associated. That he himself was a made member.

It was known that Moretti had two cousins, an uncle, and a brother-in-law who were members of La Cosa Nostra. He made no secret of that.

Moretti was investigated by the Feds, specifically by Bollinger, on suspicion of having leaked word to one of his cousins about a government informant who ended up chopped up in a Staten Island landfill.

Moretti pointed at Bollinger. "You know damn well I was exonerated at a departmental trial. And the Justice Department never had a wet dream of pulling me into an indictment. If I was a made man, I'd have had you whacked a long time ago."

Commissioner Riley stopped him. "Moretti! Relax."

"He comes into our house and insults my honor?"

Bollinger smirked.

The mayor practiced his "speak softly" policy.

The commissioner said, "Lieutenant, were you tailing Gator Moses?"

"We followed FYSHBone's lawyer to Brooklyn. He met with Moses, so we had a chat."

"Learn anything material to the investigation?"

Cassandra jumped in. "It's too early to say."

Riley ignored Cassandra and addressed Moretti.

"Is this lawyer, Guzmán, a suspect?"

"A person of interest," said Moretti. "We interviewed him at the vic's place of business. He seemed cagey, so we tailed him."

"Is Gator Moses now a suspect?"

Cassandra wanted to say yes. Moretti picked lint off his lapel.

"We have not eliminated him at this time."

"Does he have a motive, opportunity, and no alibi?"

"We're working to establish those facts."

Commissioner Riley stopped him there. "Agent Bollinger?"

"Gator Moses does have an alibi for last night," said the agent. "Me. I'm his alibi."

"You?" said Moretti.

"That's right."

"You were alone with him sharing pillow talk?"

Bollinger let that one slide. "He was under observation by my agents all night. He never left Brooklyn."

Cassandra thought about that. "Where was he in Brooklyn?"

"That's on a need-to-know basis, Butterfingers."

"Have any of your informants talked to you about FYSHBone?" she said.

"They talk to us about everybody."

"Anything that might have led to his murder?"

Bollinger said, "I'm not here to give away state secrets."

It was useless.

The mayor looked over his shoulder at his commissioner. He looked at Cassandra and Moretti, who had never been offered a seat. He looked at Bollinger.

"I don't think we have a problem. If the FBI says he was in Brooklyn, he was in Brooklyn."

The agent stood and shook hands with the mayor.

Cassandra said, "Bollinger. Do you know who Clementi was?"

He thought for a second. "Is he a member of the Five Families?"

"I don't think so."

The mayor tilted his head. "Wasn't he one of the top lieutenants in *The Godfather*?"

Moretti wagged his finger. "That was Clemenza."

Bollinger pointed at Cassandra. "Good luck trying to hold on to your new appointment."

He smirked and split.

The mayor dropped into his soft chair. He reached for a large aspirin bottle.

"Are we close to an arrest yet on this rapper case?"

You just gave one suspect a free pass, thought Cassandra.

Moretti kept a respectful tone. "Your Honor, it's still early. It's barely day one and already Maldonado and I have been all over the Bronx, at Bellevue, in Midtown, three neighborhoods in Brooklyn. We got shot at by a big boy who was head of the vic's security detail, and between me and Maldonado we took him down and recovered one possible murder weapon that's being tested. I have the rest of my team working every angle. We're canvassing and doing interviews. We searched the victim's primary home, splash pad, recording studio, his office, his vehicle. If there's a lead somewhere, we're gonna find it."

"Just make an arrest," said the mayor. "My sources in the black community tell me there's a rumor FYSHBone was thinking of jumping into the primary against me. I don't need the implications."

Moretti pursed his lips. "Your Honor, that's ridiculous."

"Is it? Did you know that this FYSHBone character had a political action committee? And that he has been spreading money all over the place to every elected official and party boss of consequence? He could have financed his own campaign and been a genuine threat."

Cassandra kept learning.

"It's the summer. It's been hot, Lieutenant. I don't need the people in a lather over this case."

"Understood."

Commissioner Riley tugged at his cuffs. "Maldonado, you hear we got a problem with the Marathon Slasher file?"

"Problem, sir?"

"Yeah, several. Not only is Salazar's lawyer threatening a civil suit—"

"For what?"

"Abusing his client. He's threatening to take you back to the Civilian Complaint Review Board, where you're a regular customer."

"I've won every complaint brought against me."

"Your streak is about to end. The lawyer also promised a motion to exclude the scalpel."

"C'mon, every lawyer files a motion to exclude in every case."

"We'll see when he files it how routine it is. If your search and seizure ain't tight, Maldonado, the chain of custody, we got a giant tumor of a problem. No scalpel, no hard evidence, no case."

"We have witnesses." Cassandra remembered the women's shredded faces. "What about the victims? They picked Salazar out of a lineup."

"Their word will be as good as their immigration papers in the hands of his defense attorney. Plus you got another wrinkle."

"What's that, sir?"

"Salazar has petitioned the court for a psych evaluation."

Cassandra thought she knew where that was going. "A not guilty by reason of insanity defense? Bronx juries don't buy that."

"Well, first we'll see whether Salazar is even competent to stand trial. That will depend on a judge."

The mayor popped three aspirin without water.

Cassandra kept her mouth shut.

The commissioner nodded. "I told you that your reign on top would be short, Maldonado. Soon as this or any other case you touch blows up, it does so in your face. I'm just waiting for my chance to take you down. Now get out of His Honor's office, both of you. This ain't a garden party. Go earn those paychecks."

CHAPTER 26

Headquarters

Moretti was full of pepper after the meeting in the mayor's office, especially about Bollinger's interference in his case, but there was no time to whine. The squad meeting at HI-PRO was underway across the street from City Hall at One Police Plaza.

"We'll have to take a meal after," said Moretti.

It was around seven. Cassandra had been hustling for twelve straight hours. They had done so much, it felt like longer.

The meeting was held in Captain Vargas's office. It lasted almost an hour.

Cassandra was introduced to the other members of the squad: Detective Goines, the British banker dressalike she had met at the crime scene; his partner, Lo, who resembled the host of a Chinese cooking show; Detective Freeman, a freckle-faced middle-aged African-American woman; and her partner, Brinkley, who looked like an aging surfer in a pink polo.

They went over what had been learned. Goines, Lo, Freeman, and Brinkley reported no leads from the canvass in the area of the crime scene.

As usual in the South Bronx, "nobody saw nothin'."

Goines and Lo described the victim's huge penthouse in DUMBO, one of the most expensive neighborhoods in the city.

The keyed elevator rose into and through the center of the apartment. FYSHBone's foyer had murals of the Hanging Gardens of Babylon.

There was a room with a triple high ceiling and a large, ornate gold candelabra chandelier in the center with melted black candles. On the ceiling was a Baroque mural of a little black boy in rags playing piano for white people in French Revolution–era outfits and powdered wigs. The room's large windows were draped in red velvet that blocked all sunlight.

In the center of the room was an antique piano before a dozen black marble busts of ancient philosophers arranged like a jury.

"That room felt *creeeeepy*," said Lo. "You could feel the bad vibes. But the gym has an infinity pool in front of a big window facing New York Harbor. Looks like you could swim off the edge and right out to sea."

"I'm partial to the library," said Goines. "Lots of books. A wall of awards. I counted seventeen Grammies. The entire room has an Egyptian theme. There's a sarcophagus, one of those golden coffins like King Tut's. FYSHBone's doorman says it's real. Supposedly, FYSHBone sleeps in it with the top down."

"Like I said, creepy," said Lo. "But the terrace wraps all the way around so you get the 360-degree view. My favorite is the big blue Manhattan Bridge right in your face."

Goines said, "FYSHBone recently installed a helicopter pad on the roof. Instead of painting an H on the surface like they normally do, he has the KUTTHROAT smoking fish skeleton."

Cassandra asked if FYSHBone even owned a helicopter.

"The doorman said he'd won a battle with the other tenants because he planned on acquiring one. He was taking flying lessons."

That was something to ask Guzmán about.

"Did FYSHBone live alone?"

"According to the doorman, Princesa De los Santos, the supermodel, comes over late sometimes. She has a key, lets herself in, and usually leaves after noon. Other than that, he lives alone."

"Was the girlfriend there last night?" asked Vargas.

"The doorman says no."

Cassandra volunteered that she had interviewed De los Santos and reported that cell records and undeleted texts showed that De los Santos was angry with FYSHBone for cooling to her and had texted him relentlessly.

"She claims she was home sick; we're going over later to check with her doorman."

Freeman said, "De los Santos was engaged to that cutie from the soap opera who ODed on LSD and stroked."

Captain Vargas asked what the doorman had to say about FYSHBone and Princesa's relationship. "Were they known to fight? Did the neighbors complain?"

"The doorman said they seemed fine, but none of his neighbors wanted to speak. I got the sense they were intimidated."

"Why?"

"When was the last time you knocked on every door in a New York City building, talked to everyone, including the help and the guys who park the cars in the basement lot and the people running all of the local businesses, and every last one of them refuses to answer even one question? It was like the entire neighborhood did not want to mention FYSHBone's name."

"Maybe they are just private."

"I don't know. The doorman was the only talkative one, and he was unreliable on account of the fact we had to grease his palm with a fifty. He seemed a little too eager to please. Especially in light of the way everybody else reacted."

"Anything else at the primary residence?"

"We collected a computer and should be getting a report after this meeting."

"Good. Anything else?"

"That's it."

Captain Vargas moved on. "What about his place in the Bronx?"

Detective Freeman threw her braids over her shoulders. "We recovered computers there, too, although most of that was for running his studio, and it was all open so we looked at his files right away. A couple thousand hours of video and audio recordings. Tons of music, but also just FYSHBone rambling."

Brinkley the beach boy had his hands clasped behind his head. "This guy was deep into the stream of his own conscious."

"We found a security camera over the front door on a live dedicated digital feed to a computer that recorded all comings and goings," said Freeman. "It did not capture the homicide, but it does show a visitor at his front door about fifteen minutes before FYSHBone goes out to walk the dog."

Detective Freeman passed around fuzzy black-and-white stills taken from the security video.

She said, "As you can see, unfortunately, it's not a high-quality image. You cannot see anything about the individual's face. He's wearing a black hat and the camera angle is from above pointing down. He looks broad-shouldered."

Detective Lo turned the picture and cocked his head to the side.

"A person of interest," said Captain Vargas.

They all looked at the image.

"Besides the loft and the studio we did not see anything else of note in the rest of the building," said Brinkley. "It's big and empty and has one big room with a long hallway and two rows of doors facing each other. Small offices. Felt like a hall of mirrors without the mirrors."

"We checked with Department of Buildings," said Freeman. "It's a former piano factory. Belongs to a corporation. The records show that FYSHBone is the owner of that company."

"That it?" said Vargas.

"Yes, Captain."

Moretti reported on what he and Cassandra had been up to. He summed up their entire day, including a comic rendition of their battle to take down Slow Mo, and mentioned the fact that the weapon recovered was being tested.

Moretti recounted their visit to the KUTTHROAT offices, the information about FYSHBone's many family court lawsuits, and his opinion that the victim's attorney, "a man with broad shoulders, by the way, like your John Doe on the security camera," was unusually evasive.

He reported on the rare .50-caliber gun recovered from the victim's waistband, plus the .50-caliber shell casings ejected from the murder weapon.

"Forensics is on it, but I imagine they won't find prints. As we all know, that's next to impossible with these surfaces. Maybe there'll be a little oil or sweat from the perp's fingertips to make a DNA strike on the CSI computer. But our victim had a hundred of these .50-caliber monsters custom-made. Presented them to friends and business associates from around the globe. Maldonado and I got a list from the record label. By the way, the cagey lawyer was one of the lucky recipients."

Cassandra opened her folder and handed a copy of the list of gun recipients to Captain Vargas, who slid on the bifocals that hung on a chain around her neck. Cassandra handed copies to the other detectives.

She said, "The lawyer does own one of these weapons, but he's also the one who told us about the list."

"The better to throw us off," said Freeman. "You know how men are."

Lo said, "This is a lot of names."

"If you'll notice," said Cassandra, "I asterisked the people who live in the metropolitan area. I figure if we're gonna start interviews, we may as well hit locals first."

Moretti raised an eyebrow as he went down the list. "Right. We'll leave the Sultan of Brunei for later."

Brinkley read down the list. "This lawyer is sending us on a fishing expedition. Did the victim really know the vice president?"

Goines adjusted his glasses. "I don't see the supermodel girlfriend's name on this list."

"No," said Cassandra, "but that don't mean she could not have gotten her hands on one of those guns. FYSH-Bone had so many and only gave away half."

"Where are the rest?"

"In a bank safety deposit box he rents downtown."

Detective Freeman spoke directly to Cassandra. "Think the supermodel could handle firing such a large weapon?"

Freeman had a point. Guns are designed by and for masculine hands. Firing a handgun is a slightly more challenging exercise for most females than it is for most men. The murder weapon was such that it would have posed a major problem for the average female.

Cassandra said, "She does have very bony fingers. And she seems a little sickly in person."

Everyone thought about that.

Captain Vargas let her glasses hang from her neck again. "The lawyer controls much of our information."

"Isn't that what lawyers do?" said Cassandra.

She didn't mention that Guzmán had dated Princesa before FYSHBone. She was not sure why.

Moretti moved on to their encounter at City Hall with Agent Bollinger.

He said, "The fact that the Feds have Gator Moses under surveillance doesn't surprise me. But the fact that Bollinger jumps in to alibi the guy? This tells me Gator is of greater value to the Feds on the street than he is in jail."

Cassandra knew where Moretti was going.

"Ipso facto, Gator Moses must be a rat," said Moretti. "The Feds must have finally built a decent case against him and flipped him and now he's informing on his coconspirators."

Cassandra had searched Gator and knew he was not wearing a wire. This of course did not mean that he was not informing; it was just a point, but she did not make it in front of the full squad. Maybe she would mention it to Moretti in private.

"What does this have to do with our homicide?" said Vargas.

"I don't know, Boss, but I can tell you that the day I start believing in coincidence, I'll turn my shield in, buy some golf clubs, and hold my breath waiting for that hole in one."

"What's the coincidence here?" said Brinkley.

"That a rich, famous guy gets his brains blown out, which leads to a shifty lawyer, who leads us straight to a thug, who gets alibied by the FBI. No connection?"

"What might the connection be?"

"I don't know," said Moretti. "The Feds are always looking for structure. A conspiracy. That's what they need to activate their powerful RICO statutes. Racketeering conspiracies. Money flowing up. Orders flowing down. If they flip somebody, that generally means there is somebody bigger, somebody higher up on the flowchart."

"Somebody more powerful and dangerous than Gator Moses," said Goines.

"In the eyes of the FBI. Yes."

"And FYSHBone's role in all of this?"

"That's the rub," said Moretti. "Can't imagine what it was. And now I really wanna know."

CHAPTER 27

Paperwork

Everyone went off into their corners to work the different angles on computers and phones. They ordered dinner from Kwong Seng Lo's in Chinatown, where Moretti was known as "Lieutenant Hollywood."

"They know to make it extra spicy."

Though it was an elite unit, HI-PRO's furniture was standard NYPD green—gray metal desks, simple padded chairs, and thick prehistoric desktop computers with faded screens.

The décor qualified as NYPD modern because the cushions did not yet look worn, the rolling chairs retained most of their wheels, and the technology looked to be around ten years old.

Moretti showed Cassandra to her bare desk.

"Really, Lou, last exit before the men's room?"

"Manhandle your way onto a squad, young detective, don't expect the best seat in the house."

Cassandra dropped her bag.

"Anyway, I was housebroken by the old-time Irish lieutenants," said Moretti. "They taught me real police work is done on the street, shaking trees, not indoors. We won't be here much."

Cassandra had a gift for banging out DD-5 reports. She took ten minutes to produce the ones to cover her day so far.

She found an available computer with Internet access and researched FYSHBone, mostly news accounts of his death and the reactions around the world. The Dalai Lama, who had worked with FYSHBone to fight a famine, had issued a statement saying the world had lost a poet.

Cassandra watched a couple of FYSHBone videos online and remembered how good and infectious his music was.

She researched Clementi.

Muzio Clementi was a late-eighteenth and early-nineteenth-century Italian composer, pianist, piano manufacturer, instructor, conductor, and music publisher, who in his day was known as "the father of the pianoforte" and "the father of modern piano technique" as well as "the father of Romantic pianistic virtuosity."

As the pathologist had mentioned, Clementi wrote sonatas and sonatinas that were used to train young, serious piano students. His improvements to piano construction became standard and remain so to this day.

Cassandra did not find too many parallels between Clementi's and FYSHBone's biographies except that both were child prodigies who reached crossroads of musical instruction at age seven, and both were very productive and successful because they were talented but also because they diversified their interests and were driven geniuses of self-promotion. Mozart was jealous enough to call Clementi a charlatan. Unlike FYSHBone, Clementi had died of old age.

Cassandra did not understand. She decided that she would question FYSHBone's mother again about her son's childhood, if she had a chance.

Cassandra checked out some of the material recovered from the computers at FYSHBone's studio.

She popped in and out of song after song after song, each one catchy from the first beat, flowy from the first hook, all of them unknown. She found hundreds in a file labeled UNPUBLISHED and hundreds more in a file labeled STRAIGHT TRIPPIN.

The video footage was mostly webcam stuff, like a diary, with FYSHBone talking directly into the lens, presumably alone, as no one else appeared in the frame or was heard, and he did not appear to address anybody else in the room.

Instead FYSHBone focused on the viewer, musing on whatever topics caught his fancy. Politics and public policy were favorites. Literary criticism. Women. The state of hip-hop.

At times FYSHBone seemed depressed. In one entry he did not look at the camera and said things like, "This city ain't nothin' but a diamond-studded muffin!... Who's gonna catch *me* when I fall through the rye? Y'all phony!"

FYSHBone began to cry and shut the camera off. Cassandra stopped right there.

Thousands of hours of material, they said.

Someone else would have to sift through it all.

Cassandra got the call she had been waiting for. She reported to Moretti. The Chinese food had yet to arrive.

"Gonna have to miss dinner, Lou. I'm gonna step out and go meet with my contact from the Hip-Hop Squad."

"You need backup?"

"I'm good. I'll call when I'm through."

CHAPTER 28

Still Not a Player

There was little traffic at twilight, and Cassandra made it to her destination in minutes. She managed to watch the very last of the sun go down behind the cliffs known as the Palisades across the Hudson River from Riverdale, an upscale section of the Bronx.

It had been a long, hot day.

On a quiet tree-lined hilltop the trees smelled fresh and green and suprisingly damp considering the recent heat. The view of the forested cliffs across the water created the illusion that the land to the west was still wild and unsettled.

A yellow Mustang drove down the curved road. It honked.

Cassandra looked up and down the block to make certain she was not being watched. She climbed in. The car took off.

The woman behind the wheel smiled, leaned over, and kissed Cassandra on the cheek. "What up, ma?"

She smelled of a man's cologne. Her street name was Cuca, and she was a chubby, pretty, Puerto Rican, butch lesbian NYPD undercover. Cassandra had worked with her in Brooklyn.

Cuca dressed straight hip-hop 24/7 and was currently assigned to the secretive Hip-Hop Squad, which was housed in the Intelligence Division.

As an undercover, Cuca played the part of a frustrated rapper still trying to break into the game, which was actually true.

She had recently had an underground hit with a remake of Jay-Z's "Hey Papi," retitled "Hey Mami," which was a song about a player trying to change his player ways.

Cassandra congratulated Cuca for the music, because it was raw and it was real and it was not a front. She had known Cuca since the academy, but met her in that dark, private locale because an undercover cannot be seen talking to a known cop. Cuca had spent her entire career in deep, deep cover.

Cuca could hardly contain herself. "Yo, you're on the front page of the paper, B! Your cover's blown!"

Cassandra shrugged and said that it had to be done.

"Guess you really are ready to be on the straight and narrow. Look at that suit. Me, I couldn't live without my cover. That's my security blanket."

Cuca was tough and had a reputation for always having fine-ass femmed-out females on her arm. Back in the day in Brooklyn South, Cassandra and Cuca had pretended to be girlfriends who were also drug dealers. They took down whole operations because men did not fear them and never imagined they were cops.

"How's my baby Jason?"

"Getting big."

"God bless. He still play with that jack-in-the-box I got him?"

He didn't. "Oh, he loves that thing."

Cuca laughed. She was dressed in baggy, full-length jeans with a dozen pockets, construction boots, and a KUTTHROAT smoking fish jersey under a tilted Yankees cap. She kept the music on.

Cassandra removed Cuca's cap. "Girl, your braids look nice."

"Yeah? Wanna run your fingers through?"

On more than one occasion Cuca had gone a little farther than she needed to to convince the audience that Cassandra was her girl.

Cassandra put the cap back on Cuca's head. "Keep your hands where I can see them, lady."

"Don't blame me, Cassie. You're a beauty."

"It's cool."

Cuca drove the Mustang low, stretched, leaned back on her elbow. Her fingers were close to the blunt in the ashtray.

"Just a prop for later," she said. "You know how it is out here trying to get into character."

Cassandra did know.

Cuca circled the dark, quiet hills. "So now you're on the FYSHBone file."

"Yeah. Cuca, what do you know about him?"

"We tailed him regularly, of course. Not me. The unit. Actually, these plainclothes boys who stick out like Boy Scouts."

"How'd FYSHBone get on their radar?"

"I wasn't in his circle. You know I rock Harlem, but it could be anything. Something they read on a blog. FYSH-Bone could've had a snitch in his camp. I don't know if the squad has any other undercovers in the field that might have been around him. I fly solo and report to just my handler."

"You couldn't see his file?"

"I tried to get my girl inside the unit to sneak a peek for you. She tells me it's gone."

Cassandra thought about that. "You hear anything on the street?"

"People spit rumors."

"Anything a veteran like you might consider?"

"Been hearing a lot that the Feds were onto FYSH-Bone."

"For?"

"Nobody knows."

"Well . . . *some*body knows." Cassandra told Cuca about the trail to Gator Moses and Agent Bollinger's providing an alibi.

"Your federal tax dollars at work," said Cuca.

Cassandra wondered about the connection and shared Moretti's theory about Gator's being a rat, and there probably being somebody further up the food chain of a criminal enterprise.

Cuca theorized, "Maybe FYSHBone was the head of a criminal conspiracy that includes Gator. Maybe he was Gator's boss. FYSHBone always banked on his reputation of having started in the dope game."

"Gator claims that was just hype."

"Ma, what if he said that to throw you? Either because he was broken into never speaking ill of the boss, never implicating him, like a master trains her dog, or because this is a political assassination, a power grab, and Gator is part of it. Or he's aligning himself with the new guard. In any case he wants you to look elsewhere."

"Those are a lot of chess moves, Cuca. Gator doesn't seem that smart."

"The dumb ones are the dangerous ones."

"You hear anything about FYSHBone's girlfriend?"

"Naw. Supermodels are too skinny for me. I like mine with a little beef. Speaking of which, you lost weight doing all that jogging."

"It'll come back if I don't keep it up."

"You found Mr. Right yet?"

"Honestly, Cuca, I haven't been looking."

Cuca had a colorful, actual-size Queen of Hearts playing card tattooed on her forearm, and on the inside of her wrist the double female symbol. "Cassie, you might not even know what you like."

"I know what I like all right, Cuca. I just don't know where to find it."

"Ain't that the truth. One thing about conspiracies, though, to get back to that: If FYSHBone was part of an enterprise, whether he was up the chain or down the chain from Gator, or even on the same plane, the cats around FYSHBone are likely to be a part of it. Focus on them. Especially the ones you know for sure were under his thumb."

"Cuca, you could teach a class in political science."

"Ma, that's just common sense. I mean, that's only so much speculation. You and I tore through Brooklyn South like cowgirls and never penetrated the Red Hook syndicates. The crack structure—the heirarchy—it remains real murky over there. Who's the boss? Nobody in law enforcement has been able to decode it. It's been decades. And it is still a thriving market. Better than Wall Street."

"The people still wanna get high," said Cassandra.

"Yes, they do."

"Moretti also thinks, with the Feds involved, that it's about structure. Power moves."

"Stands to reason," said Cuca. "And if Moretti's right, that Gator is a rat, and that he and FYSHBone were part of a consortium, then whoever took out FYSHBone may be gunning for Gator next. Rats usually don't do so well in coups."

Cuca had given Cassandra plenty to think about.

"So you're partnered with Moretti now, huh? He's an underground legend."

"Yeah? FYSHBone's bodyguard rolled him like an unripe tomato down the grocery aisle."

Cuca cracked up.

"You should have seen him trying to act like he was going to plant a snub .38 on Gator. What if I didn't back him?"

"He knew you would. You're true-blue and it shows."

The ex-partners rode around in slow motion. Cassandra listened to Cuca rap along to "Twinz (*Deep Cover* 98)," Big Punisher and Fat Joe's cover of the theme song from *Deep Cover*. Cuca did both parts flawlessly. She got to the part in Little Italy where she riddles middlemen who don't do diddly and did not fall off beat. The way Cuca shaped her lips to form and emphasize the words into an imaginary microphone was fascinating.

Cassandra said, "Girl, you still flow."

The two quickly relived some of their highlights. Cuca was a badass who loved to scrap toe to toe with males and win. She was also funny as shit and had kept Cassandra in stitches during their late nights and endless stakeouts.

A couple of times they had run laughing from scenes where it was *they* who had broken the law. Cuca was really an outlaw who had found a place to put it all.

She turned the music down.

"You know what really hurts about FYSHBone, B? Already the lyrics carry a different feeling. You realize the music was fun, but there was always a subliminal sadness that his swagger couldn't master. Such delivery and breath control. Such passion. It turns out FYSHBone was a sad soul."

Cassandra was discovering that.

"It breaks the heart," said Cuca. "You know how deep into his music I've always been. Remember the night we spotted him break-dancing at the Copa? The way he spun on his head?"

"I knew today would be tough for you."

Cuca was a hip-hop historian, who believed that it was a vital cultural movement like any other, including the Jazz Age and the Rennaissance. She had issues about the many ways in which the culture had been co-opted, commercialized, and homogenized.

For example, it bothered her that hip-hop and rap had mistakenly come to be viewed as originally and mainly a black thing. Rap had started in the South Bronx, the Boogie Down Bronx, in the seventies. That meant one ethnic culture above all others: Latinos, predominantly Puerto Ricans—Nuyoricans—though there had been others. Hip-hop had been born in the cradle of "*El Condado de la Salsa*." One begat the other.

Regardless, Cuca was convinced that FYSHBone had been a maestro like no other. She once said that if she were forced to lie with a man, FYSHBone was the only male she would even consider.

Cuca circled a little more, then dropped Cassandra off.

"All right, *Boricua*."

"Aw'ight, *Morena*."

"I'll call you."

"Whenever you need a friend, ma. You know I always come up to the surface for you."

Cuca winked. The Mustang prowled.

It was past ten. Cassandra headed back to the office.

CHAPTER 29

Assault and Battery

Much earlier that same day Sabio searched all over Manhattan for a charger for FYSHBone's old laptop. The first place said they don't make them anymore, buy it used. The used place said used ones are in short supply, call the manufacturer. The manufacturer said it would have to travel from deep inside China and would arrive in four to six weeks, how would he like to pay?

Sabio hung up and went back to the label and into FYSHBone's office.

The original charger had not been left in any outlet. It was not in a drawer. It was not in the closet. It was not under the couch or behind the couch or under the cushion where Sabio had found the laptop. It was not stashed inside the grandfather clock.

Wait.

Sabio removed the cushions again and jammed his hand inside the couch, the way you dig for dropped coins.

Yes!

FYSHBone had stashed the charger inside the fold.

Sabio, you persistent prick. Sweet.

He took the laptop and the charger into his own office and locked the door.

The thing took a long time to boot. The whole time Sabio went in circles and thought about his dilemma.

He was at the center of a triangle between billionaire Bishop, FYSHBone's mother, and Gator Moses. Hundreds of millions of dollars were at stake.

The fact that he was no longer in a position to get a taste of it all ate at him.

How could he bring the two sides together so he could get out from under Gator? Was it possible to get more than what Bishop offered? Could he still get what he had in play before all of this went wrong? Was it possible to do *even better* than before?

The optimist and the hustler inside Sabio did not want to quit.

But the realist in him knew that he was in deep, deep trouble. If he was not very, very careful, he could wind up with his throat cut and his tongue pulled out through his neck.

The laptop was ready. Sabio logged on with the dog's name again.

He went through folders and files.

This was FYSHBone's oldest computer, the one on which he kept his most cherished documents. There were poems and an abandoned novel. Legal letters. Saved emails.

A letter to his mother.

It began, *I've been waiting my whole life to tell you . . .*

Sabio felt a twinge of embarrassment. He was not a voyeur and this was clearly private.

But he needed every advantage.

Dear Mother: I've been waiting my whole life to tell you how much it hurts. It was never right what you did to me. The way you forced me. The way you made me bend to your will.

I never wanted to be a concert pianist. I never wanted to play with the Philharmonic. Why did you push your dreams on me? How come you couldn't just love me? I just wanted to be from Red Hook.

Now I'm doing my thing and you don't even show respect? How come you never been to any of my shows? You won't listen to my music or watch my videos. Do you know how much people around the world feel me? And you won't take my money?

Can't you see all I wanna be is good? I just want you to be proud of me, Momma. Be proud of me! Be proud, I order you! That's all I ever wanted. Why can't you be proud? When daddy died—

Sabio stopped right there. He was intruding and there was no need and his shame was finally enough to make him turn away.

He looked in other folders. Finally a file with the right title.

Please let this be it.

He double-clicked to open it.

Sabio pounded his knee. The file was in French.

Are you kidding me? I fucking failed French!

The computer was too old for wireless Internet so there was no way for Sabio to find a translation program online. For that he would need to find some old dial-up to plug into. Good luck with that.

Sabio was not very technical, so he did not know how

to transfer files from this computer to the more modern ones and would need help. He couldn't have any of the tech guys at the office look at it because they would then know too much. He needed to think about this.

Sabio went out to the office to deal with the many things that needed to be handled, including putting to rest the fast-spreading rumor that, grief notwithstanding, the real pain resulting from the death of FYSHBone would be the instant loss of all of their jobs.

Sabio managed to get the other execs to form a battle plan for keeping day-to-day operations going. Then he gathered the staff in the conference room, including the Miami office, via videoconference, to give a rousing speech that was part eulogy, part information session, part question and answer, rememberances, and finally, "Let's win one for FYSHBone!"

The staff dispersed. Dulles was nowhere to be found.

Done with that obligation, Sabio checked online.

Miracles never cease!

The Cubs won super-big on the road. Sabio had staked the few thousand he had left on his long-shot home team of lovable losers to do precisely that, and now he was flush enough to keep Gator Moses off his back for a month.

Eat a dick, Gator! You, too, Bishop!

Sabio split to pick up his big winnings and smoke a victory blunt.

Apple was an aging stripper who plastic-surgeried herself back in the eighties to look like Apollonia from Apollonia 6. She still worked day shifts at a strip club on Queens

Boulevard where she doubled as a bookie, one of the few who still took Sabio's action.

Sabio showed up just as Apple took the stage. She did a well-worn and bored solo performance to "Sex Shooter," in which she made a finger gun and pretended to shoot "love" in the direction of the two or three guys sitting far from the stage getting lapdances in the middle of the workday in the shadows of the cavernous club.

When Apple was through, she collected the three to five crumpled dollars that had been tossed on the gummy floor. She stepped off the stage and came toward Sabio with the usual swinging hips.

She leaned over and whispered, "Ready for the Champagne Room, daddy?"

Apple never conducted gambling business in the open, but in the dark, private lapdance room in the back, with the curtain pulled.

Sabio sucked the last of his rum and Coke. "Bet."

They went in the back and conducted the transaction in the usual manner. When Sabio made a bet he whispered it to Apple while she leaned over and either pretended to give him a lapdance or actually gave him a lapdance, depending on his mood.

Lately he had passed on the lapdances.

After he whispered his selections, he left the cash under the cushion. When he won he came back and his winnings would be where he had left the wager.

Today it was a fat envelope for pickup, the fattest in a very long time. Sabio kissed it. Out of habit he peeled a thousand in cash and folded it into his pocket.

"You're the apple of my eye, Apple."

"My pleasure, baby. Want a dance?"

"I'm okay." He put a crisp hundred in her garter.

"You keep rejecting me I might take it personal," she said.

"It ain't that." Sabio needed more these days than just the physical. But this wasn't the moment to talk about it.

Apple disappeared the hundred. "It's okay, baby. You know where I'm at."

Apple turned and pulled the curtain.

Leland Bishop and his man Hegel stood on the other side. They formed a wall that filled the narrow doorway to the cubicle.

Apple threw a hip. "Get away, freaks, this ain't no freak show."

Without a word Hegel, pressed a thumb into her naked rib at just the right point to make her widen her eyes and freeze her mouth open.

Bishop said, "We know where you live with your children, Apollonia. Scream and my man will get messy. When he releases, go back to the main room and service customers. Do not call the bouncer. He will get seriously hurt. After that I shall phone the mayor and shut this place down. We only want to speak to Mister Lucky."

Hegel released Apple and she gasped.

Sabio did not want to be left alone with these two. "It's okay, Apple, go."

She took off.

Bishop's accent scraped nails on Sabio's chalkboard. "I say, old sport, all in a day's work, is it?"

Hegel rubbed his wrist.

"What are you doing here, Bishop?"

"We need to speak."

"Now?"

"What of your conversation with FYSHBone's mother?"

"She's at a different price point than you. She's grieving."

"Guzmán, do you believe that money sleeps?"

What kind of a question was that? "I don't know, Bishop, I haven't—"

"Do you need me to give you an English lesson?"

"Excuse me?"

"Shall I teach you some English?"

Sabio had a bachelor's degree in social work *and* a juris doctor. "Listen, Bishop, I—"

"Today's word is 'motivation.'"

"What?"

"Motivation, Guzmán. Do you understand?"

"Bishop, I'm getting sick and ti-*ahhhhhhhhhh!*"

Sabio was suddenly racked by a wrenching, intense pain in his penis and testicles.

"Ahhhhhhhh!"

Sabio's teeth chattered. His whole body spasmed.

"P-p-pleeze! Stuh-stuh-stop!"

Hegel gripped a weapon that delivered an electric charge. He pressed it to Sabio's balls.

"F-f-fuuuuck!"

"Motivated now, old sport?"

"B-B-Bishop, you suh-suh-son of a bi-bi-*ahhhhhhh!*"

"Do you understand?"

Sabio hyperventilated. "I do, I do, I—I—I'm motivated, I'm motivated."

"Can Sigmund put it away?"

Sabio nodded.

Hegel stood back with the stun gun at his side.

Sabio caught his breath, covered his jewels, and harpooned Hegel with his eyes.

One day, motherfucker.

Bishop showed his bicuspids. "You will secure FYSH-Bone's mother's signature, yes?"

Even in a stupor of pain, shock, fear, and desire for vengeance, Sabio knew rationally that what Bishop wanted was impossible.

"I'll do it, Bishop. I'll get her signature."

"Splendid." Bishop reached down and picked up the laptop. "We'll take this for now."

Should have known you wanted that.

"And this." Bishop reached into Sabio's inside pocket and removed the stuffed envelope.

Aw, c'mon, no way. "Bishop, that money is mine."

"Wish to file a report?"

Sabio did not.

"I told you that you would earn your way out of this or perish, Guzmán. You are not about to escape by risking it all on one turn of pitch-and-toss."

Sabio did not quite get that.

Bishop clarified: "Did you really think you'd be bailed out by the Chicago Cubs?"

Sabio's dick was shriveled and his balls felt swollen.

"Go now, Guzmán. Work. Negotiate. Make it happen."

Sabio eyed his fat envelope. "That's all the money I have."

"It was?"

Bishop peeled off one hundred out of the several hundreds of hundreds inside the envelope. He folded it and stuffed it into Sabio's breast pocket.

This was too much. "Bishop, you're not serious."

"Do you need Sigmund to demonstrate how serious?"

He didn't.

"Go now."

Sabio did not need to be told twice.

He pushed past them and through the main room where another dancer gyrated just as certain as the world turned on its axis. Sabio went out to his car, sat in it, watched the front of the club, and saw Bishop and Hegel exit and climb into a limousine.

Sabio waited a bit longer and checked all mirrors. Convinced he was alone he checked the secret compartment under the passenger seat to make sure it had not been breached. The compartment was designed to hold a large gun case loaded with a custom KUTTHROAT AVENGER.

Sabio had left the charger for FYSHBone's old laptop in the car.

Bishop was unlikely to run into as many barriers as Sabio in trying to get the old laptop operational, but someone would have to do some legwork. Sabio still had time.

He could not believe they had gangstered his big winnings. Long shots like that do not come in often. Sabio would have to start again from scratch.

He took half of the thousand that he had peeled from the envelope before Bishop showed up and added the hundred that Bishop had tried to humiliate him with.

Sabio then marched right back inside to Apollonia and placed another bet, this time on the Mets to win big that night at their new stadium, another long shot.

Apple took Sabio's action. But this time she did not smile, she did not blow in his ear, she did not call him daddy or baby, and she did not offer him a lapdance.

CHAPTER 30

Hall of Mirrors

Late that first night the HI-PRO Unit was back in the area of the crime scene. At Cassandra's urging, Moretti had ordered the other HI-PRO squad members to spread throughout the area and canvass again and cast a wider net, five additional blocks in three directions.

They were past the eighteen-hour mark on their shift.

She and Moretti were under the viaduct about one hundred yards from where FYSHBone's body had been found on the sidewalk in front of his recording studio. Cassandra scanned the gutters and sidewalks with her flashlight.

Moretti pitched in on the opposite side of the street. "You're gonna make me work for this, huh, kid?"

Cassandra did not respond. She found nothing in one sewage drain. The others were covered with garbage that looked settled. Just to be sure she kicked away empty bottles with her pump. She peeled damp, moldy newspapers, plastic bags, and strip club flyers with a fresh pair of latex gloves.

Nothing underneath.

Morettti's voice echoed against the concrete walls. "Not so glamorous, is it?"

"Oh, it's everything a little girl dreams of."

They met at the far end of the viaduct.

Moretti put away his flashlight. "Well?"

Cassandra looked eastward toward the crime scene. She looked up toward the railroad tracks. "What about up there?"

"What about it?"

"Perfect hiding spot."

Cassandra pointed at a fence that ended at the concrete abutment but was not as high. At the top of the ten-foot wall was a jungle of brush, trees, and weeds plus years' worth of garbage that sloped up toward the tracks. Moretti got her drift.

"You must be out of your mind if you think I'm climbing up there, sunshine."

One of them had to. Cassandra shook her head. "You had to send the strong *young* cops off on a canvass?"

"Oh, you're just a peach."

Cassandra removed her jacket and hung it carefully on the fence. She looked at Moretti. "I'm gonna need a boost."

"I got three herniated disks!"

"Don't be such a wet noodle."

Cassandra positioned him where she needed and worked her way up. It took work. She used the fence and Moretti as far as each would go, reached for some exposed tree roots, and found them solid enough.

It could not be avoided: Cassandra's butt was in Moretti's face.

He laughed. "Maldonado, I like you more and more."

"Don't enjoy it so much. On three."

Cassandra counted. Moretti heaved and she pulled, and

even though her pump slipped on the concrete wall and she almost tumbled, they exerted again and she tugged herself up.

She dusted herself off and relit her flashlight.

Moretti warned Cassandra to watch for rats.

Look at that, she thought.

The exposed roots right next to the ones Cassandra had just used were visibly pulled from the dirt more than hers were. A little fresh, black earth was loosed and peppered.

That had to have been after whenever was the last rain—two weeks ago, as Cassandra recalled—because rain would have washed the dirt away or mixed it back into the soil.

One root was even cracked, and the pulp was light yellow and clean, which meant it was a fresh fracture that had not had the time to get dull.

Someone much heavier than Cassandra had recently pulled himself up by those roots.

She got down close to the branches with the flashlight and really scanned them, especially near the point of the break. She used the small magnifying glass from her keychain to methodically scan the rupture in the branch.

Aha. What *is* that?

Cassandra moved the magnifier in and out to focus.

The fiber of some bright blue material.

Come here.

Cassandra got out her Swiss army knife, also from the keychain, and used the tweezers to collect the fiber, which she then safeguarded inside another latex glove out of her pocket.

This was going great. She felt like a real detective.

She hiked up the slope to the tracks, which extended

south in the direction of Randall's Island to Hell Gate and in the other direction to parts unknown. From this height Cassandra could see the spires of Manhattan lit like the constellations.

She carefully crossed the tracks to the side closest to the crime scene. Cassandra looked up and followed a descending jet that was not so low as to rattle windows, but was close enough that one could make out the logo.

A late-night flight into the city of blinding lights. They were under one of La Guardia's approaches.

Cassandra walked a little south. *Jackpot!*

From her vantage Cassandra could now see directly into FYSHBone's recording studio and loft. The elevated train tracks were not just an excellent spot to lie in wait, they were also the perfect spot for spying on FYSHBone!

Cassandra felt like a kid unwrapping presents.

She spoke aloud: "Okay, so you came up here and you watched and you waited and you stalked poor FYSHBone like a hawk waits for a simpler bird. So now what?"

Cassandra methodically scanned the ground in the immediate area but found nothing of consequence. She aimed her flashlight across the street and scanned the darkened loft. Her patch of light reflected off the large mirror and—

Whoa! A scary pair of glowing eyes! They spotted Cassandra spotting them through the reflection and spun away into the dark.

"Lieutenant!"

Cassandra swept the loft with her beam. A shadow jumped through an open door.

Whoever it was, was fleeing.

"Lou, there's somebody up there!"

"What?"

"In the apartment!"

Cassandra ran down the slope, almost tumbled, got to the branches, and lowered herself.

"You can see into the apartment from up there. There was somebody up there watching me and now they're running!"

They ran. Moretti had the keys. He called for the other HI-PRO members who were on the canvass to converge on FYSHBone's abandoned warehouse.

The sticker between the door and the door jamb that identified the building as a sealed crime scene and warned of the penalties for trespass had been broken. The detectives ran into the darkened lobby.

Oh, man.

The elevator descended. Its clanking echoed inside the elevator shaft and got louder as it approached. Casandra and Moretti waited off to the side with their flashlights pointed and their guns drawn.

Cassandra's heart bounced around her chest.

Moretti gave her the silence signal.

The elevator landed and they raised their guns.

The door slid open.

Nothing. The elevator was empty and the light was off. It had been broken. Whoever was in the building was on another floor and had sent the elevator down.

"Squeeze play," said Moretti. "I'll start down here and take the stairs, you ride to the top floor and work your way down."

Cassandra got in and pushed the button. The motor sounded extra-loud. The person could be anywhere in the dark shadows of that massive building.

Cassandra remembered the report by Detectives Freeman and Brinkley. How the building "felt like a dark hall of mirrors without the mirrors."

She breathed and kept her gun and her flashlight in front and asked God to watch over her.

The door opened to the top floor.

Cassandra held her breath, waited a second, heard nothing, and waited a second more. Other than what shot out of Cassandra's flashlight, there was no light in the hallway except what leaked in from the street through one grimy window with several missing panes.

Cassandra bent at the knees, stepped out, and quickly pivoted left, then right, to catch an ambush.

Nothing.

The studio and apartment were to her left. Cassandra had glimpsed the person ducking out but he could have gone back inside for some reason.

Cassandra quietly tried the door to FYSHBone's compound. It was locked. Moretti held the keys and he was somewhere else inside the building.

How she hated these dark places.

There was a door to her right. Cassandra had peeked into the room beyond it during her first visit to the crime scene. It was a big, empty, dilapidated suite of what must have been the piano factory's offices.

The windows were filthy enough in the daytime to barely allow light. That was doubly so late at night, and the windows were inside the offices, so that the hallway especially had zero light except for Cassandra's.

She crept down the hall, being extra-careful not to make noise on the dried old wooden floorboards. It smelled musty and dusty and of moldy plaster.

Two rows of doors faced one another. The person who could be behind any one of them could also be FYSH-Bone's killer with a powerful weapon. Cassandra was afraid.

She tried one door, careful to stay out of the line of fire, although the slow creaking of the rusty hinges could not be helped.

Nothing happened.

Cassandra shone her flashlight inside and found a dusty old desk. She tried the opposite door.

Same thing.

Slowly, carefully, she made her way down the dim hall.

Moretti, where are you? Where is the rest of the team?

It had only been a minute, but it felt like forever. This was such a big building.

Cassandra finally opened the second to the last door and—

RRRRREOW!

A cat Cassandra never saw bounced off her leg, startled her, and made her swing the flashlight without knowing, so that the bulb smashed into the desk and burst, which threw the room into pitch darkness.

Cassandra spun, frightened, and immediately plowed her face through a giant cobweb. She gagged and slapped away at the sick, sticky, silky threads and swallowed a scream.

She heard footsteps running down the hall toward the stairs.

Crap!

Cassandra ran out into the dark hall and saw a shadowy figure hauling toward the thin light that was visible through the doorway where she had entered the suite.

"Stop! Police!"

Cassandra caught a flash of a figure in a hood as it ducked out the door and to the left behind the wall out of sight and toward the elevator.

No!

She heard the elevator door open and the button being banged repeatedly as she ran full speed in her pumps on the old wooden floorboards with her gun in one hand and her useless flashlight in the other.

"Stop!"

Cassandra heard the door slide and got to the elevator just in time to see it go the last eighth of an inch and hear the engine begin to hoist the elevator car down.

No you don't.

Cassandra dropped her flashlight, took the stairs that were right there, and ran down floor after floor to keep up with the elevator.

She called down into the the stairwell for backup, unaware of Moretti's location inside the building.

"Lou, the elevator!"

Cassandra kept up with it, breathless. She got to two. The elevator kept going to the lobby and so did she.

Never thought I'd be down here waiting, did you?

Cassandra dropped down into a combat shooting position at a safe angle and out of breath.

Come on, come on.

The elevator hit the ground floor.

Bring it!

The door slid open.

Nothing.

"Come out with your hands up!"

Still nothing.

Cassandra sweat and breathed hard. The door closed again. She approached slowly with no light but with her gun pointed. She hit the UP button to reopen the door.

There was no one inside.

How could I fall for that again?

Cassandra heard breaking glass on the floor above.

What the—

She ran upstairs one flight and boldly kicked open the only door. Behind it was a dark, empty, very large high-ceilinged room where the piano manufacturing must have taken place.

At the far end was the window she had heard smashed. It admitted a pale yellow light from the street. Cassandra ran to the broken window and looked out.

The hooded figure was gone.

One flight down on the broken concrete was a chair that had been thrown through the window and shards of broken glass and splintered wood from the windowpanes.

There was some kind of metal drain or pipe that was bolted to the brick exterior. It ran the height of the building and was within reach of the broken window. The person had probably used it to climb down, since this was still a great height for jumping only to land on broken glass.

Cassandra ran downstairs and called the other HI-PRO detectives on the radio to alert them to the runner in a hood. Maybe the person was in a car by now. There was no way of knowing.

Cassandra put it over the citywide band as well, so that the local cops would be on the lookout, but there was just not much to go on.

By the time Cassandra got outside and around the corner to the back of the building, where the runner had exited, it was clear there was no sign and that the runner was gone gone gone.

"Damn it!"

She holstered her gun.

Moretti poked his head through the window and looked down at her.

"The subject escaped through here?"

"I think he used that pipe to shimmy down."

"That's pretty motivated. This is still pretty high. You get a good look?"

"A person in a hood."

"What color hood?"

"Navy blue, maybe. Black, maybe. Maybe dark gray."

"Male or female?"

"I can't say."

"Black, white, Hispanic, Asian?"

"I don't know, Lou."

"Tall, fat, short, skinny?"

Cassandra shook her head.

"Maldonado, are you kidding?"

"I only glimpsed a quick shadow. It was dark."

"Wow. Well come back inside. Let's check out the apartment. See if he ransacked it or something."

The other HI-PRO detectives screeched their vehicles to a halt out front. Cassandra gave them the quick, non-descript description and they took off, engines racing, to comb the area, which might as well have been the bottom of the wide Sargasso Sea.

Cassandra felt defeated. She rode the elevator up.

The bright lights and big white walls that dominated FYSHBone's loft were a shock to the eyes after all that blight.

Cassandra was tired. It had been a very long, difficult day. She was sweaty and dusty and had not gotten all the cobwebs out of her hair.

Worst of all, she wondered whether by playing hardball to get onto this squad she had not bitten off considerably more than she could chew.

Cassandra thought she might walk to FYSHBone's floating bed and lie on it and fall fast asleep if she was not careful. God, she was tired.

There was still work to do.

What was that intruder doing up here?

FYSHBone's splash pad looked as it had so many hours earlier.

Cassandra did not see anything unusual. Then she noticed the bed.

"See that, Lou?"

"What about it?"

"The bedsheets. They look wrinkled. Like somebody's been sleeping on them. Rolling around even. They were military-style neat this morning."

"You sure?"

She was. Cassandra went over to walk around the bed. On the other side she found something.

"Lou, look at this!" She picked it up with a pen.

"Maldonado, is that what I think it is?"

A G-string. There was light spotting.

CHAPTER 31

Late Late Show

CSI was called in to dust for new fingerprints and collect the G-string. Otherwise, the whole thing was too much to guess about and go in circles over at that late, late hour.

Moretti called a quick meeting in the street, to learn that the other members of the HI-PRO team had not discovered anything new with the expanded canvass.

Precinct detective squads generally have sleeping quarters where members of the force can sack out during extra-long shifts and keep going, but this was not one of those situations. Moretti sent everybody home to their own beds to refresh and be back early.

Cassandra was more than happy to drop it for the night.

Once home, she checked on her sleeping son and found him breathing normally with the air on. Cassandra wished she could lower the air so she could lower her utility bill, but she knew that if she did and the heat pulled him from sleep early it was going to be a slow boat to suffering for all.

She kissed her son on his smooth, beautiful forehead.

Cassandra's mother slept on half of Cassandra's bed, as she usually did when she cared for her grandson late into the night. She was a very light sleeper, but she might not hear from the basement if the boy got up. Cassandra did not know what on earth she would do without her mother.

Cassandra kicked her pumps into a corner of the closet, peeled her suit and hung it, put on light pajama shorts and top, then removed her bra through the sleeves and scratched herself under the breasts where the underwire dug in all day.

She brushed her teeth and washed her face and finally climbed into bed next to her mom.

Cassandra's mother was awake with her eyes closed. She didn't whisper but she spoke to her daughter in Spanish, very low.

"Are you okay?"

"Yeah, Mami."

"Did you eat?"

"Yeah."

"You want me to heat some rice and beans and *pernil*?"

Cassandra's eyes were already closed. "No, Mami, I'm fine. How was Jason?"

"*Bien*. He sang himself to sleep. He really does have a beautiful voice. He inherited that from you."

"And I from you."

"You don't have to say such things. I'm not a señorita in the plaza anymore, dying for men's *piropos*."

Maybe not, but her mother deserved to have whatever side of the bed she wanted, even if it was the same one Cassandra liked.

"I'm going to sleep now, Mami. Good night."

"Good night, *M'hija*."

After a minute her mother got up and went downstairs to her own bed. She left the night light on.

*   *   *

In the morning Cassandra was up with no problem.

Everyone went through their routine, except that her mother had gotten up and made breakfast so Cassandra could sleep a little later. She had the paper waiting when Cassandra came out of her room fully dressed and refreshed.

Cassandra hugged and kissed her son and combed his hair, as he was already dressed and fed. She sat calmly with a strong cup of coffee and some eggs and the front-page news of FYSHBone's death. Police reported no early leads.

Reporters had teased out some facts through their contacts. That FYSHBone had been in talks to make a deal with KAMIKAZE Vynil was now public.

Leland Bishop had issued a statement that his company had been in talks, which he refused to characterize, but he said, "The rumors that it was a 'bailout' of KUTTHROAT are entirely exaggerated and we will not confirm or deny those at this time."

Lord knew Cassandra was no financial genius, but that sounded like double-talk. Guzmán had not said a thing about the company being troubled, but she and Moretti had not asked. She needed to interview Sabio again.

And maybe again.

She ate her eggs and recounted the previous day's adventure for her mother without the graphic, gory details or the part where she got shot at and almost went over the edge of the roof with Slow Mo. Neither did she mention how she ran around alone in a dark, abandoned building chasing somebody who could very well have been the shooter.

One of the unspoken fears about Cassandra's work was not only the danger to her, but what would happen to her son if anything happened to her. Cassandra was able to put that fear out of her head most days, but she knew her mother worried over that, as any mother would.

Her mother did not know FYSHBone's work. Cassandra named a few songs and his movie roles.

"No."

The Mexican pop singer FYSHBone dated.

"No."

The Venezuelan beauty queen he impregnated.

"Tampoco."

Cassandra hummed and did the hooks from "This Nigga Don't Play," "Tarantulas," "Legacies," "The Street King," and "Night Moves."

Her mother knew none of it.

"Anyway, he was a big star, Mom."

"I believe you. Are you going to be working such late nights every night again?"

Cassandra did not know. She hoped not. Again, she understood her mother's concern.

But the bills that arrived the day before waited on the edge of the table. Cassandra passed a hand over her son's head.

"Mami, I think this is a special case."

Cassandra's mother nodded and continued with the dishes. She prayed aloud for Cassandra to hear and accept the blessing that God should protect her daughter and all of her new colleagues, including Señor Moretti, and that the Holy Spirit would illuminate their path and lead them to the troubled person who did this, with no more violence and no more senseless loss.

Cassandra put her hand up. "Amen and amen."

Her mother packed some fruit for the road.

CHAPTER 32

Seven Little Notes

Evidence came in during those first few days but nothing hit Cassandra in the head like Newton's apple. She went in circles between FYSHBone's personal life and his business affairs, and no clear picture formed.

Detectives worked phones and conducted in-person interviews of many of the people who had received guns from FYSHBone.

No suspect emerged from that effort.

She tried to reach Leland Bishop to schedule an interview and was repeatedly blown off by his scheduler.

Ballistics eliminated the two guns recovered so far—the one from FYSHBone's waistband and the one Slow Mo shot at Cassandra and Moretti with—and each was proven to have not been the murder weapon.

They did not find any identifying evidence, such as DNA or a fingerprint, on any of the casings recovered at the crime scene. Each was squeaky clean.

All of the fingerprints that had been collected came back, but nothing was solved.

Slow Mo and other members of FYSHBone's posse, each of whom had unremarkable criminal records, had been inside their boss's vehicle, his loft and studio, and even in his luxury penthouse.

But again, Slow Mo's gun was eliminated, and the ex-cons in his circle all had solid alibis.

Princesa De los Santos had of course been in FYSH-Bone's car. The supermodel was once arrested for allegedly cutting an assistant's ponytail off with a knife during a photo shoot that went awry, so her prints were on file.

Princesa had left plenty of fingerprints in FYSHBone's penthouse but did not leave a single print at his secret hideout in the Bronx. Maybe the panties Cassandra had recovered there were not hers.

The blood on the panties was found to contain traces of uterine tissue cells, which meant it was in fact menstrual blood. Whoever was in FYSHBone's apartment the night Cassandra ran around in the dark was a female, and they now had a DNA profile for this person, if no match.

Was it Princesa's blood? Could they get a warrant to test her DNA? What would that prove? A judge would require more.

Cassandra called the dog pound. No one had rescued FYSHBone's mutt. Cassandra really did not want to hear that the dog had been gassed.

The tiny bit of blue rubbery material that Cassandra recovered from the jagged tree roots up on the train tracks came back as neoprene, a material with a million commercial uses.

The court records of FYSHBone's many litigations did not provide a way out either, as they merely corroborated that FYSHBone had exes who bore his children and sued for support.

Papers showed that FYSHBone somehow always managed to plead that he was broke and managed to keep all of his unclaimed children away from any real money.

To Cassandra, the struggling single mother, it seemed petty if not selfish and callous in light of FYSHBone's evident wealth, but none of it felt like a prelude to his spectacular murder.

Cassandra fast-forwarded through hours of FYSHBone's video recordings. She found him funny, angry, insightful, but also at times surprisingly boring.

Sometimes he was hysterical. At times he sounded especially angry at his mother. He spoke directly to her and did not check his tone.

"It was all your fault, Momma! You tried to make it seem like it wasn't you, but you know that it was. You tried to make me someone I was not. Why did you make me restring it? Why? You knew that I didn't want to. How could you be so cruel?"

Restring it?

Cassandra wondered whether FYSHBone had ever gotten treatment for mental illness, but found no record of such treatment in what had been collected.

The HI-PRO detectives hit the streets to visit the ex-girlfriends and mothers of FYSHBone's children who lived in the tristate area, which was several.

Most of his exes had alibis and either said that FYSHBone was a loser and a deadbeat and lousy in bed or that he was unforgettable and took them on picnics and safaris and—the most common—wrote and sang love songs to them with an old accoustic guitar over breakfast. One said he was a genius of the Kama Sutra. These women never understood what went wrong.

Foolish games, one said.

In any case, all of FYSHBone's exes were determined to get their kids or themselves their due out of his estate, and all expressed concern about what would happen with his money now that he was gone.

Cassandra wanted especially to pursue family angles, so she and Moretti kept FYSHBone's sisters' interviews for themselves.

FYSHBone kept one sister in a Staten Island mansion he had paid for in cash. That sister complained that the taxes out there were such that even though she had no mortgage, she would never be able to keep the property unless FYSHBone had left her something additional in his will.

Did the detectives know anything about that?

"No," said Moretti. "Ever consider getting a job?"

FYSHBone's sister dirty-looked Moretti as if he had suggested she sacrifice a vital organ.

FYSHBone had left her a lot of space, a great yard that would be any doggy's delight, but Cassandra did not bother to ask if the woman wanted to rescue her fallen brother's stranded pup.

The other sister called herself Billie even though that was not her name. She lived surrounded by jazz memorabilia in a Harlem brownstone that doubled as a bed and breakfast. She always wore diamonds. FYSHBone had also paid for that in cash.

Billie kept Miles Davis on in scratchy vinyl in the background. She appeared more hurt by her brother's death than the first sister.

"All my brother ever wanted was to be true to his music. This world never let him."

Moretti sniffed. "With all due respect, miss, your brother seems to have made out quite well behind his music."

"You think money fixes what's inside?"

Cassandra asked Billie what she meant.

"There are spaces so empty, Detective, no amount of consumption fills them."

Billie talked about FYSHBone's father, LeRoi, Jr., who she called Daddy even though he wasn't. He was an aspiring jazz pianist and composer. He had an antique piano in the Red Hook apartment, at the window with the view to the city.

"Daddy sat at that piano night and day and worked on just that one piece, 'Magnum Opus.' Daddy's masterpiece. He dedicated it to my little brother. Started it the day my brother was born. Daddy was almost finished, too, but it just had one little missing signature. A little something. Seven notes that would lock it all into place. But it was those last elusive seven notes that did it."

Billie hooked an arm over the backrest of her chair, took a drag on a cigarette, and brushed her hand through her lustrous hair.

"On my brother's seventh birthday he walks past the piano, takes a look at the wrinkled sheet where Daddy marked and erased a thousand random notes. Little LeRoi just sees it. He just sees the missing notes. He can't help himself. He wasn't being mischievous or a showoff. He really was the sweetest boy. God, how he loved his daddy!"

Billie dragged deep. She blew a funnel of smoke into the ceiling.

"Daddy gets back to his piano. He sees what my brother has done. He plays the seven notes. Breaks into a sweat. He plays the entire piece forte. Gets to the seven notes again: Da-da da-da da-da da. Proceeds to the coda and the final note, then lets the silence grow. Seven notes. That's all it took. Something in Daddy cracked. He didn't say a word. My brother waited for praise that would never come."

Billie gulped three fingers' worth of rye. She leaned forward, elbows on knees. Cigarette smoke rose in a line that vaporized as it passed her face.

"Our daddy waited until he was alone with that piano. He ripped out the wires. Fashioned himself a noose. Lynched himself with piano wire for whatever crime he felt had been committed."

Cassandra swallowed. "That's awful."

"My brother found him. You never saw another purple quite like Daddy's tongue. FYSHBone carried that guilt the rest of his life."

Perhaps he has peace now, thought Cassandra. *Or maybe not until his affairs are put in order. His killer is still on the loose.*

Billie poured herself three more fingers' worth of whiskey. "Worst part, it didn't have to happen. Daddy wasn't even the real father. We all knew that, no matter how much my mother tried to pretend. Nobody knew who that child's father was. But it wasn't the man FYSH thought he drove to suicide."

Moretti asked Billie whether she had any idea who would want to hurt FYSHBone.

"I guess in some ways I'm saying *he* always did. But I really can't think about this anymore. Can you please leave?"

CHAPTER 33

I Just Want You Close

The detectives headed to Midtown again to interview the rest of the staff at the record label. It had been a couple of days. Cassandra was intrigued to learn a source of FYSH-Bone's pain, although it was not likely to help her solve his homicide.

Before the detectives left Billie's place, Cassandra showed her the drawing of the seven notes tattooed on FYSHBone's forearm. They were the same ones added to his father's tragic masterpiece. He did carry it with him.

What does it all mean? thought Cassandra.

She was excited to return to KUTTHROAT. She wanted to look at Sabio Guzmán.

The lawyer did not disappoint, in an athletic-cut beige suit, canary yellow shirt with no tie, open at the collar. He made a pain of himself by insisting that as general counsel he be present at each interview.

Guzmán interrupted and instructed staff to not answer questions related to "trade secrets" or any knowledge employees had of FYSHBone's affairs. He allowed staff to give only their personal impressions of the man.

Apparently the departed was universally regarded as

a relaxed, fun, generous boss who encouraged staffers to be creative problem solvers and to work and play together as a team, which he cemented by doing things like taking the whole staff on a Caribbean cruise.

Each staffer sounded more wooden than the last. Many used the same words and phrases.

Left alone for a second, Moretti said, "These people have been coached."

Cassandra thought, *No shit, Sherlock*, but did not offer an opinion.

She was particularly interested in talking to the label's financial man, Dulles. She was thinking about Moretti's theory that the Feds always look for the structure of a criminal enterprise, a hierarchy of coconspirators where money flows up and orders flow down.

She was also influenced by Cuca's concern that FYSH-Bone might have been embroiled in a racketeering conspiracy and that his death could be related. Cuca's advice about FYSHBone's underlings led Cassandra to want to speak with KUTTHROAT's money man.

"I'm afraid he's unavailable," said Guzmán.

"Where is he?"

"He has taken a mental health day. This is all very upsetting."

Guzmán had an answer for everything. Cassandra wondered what his breath smelled like.

She drew a small heart on her notepad. "The more we dig into FYSHBone's private life, the more it seems he never had any one major love affair. No marriage, no long-term girlfriend. You have any insight into that, Counselor?"

"FYSHBone had unrealistic expectations."

Moretti sucked his teeth. "You mean like expecting that just the one woman can fulfill all of your needs?"

Sabio made eye contact with Cassandra. "Jeez, I hope not, Lieutenant. I mean, I hope *I* never feel that way. I really want there to be that one woman. Obviously I've been wrong before, chose poorly, but...I still believe the right one is out there."

Cassandra liked what she heard. "So what do you mean FYSHBone had unrealistic expectations?"

"Alicia Keys, for example."

"The singer? What about her?"

"Remember the single 'No One'?"

"Beautiful song."

"Too beautiful. The minute it dropped, FYSHBone gets it in his head the song is about him."

"Were they together?"

"They never even knew each other."

"So what made him think that?"

"FYSH said he 'heard' it in the song. In the piano at the beginning and then in the 'perfect marriage of music, lyrics, emotions, and vocals.' He said it was a secret message Alicia sent for FYSHBone to rescue her. We watched the video and when he saw Alicia breathe at the beginning, he said he knew this woman was for him."

Moretti slapped his leg and chuckled. "What chutzpah."

Cassandra asked where it all went.

"Well, FYSH was set to play a benefit concert. Alicia was also performing. He figures this is the perfect occasion. He'll show up with a ring, get down on bended knee on stage at the concert in front of everyone, and pop the question."

Cassandra found this disturbing. "Even though they never dated?"

"Like I said, unrealistic expectations. FYSH even reached out to the Smithsonian about the Hope Diamond. I convinced him this was presumptuous, even for him. Alicia might want a more formal courtship. It could get really embarrassing. He decided on chocolates instead."

Cassandra crossed her arms. "Wait a minute, from diamonds to chocolates?"

"These were very special chocolates. Rarer than the rarest truffles. Had to be flown in from Switzerland. Cost the same as high-quality diamonds, comparing carats to ounces. FYSH got Alicia six carats' worth."

Cassandra remembered the microdiamond Michael had given her on the Wonder Wheel at Coney Island.

"So FYSH and I are backstage at Madison Square Garden for the concert. FYSHBone is nervous. He's set to collaborate with Lil' Kim, a whole Brooklyn tribute to the Notorious B.I.G. Down-ass, heavy metal versions with Lenny Kravitz on electric guitar."

"What about Alicia Keys?"

"She's ready to go; she's the act before them. The house lights dim, the Garden rumbles from the manic thunder of the crowd. Right at that moment, FYSHBone decides to approach Alicia, as she steps toward the stage."

"All about him," said Cassandra. "Typical."

"You don't know the half of it. Alicia's security cuts him off, rightly so. FYSH never got close. Alicia never even saw that he wanted to speak to her."

"What did FYSHBone do? Did he wait for her to come offstage?"

"No. He pulled me to a stairwell to cry and complain. He threw the chocolates on the floor and stomped on them. We heard Alicia play 'No One' to the crowd and

FYSHBone banged his head with a fire extinguisher until he got woozy."

Moretti whistled. "Somebody needed some meds, huh?"

"What happened next?"

"Nothing. FYSH returned backstage. Five-fingered a doo-rag off one of his posse to cover the knots in his forehead. Went out on that stage and gave the best live performance of his life."

"I guess adversity really is the wellspring of success," said Moretti.

"After the agreed-upon set, FYSH took out a black acoustic guitar he said he inherited from Johnny Cash. He played an impromptu, downtempo, unplugged version of Outkast's 'Hey Ya' that revealed the sorrow at the center of that song. FYSH dedicated his performance to 'a girl so beautiful, she thinks she can break my heart just by breathing. I got news for you, baby: my heart was already broke before you came along.' After that Alicia Keys never came up again."

"I guess you made your point about unrealistic expectations."

"Don't get me wrong," said Sabio. "I know he sounds deranged. What I'm trying to tell you is that FYSHBone was really an idealist. A romantic. He wanted the world to be perfect. To have that one great love affair. The ironic thing is he was too dysfunctional to live with the fact that life is full of dysfunction."

CHAPTER 34

Black Majesty

FYSHBone's viewing was at a funeral home on the Upper West Side open to the public. The line stretched around the entire block. The people waited and danced in place and broke into group a cappella versions of FYSHBone's most famous songs.

Inside there was a VIP section behind velvet ropes in a chapel with an annex and the coffin up front. The casket was silver and it was closed.

Easels held blowups of some of FYSHBone's album covers, and the close-ups revealed the oft-overlooked detail that FYSH had the most amazing hazel eyes of all time.

Four flags were posted: those of the United States, the State of New York, the City of New York, and the red, black, and green that symbolizes African liberation.

Ushers made certain that members of the public filed past without stopping. It was nighttime and the procession of mourners had begun at ten in the morning and showed no signs of slowing down.

Cassandra did not wait in line. She flashed her shield to get past the velvet ropes.

She joined movie stars, professional athletes, tycoons, politicians, pop music phenoms, and the greatest rappers of their generation in a VIP section.

She saw members of FYSHBone's family whom she had interviewed, including his sister Billie, who looked elegant despite a slight slur.

FYSHBone's children looked quiet, if not sad, and greeted each other like strangers who meet only at weddings. Everyone spoke in hushed tones.

Rumors circulated that FYSHBone's mother had not arrived and might not come as there was a fear she might have a seizure or a heart attack or a nervous breakdown.

Princesa hovered above most people with her pointy chin. She wore a black spaghetti-strap dress and large black shades. Her chubby assistant followed.

Gator Moses arrived without his bodybuilding protégés. His Russian blonde trailed him like a kite. Famous people, especially athletes and elected officials, all knew and greeted him, but quickly moved on.

Cassandra spotted Sabio Guzmán in a corner. He did not mingle or remove his shades. He looked good in the classic black suit, white shirt, black tie combo. At that distance he passed for somber but Cassandra could not tell.

Sabio saw Gator Moses and did an about-face, but Gator's woman caught that and whispered to her man and pointed Sabio out.

Gator went after him, his woman right behind.

Cassandra watched.

Moses extended his muscular arm and caught Guzmán on the shoulder. The lawyer turned and acted surprised.

Cassandra could not read Gator's lips, as he had his back to her, but his body language read like an ice pick.

Guzmán nodded and appeared to say "No problem, no problem."

The trio headed outside.

Oxana whipped out a chocolate bar and wolfed it as she walked, dropping the wrapper.

Cassandra discreetly followed and tucked herself behind a tree to watch.

The lawyer reached into his jacket and produced a thick, stiff envelope.

Gator snatched it and handed it to his woman to count but did not release Sabio from his glare. The woman counted, which took a minute, then said okay. She stuffed the envelope into her bosom.

Even if those are only twenties, that is a fat chunk of change. What is Sabio paying for?

Cassandra looked around to see if she could make out any FBI men on Gator's tail. She made none but did spot Leland Bishop and his man spying on the entire transaction from behind a parked truck.

Bishop punched the palm of his hand. "Bollocks!"

Why did *he* care about a transaction between these two? Cassandra wondered whether it could have anything to do with the deal for KUTTHROAT, but she was mystified.

Cassandra looked back at the trio. Gator's woman did a half pirouette on the balls of her feet and headed back inside with her man.

Sabio followed. So did Cassandra.

They returned to the VIP section, which was over-crowded. Sabio again moved to a corner and stood with his hands in his pockets observing from behind his shades. Gator went into another corner with his woman.

Cassandra waited for Bishop and his man to reenter and went over and introduced herself.

The tycoon said, "Ah, yes, the heroine from the Marathon Slasher incident."

"I'm on the FYSHBone murder now."

"A ghastly business."

Business? "I left several messages with your New York office."

"Yes, I've been very busy."

"Your assistant claims you've been out of the country."

"I imagine you are clever enough to have checked with customs."

"You've been in country since just before the murder."

"Correct. I do not always alert my local help. I apologize for the misinformation."

"We hear you and FYSHBone were about to become partners."

"I was set to acquire his publishing rights, yes."

"So what happens now?"

"We're trying to work something out with the estate."

"I imagine you're in a better position now that he's dead, huh?" Cassandra had no way of knowing, but liked to take stabs.

"He who develops a callus on his bottom is in the best position."

"Come again?"

"The negotiator with the most patience, who is willing to sit the longest, wins. Desperation is the enemy of reason."

That didn't explain anything. "Who are *your* enemies, Bishop?"

"Great Britain has no enemies."

Cassandra acted as if she knew more than she did. "You're not bothered by this deal between Gator Moses and Sabio Guzmán?"

"It's none of my affair."

"Do you own a .50-caliber weapon?"

"Certainly you are not interrogating me at a funeral, Detective."

"Prefer to go downtown?"

Bishop smirked but looked around, embarrassed. His man shifted on his feet.

"Let's try this again, Bishop: Do you own a .50-caliber handgun?"

"No."

"You didn't get one from FYSHBone?"

"No."

Cassandra nodded at his aide. "Does anybody who works for you carry such a weapon?"

"How would I know what my employees carry?"

"Within the scope of their employment."

"To my knowledge nobody carries a .50-caliber weapon on my behalf, Detective."

"Where were you on the night of the murder?"

"I have a right to remain silent."

"Again, that kind of talk only matters if I'm putting the cuffs on you right here, right now. Is that what you want? A strict reading of your rights under the law?"

Bishop said nothing.

"We know you were in the city and that you were not home."

"Learn that from my doorman, did you? Somebody else who's fired. I was at a fundraiser at the Waldorf."

"FYSHBone was shot after midnight."

"Right-o. After midnight I retired to the home of a Park Avenue socialite. My man Hegel here was given the night off. Let me cut you off before you ask for a name, as I will not be exposing my alibi to examination. Not unless I am at the point of an indictment. No need to stir up an international scandal."

Cassandra did not bother to use the word "warrant." She was a million miles from putting the screws to this guy.

"We'll have plenty more questions, so don't leave town."

Bishop walked off without bidding her adieu.

Cassandra spotted Slow Mo.

Look at this. Two days after he takes wild shots at two detectives and may be involved in a murder, and he is out on the street. What a system.

Cassandra kept an eye on Slow Mo.

The big man saw Sabio. They stared at each other across the crowded room.

Slow Mo was free on bail, presumably because a judge had decided he was not a threat to the community. He pointed at Sabio across that crowded room and drew a plump finger along his own Adam's apple nice and slow.

Sabio did not return the gesture or any gesture or turn away or mouth any words or act intimidated. He just faced Slow Mo with his hands in his pockets like, *Make your move, motherfucker.*

For reasons Cassandra did not understand this turned her on.

Sabio was approached by a slender, bald man with a crescent of black hair ear to ear around the back of his head like a cul-de-sac. He wore thick, outdated black glasses.

The two men appeared to argue.

The bald man went his way and Cassandra followed. His nerdy appearance made her think he must be Dulles, the label's accountant.

He went into the hall to get water from a fountain.

Cassandra approached, flashed her shield, and introduced herself. "Are you Dulles?"

His eyes got wide. Water dripped down his chin. "I am."

"I wanted to ask you a few questions about FYSHBone and your work at the record label."

"Really? Um, what kinds of questions, because—"

Dulles's phone rang. He interrupted himself and answered. "Um, yeah, okay." He looked down the hall.

Cassandra turned and saw Sabio, on his phone, turn back inside the chapel.

Dulles hung up. "See? Like I can't really talk right now. I'm all nervous and upset about all of this, and—"

Cassandra interrupted him. "Listen, if someone is trying to intimidate you—"

"I did not say that. I don't want any trouble. I'm not talking about anyone; don't even form that thought."

A bead of sweat zigzagged down Dulles's temple.

Cassandra handed Dulles her card.

"I'm going to get to the bottom of what is going on here. If you want to talk and come clean about anything, you call me, Dulles. I will be fair to you."

Dulles swallowed and made deep eye contact with Cassandra. His face went ashen. He put her card in his pocket and walked away.

Cassandra went back inside. After a moment, a hush fell over the crowd. The VIPs parted. FYSHBone music continued over the loudspeakers on a whisper. The ushers stopped the procession of mourners.

Tamora Edwards inched down the empty center of the room toward her son's remains. She wore an elegant black dress, a black hat and veil, white pearls, and low shoes. She gripped a black purse with both hands shaking. She took tiny steps and moved as if being pulled to her doom by a slow, invisible rope.

Tamora got to the silver coffin and stood before it. Her shoulders drooped. Her neck was at an angle. She stood still, with tension in her crooked back like a lonely, knotted, wind-burnt tree with no leaves.

Finally Tamora reached a black glove toward the casket. She touched it and paused.

Then the mother sobbed.

The mother wept.

The mother howled.

Tamora's body heaved as if great winds blew through it. With every wave she curled over the coffin more until at last she was draped over it, arms wrapped around the silver container that would ferry her son across the dark river.

Tamora's head rolled. She looked up at the ceiling and released the deep unnatural sound of incurable grief.

The purity of her pain infected Cassandra. She thought of her own son in a box. The destruction of *his* precious eyes.

Where does our innocence go? she thought.

Cassandra's throat swelled. Tears welled. Tamora cried and howled and drowned her son's music.

"Ooooo, my baby! Ooooo, my lastborn! My son! My only son!"

Tamora kissed the coffin and looked toward the ceiling and wailed.

Her tension paralyzed the room. There was nothing anybody could do. Cassandra did not want to feel this anymore.

She prayed for the aggrieved and the departed, then walked out.

CHAPTER 35

The Heart Is a Metronome

Sabio Guzmán was out on the sidewalk in front of the funeral home. He stood straight, with his hands in his pockets and his head angled toward the starless sky.

Cassandra was still upset by grief. She needed to calm down. She stood for a moment to compose herself.

Guzmán did not appear to be in a hurry.

Cassandra snuck a quick look in her compact mirror to make sure her crying had not demolished her light makeup.

She called her mom to check on her son and verify that everything was fine. He was home and well-fed and bathed and ready to be turned in for the night. She warned her mother that she was not sure when she would be home and told her she loved her in a way that made her mother ask if she was all right.

"I'm just grateful Jason and I have you."

"*Esta bien*. Don't worry. He's here singing for Grandma." In Spanish she said, "Go do what you have to do."

"Okay, Mami. I love you."

"I love you, too. Drive careful."

Cassandra turned and Guzmán was right there.

"Detective."

"Counselor."

"I saw you inside."

Guzmán seemed to look directly at her, but it was impossible to tell.

"A little dark for sunglasses," she said.

Sabio slid them up on his head. His eyes were almond-shaped. It appeared he had been crying.

"Tough to see FYSHBone's mother go through that. I came out to call my mom in Puerto Rico. Wish I was there with her now."

"Only natural."

Cassandra wondered whether Sabio had children, and if so why he didn't want to go be with them.

"I wanted to talk to you inside, but you looked like you wanted to be left alone," she said.

"I did," he said. "I don't anymore."

She nodded.

He looked into her.

People stood in line to proceed past FYSHBone. Celebrities and power brokers exited in teams, double-kissed cheeks, and climbed into waiting limousines.

Cassandra and Sabio stood face-to-face.

She wet her lips. "I could go for a drink."

Sabio looked over his shoulder at the exiting VIPs. "Me, too, but I need to get the hell off Fantasy Island."

"Feel like following me up to the Bronx?"

*   *   *

Cassandra approached one of the Harlem River crossings. She was behind the wheel of her minivan. She drew calm from one of her son's nature CDs, the one she had bought for him in Puerto Rico that captured the music of the rain forest. Her favorite was the nighttime call of the tiny delicate tree frog called the *coquí*.

Sabio followed in his bright blue sports car.

Cassandra checked her rearview. The man was right behind.

What am I doing? she thought. *This guy could be dangerous.*

Sabio was not quite a suspect in a homicide or even officially a person of interest, but she *had* met him during the course of an investigation. She had just watched him hand a gangster an envelope stuffed with cash. She had learned that he owned a .50-caliber handgun and that he might have had a motive to be jealous of FYSHBone over Princesa. He also interfered with her interviews of relevant witnesses. And he didn't have an alibi.

So again, what on earth was she doing?

She still had questions.

Bullshit, she didn't need to be alone with Guzmán to interview him. Certainly not at a bar.

He cut a fine figure.

But it was obviously more than that.

Cassandra felt a connection, and it wasn't just his magnetism. She somehow felt she knew Sabio, understood him. That they were alike in some fundamental way.

She knew the rule: Everybody lies.

She knew the other rule: Everybody lies to the police even more so.

Still, Cassandra *felt* on some level that she could trust

Sabio. There was no way of knowing. The trust was fragile. But it was something she believed, or wanted to. That
Sabio was okay. That he was good. That there was something genuine beneath the slick façade.

Maybe she was in some kind of denial, the way people
are the first time they smoke, shoot, or snort.

*I know this is wrong, I know I am weak, I know it can-
not lead anywhere good, but things will be different this
time because this is me, and I am special.*

It was unusual these days for Cassandra to give anybody, especially a man, the benefit of the doubt. For whatever reason, she wanted to now. She simply wanted to.

God, please don't let this be a mistake.

Cassandra crossed the bridge and made a right, then a
left, then another right, then two lefts, then another right.
They parked.

Sabio put the Porsche in neutral and shut off the engine.
He followed Detective Maldonado to some dark corner of
the South Bronx.

What was he doing here? With her? The woman was a
cop. She snooped around FYSHBone's affairs. This was
super risky.

Sabio's ex-therapist would say, "Yeah, but you *love* risk."

Not really. Not like he used to.

True, he was still invested in the possibility of the big
payout. He had developed terrible habits and those would
need to be overcome.

But all of that mumbo-jumbo about endorphins and the
reliving of childhood scripts did not explain Sabio's present condition. It did not fulfill his present needs. And it

did not explain why he had followed this woman over the river.

The answer was simple: She was fine. He could see that she was true. There was something good inside her that showed on the outside, and it had been a long time since Sabio saw that in anyone. Maybe it wasn't too late for him.

Or maybe he was kidding himself.

He sprayed his neck with cologne.

Cassandra watched Sabio swagger up the sidewalk.

He unveiled a friendly smile. "Where are we?"

"It's upstairs," she said. "Let me warn you, we're over-dressed."

"That's okay."

"This place is very neighborhood. Projects. Under-ground. That's why you can't see it from the street. You have to know someone. I grew up around here."

"Cool."

Cassandra felt like an adolescent seeking approval. It had been a while since she had been to this place, and she wondered what Sabio would think and worried frankly that he might conclude she was low-rent.

But she had no interest in pretense.

She banged on the heavy metal door. You could barely hear merengue music on the other side.

The slat slid open and the music blew out like a trade wind.

"¡Mira quién es!"

The doorman, an older gentleman who ran a domino club, hugged Cassandra and told her he had seen her on the front page of the newspaper. He gave Sabio the up and down. They entered.

The space might have started as one of those extra-large high-ceilinged prewar apartments once popular in the Bronx.

Now the interior walls were gone. It was a small night-club with tables near the front, a small central bar, a packed plastic-tiled dance floor, and a small stage a mere foot and a half off the ground.

No band, just a DJ and a large Puerto Rican flag on the wall.

Sabio said, "Is this spot even legal?"

Cassandra said, "You know the stupidest law in New York? Cabaret license. If you don't have the right license, you are not supposed to let people dance in your estab-lishment. Can you think of something more obnoxious? A ticket for letting people dance?"

"Fascist on its face," said Sabio.

The place was crowded and hot. The dance floor was dark, as most dance floors ought to be. Ages ranged from early twenties through sixties and averaged around forty.

Young men in baggy hip-hop gear leaned against walls. Older men in collared short-sleeved shirts wore their chains out. The oldest women dyed their hair and wore earrings that tugged on their earlobes, plus colorful, shimmery clothes that hugged their rolling hills.

Women from their forties on down styled multiple tat-toos, big jewelry, long nails, form-fitting jeans, and shorts that showed lots of thigh. Their blouses were technically too small, but no one complained. They danced in low-top sneakers, sandals, and flats. Many looked tough but laughed and smiled easily.

The DJ switched to salsa. They ordered rum and Cokes and when the drinks came Sabio commented on how inexpensive they were.

"For the price of one round at the Mandarin Oriental we could get tanked up here."

"At least there you'd have an exotic drink and a view," said Cassandra, privately recalling a drug deal she had solidified next to the big window overlooking Columbus Circle and Central Park.

"I got a pretty view right here," said Sabio, looking straight at Cassandra and taking a sip through a skinny straw.

Cassandra smiled but did not return the compliment.

They spoke little and let the rum find its way into their blood. Cassandra had been too focused lately to stop for a drink. It had been months. She began to get warm.

Sabio ordered another round, and by the time they toasted, Cassandra felt the sugar rise.

The DJ dropped a *bachata*.

"You dance?" she said.

Sabio put his drink on the bar and took her hand. Cassandra gulped what was left in her glass and followed Sabio to the dark dance floor.

Sabio had not danced *bachata*—or anything else, for that matter—in a very long time. He loved to dance, had grown up with it, carried it in his blood. His mother once won first place and a thousand dollars in a salsa contest that was later televised on local TV—in of all places Pasadena, Texas.

Sabio was tipsy, but when he got to the dance floor he

ignored all other movement in the room except for the
beat and did the one two three-*up* that is the basic bachata
step, a modified cha-cha-cha. Once Sabio had the basics it
was off to the races.

He held Cassandra's hands lightly to start. She let him
find his beat, then joined him.

Sabio pulled her close, put his arm around her waist
and his hand on the small of her back and guided her in a
smooth, slow circle, the first of several.

They pivoted together easily, gracefully. Sabio raised
Cassandra's arm and released her waist and she turned
in the direction he wanted her to, so elegant it made him
smile.

They went around the dance floor like two swans
around a glassy lake.

The bachata ended and they danced another, then a
third, until they finally wore out. Sabio led her back to
the bar and his only thought was that he could not wait to
dance with Cassandra again.

She was really something.

Cassandra was really hot but very pleasantly surprised by
Sabio on the dance floor. He had a strong beat.

He passed her napkins to dry herself. "Cassandra, you
dance like a feather."

It felt good to hear him say it. She liked his footwork
and the way he hovered over her when they were close.
The smell of his neck made her want to run her hands
over his bare chest.

"I like what you do with your hands," she said.

Sabio "listened" with his fingers to where she wanted

to go, then led her there. It was subtle and it was intuitive and it was very nice. "You must be the sensitive type."

"Last time a woman called me sensitive it was a complaint."

Cassandra bumped him with her hip.

They ordered another round.

"Why did you become a cop?"

Cassandra thought about the ring on her necklace underneath her dress, out of sight. It was not the time to go into all of that.

"The usual reason. To make a living."

Sabio said, "I saw you answer that at the press conference. There must be more."

Cassandra had been pregnant with no prospects when she signed up for the police exam. She needed a job.

"I wanted a backup career. I was trying to break into entertainment. I didn't want to be a starving artist."

"Are you an actress?"

"Sometimes. I dance and sing."

"You go to school for that?"

"Yeah. Performing Arts."

"The high school from *Fame*?"

"I majored in dance."

"That figures."

"I wanted to go to Julliard after but things didn't work out."

"What happened?"

Cassandra's father had beaten her the night before the audition and bruised and swelled her eye. She felt self-conscious during her entire performance. She was not about to share that with Sabio or anybody else right now.

"I blew the audition."

"That sucks. How'd you end up in police work?"

"I saw a young female uniform walk out of the local precinct. Three jerks I knew from my building stepped right out of her way. I thought, *I want that*. I went in, I asked, it just so happened the exam was coming up."

"Serendipity," said Sabio.

"So they say. How did you become a lawyer?"

"I was in social work. Failing at reforming gangbangers in Chicago. I wanted to make a better living."

"So why New York?"

"My father lived here. I needed to find him."

"Did you?"

"In Bushwick."

"How is that going?"

"He passed away."

"Sorry."

"Don't be. It was great. He was funny and warm. Told me the story of his life. I learned a lot about what makes me tick."

"Your idiosyncracies."

"Yeah."

"Was that helpful?"

"It was. It still is. I mean, I'm still a work in progress."

Cassandra wanted to ask so many more questions. Like how Sabio got mixed up with FYSHBone and why he gave Gator so much money and whether he had really seen something to hold in Princesa De los Santos.

She did not want to hear anything that might ruin the mood.

"Is there a woman in your life, Sabio?"

"No."

"Do you have children?"

"A daughter. She's grown. I had her when I was eighteen. She's . . . well, she's in Iraq."

"Doing what?"

"In the army."

Cassandra nodded but was careful not to communicate too much concern.

"She's barely old enough to order a drink," he said.

Cassandra had wished so often, especially in the early years of Jason's diagnosis, that her son would have a chance to lead a normal life, to make choices like any other person. At least she would never have to face the prospect that her son might choose to be in a war.

"That must be hard on you. Her being so far away."

"She grew up in Chicago. She was seven when I came out here to go to law school. I keep a picture of her in my car from when she was little. I realized recently she doesn't smile in pictures anymore."

Sabio eyes traveled to some place far within. It was time to lighten things.

Cassandra said, "Chicago, huh? Let me go talk to the DJ."

Sabio watched Cassandra speak into the DJ's ear. They high-fived each other. She came back pleased with herself.

"I put in a special request for you. Let's see if you can figure it out."

The whole party was in reggaeton mode. The older folks hung around the bar and refreshed their drinks or went to the bathroom, but the middle-aged ones and the younger ones danced in place or in pairs on the dance

floor against one another. All the reggaetoneros swayed
their hips suggestively.

Sabio and Cassandra remained posted at the bar but
danced next to each other without linking. Sabio had a
strong urge to get behind the woman and start *perreando*,
a word that has its roots in the Spanish word for dog. It
literally means to bump and grind doggy-style and is a sta-
ple in reggaeton. Sabio did not want to make any sudden
moves and come on too strong. He really liked Cassandra.

"So, Detective, is there anybody special?"

Cassandra sipped her drink.

He asked again.

"Just my son, Jason. He's ten." She paused.

Sabio figured she was gauging his reaction. He nodded.

"My mom lives with us and helps me take care of him."

"You don't have a man?"

She grinned. "Haven't had one yet."

Ouch.

The DJ let the last of the reggaeton fade, then dropped
a classic that Sabio had not heard in years.

The Jungle Brothers. "I'll House You."

"No way!"

"Yeah, Sabio! House music!"

House is uptempo electronic dance music that origi-
nated in Chicago. It is descended from disco, mixed with
funk and soul, plus a prominent bass drum to keep the
beat, and usually a high hat. It is intense and fun to dance
to. This particular song was an anthem.

Sabio said, "This was your special request?"

Cassandra nodded and bounced in time to the congas.
She placed Sabio's drink on the bar, grabbed his hand,
and pulled him to the middle of the dance floor.

One of the main fun things about house music is that anybody who can even remotely pick up a beat can dance to it because the beat is so strong and the basic step is so simple.

Just bend at the knees and move up and down or side to side to the beat, then do with your hands whatever feels natural. You can do that, you can dance house.

Of course a veteran like Sabio could find so much more. He and Cassandra found the beat instantly, as if the song had always played and they had always been on beat. Simulated cowbells gave the song a Latin feel.

Sabio wanted Cassandra. He wanted to hold, touch, feel, and squeeze her. He wanted to know her. He wanted to wake up and smell her. He wanted to make her smile.

They jammed up and down, side-to-side and face-to-face, eyes locked, in tandem.

They got groovy.

They got funky.

They got down.

It was nighttime in the Boogie Down.

CHAPTER 36

Islands in the Stream

They stumbled out onto the sidewalk laughing. Cassandra felt light. It had been a long time since she danced like that. A long time.

It was a natural moment for the pair to separate.

Or not.

Sabio's car was very blue.

"Looks fast," she said.

"Like a beam of light."

"You should offer me a ride."

"Where do you wanna go?"

Cassandra took the keys, popped the locks, slipped in behind the wheel.

"Gonna stand there all stiff like a statue, Sabio? Get in."

He hesitated. "Know how to drive a stick?"

Cassandra laughed sarcastically. *You'll find out.*

Sabio went around.

She started it. "It really does purr, doesn't it?"

She found reggaeton. Arcangel's *"Pa' Que La Pases Bien."*

Sabio pushed the button to take the top down.

Cassandra edged out of the tight space and burned rubber.

High speed through changing lights. Her bronze locks smacked through the wind. Cassandra felt in tune with the music, especially the violin.

Over the Third Avenue Bridge. Like a bullet to the access ramp to the Triboro.

"We going to Queens?" he said.

"Does it matter?"

Cassandra flashed her badge at the toll booth and drove through without paying. She shot all the way across several lanes to barely make a little-used ramp down to a little-known island.

Sabio looked around. "I've never been down here."

"I did a million drug deals here as an undercover."

Isolated. Dark. Undeveloped.

Cassandra peeled onto the paved straightaway underneath the high, elevated road to the Triboro Bridge.

Tall cement pillars flew past.

Sabio put his hand on the dash. "Slow down."

You scared, little boy?

Cassandra downshifted, ripped a left, pulled the wheel into a crazy-eight pattern.

Tires screeched. She threw her head back and felt the rush.

The car slid sideways in gravel toward one of the giant columns.

Sabio jammed both hands on the dash. "Stop!"

They slid to a stop just four inches from impact.

Cassandra eased the vehicle into first gear and moved at a nice, controlled speed.

"Did I scare you?"

He swallowed. "Just didn't want you to scratch it." Sabio laughed and so did she.

Cassandra looked at his profile. *Damn, you look good.*

She explained about the NYPD's behind-the-wheel training and how in her role as a high-profile drug dealer she drove a confiscated Maserati to its limits.

She pulled onto a lawn grown wild under a tree at the edge of the island.

She shut off the engine, turned up the radio, and got out.

It was totally dark.

There were big rocks and a concrete barrier that separated them from the black, treacherous water. Cassandra jumped down and climbed onto rocks wet with moss. She perched one foot on one rock, one foot on another.

If you slipped, the determined current would ruin you.

Cassandra climbed back toward Sabio. He pulled her up with a strong hand and did not let go.

She stood in front of him.

"Sabio."

"You really like the open flames, don't you, Cassandra?"

She watched his lips. He moved ever so slightly forward.

She moved in and put her mouth on his.

Is this really happening?

They kissed. His mouth felt full. His tongue was soft and strong. She could not believe she was doing this.

Sabio held her face, pulled back, looked into her eyes. He was one of those dramatic types. His mouth felt like velvet.

Cassandra put her hands on the back of his bare head and pulled him in. He let out a soft moan. Her blood rose.

Cassandra whispered, *"Muchacho malo."*

He grunted.

She felt him through his pants.

Mm, can I get some of that?

Her backside was against the car. They kissed and he pressed into her.

She thought, *We better stop. This could be trouble.*

They didn't.

Sabio reached and unstrapped her bra.

He pulled up her shirt and peeled off the C cup.

Ay, Sabio.

He put his mouth on her.

Oh, God.

Reggaeton on the radio: *"Métele...caliente...métele... caliente."*

Sabio's head was smooth and shiny.

Cassandra knew she wasn't supposed to.

She unbuttoned her jeans, pulled the zipper down, wriggled free with gyrating hips.

Sabio hooked his thumbs through her belt loops and pulled.

Yes.

He pressed his weight against her, wet his fingers, touched her the way she touched herself.

Wow. She moaned.

Cassandra wanted to feel Sabio inside. She wanted him to make her eyes flutter.

She became engorged. Her spine curved. She could not wait for the release.

Where was it?

"¡Cassandra!"

What? Her mother?

BAM BAM BAM!

"¡Levántate! Time to get up."

Mom?

Cassandra rushed to the surface.

BAM BAM BAM. "¡Sandra!"

"Huh?"

Cassandra opened her eyes. A flood of light. Her bedroom. She felt woozy, dehydrated. Pressure inside her head. She was hung over.

Her mother banged her bedroom door and called her name.

Cassandra was in bed alone. Her panties were moist. She was under the sheet.

She shaded her eyes and told her mother to come in.

"What time is it?"

"You dropped your phone downstairs. Were you drunk? It keeps ringing. Señor Moretti. I picked it up finally and told him you were sleeping and he said you better wake up and call him, that there's trouble."

Great.

"C'mon, get up and get ready."

"All right, Mami."

Her mother smirked. "Were you dreaming?"

Boy, was she.

After the club she had left Sabio on the sidewalk with a handshake and an awkward hug, but eye contact that said maybe in some other context, at some other time, if the investigation worked out right, something could happen.

Her mother pushed. "And what were you dreaming about?"

A fast car, Mami. A very fast car. "Nothing."

"Fine. Keep your little secrets. I'll make breakfast. Any requests?"

Cassandra pulled the sheet over her head. She took a frustrated breath. "I could go for some sausage and eggs."

CHAPTER 37

The Harder They Come

After Sabio and Cassandra parted on the sidewalk in front of the club, Sabio drove and thought about her.

What a dancer. What grace.

He dug how easy it was to lead her. Really to share the lead. The way he could touch the tip of one finger and know what she wanted.

Rare.

Actually, he'd never felt that. Certainly not that he remembered.

The little mole over her lip was in just the right place.

Sabio wanted to stay with Cassandra that night, to whisk her away, but it would not be right.

She was on a mission and so was he and they were at cross purposes and that is not the place to begin any relationship.

Relationship?

The word usually caught on Sabio's tongue, even when it was only a thought.

But Cassandra was worth it. A little revealed a lot. He was already certain she had something he wanted. Maybe something he needed.

Sabio wondered about her son. What kind of boy was he? Did he need a father figure? Was shooting hoops in the driveway still in Sabio's cards?

This was madness. What was he thinking?

There was nowhere to run and nowhere to hide.

Sabio was in a deep hole, almost as deep as the one waiting for FYSHBone.

He glanced at the picture of his daughter next to the speedometer. God, how he missed her.

She only had a few months left of her enlistment. Sabio wanted so badly to receive her with a packet full of cash.

The only reason Sabio's daughter even joined the army was that she needed money for college. And the only reason for that was Sabio's failure to manage his finances. Sabio's failure. His inability to grow and provide.

When his daughter told Sabio her plans, he tried to convince her otherwise. At that moment, the way his luck had run, he didn't have the solution to place on the table.

His only chip? Sign up for two years instead of four, Mamita, give your father a chance to get his house in order.

She agreed.

Instead of getting better Sabio tried to dig out the same way he had dug in.

Now his baby was in a war zone. She never smiled in pictures. She rarely emailed. She was at risk every day of great injury, pain, and psychological trauma, if not death.

Sabio felt anger, guilt, frustration, and shame. Above all, worry and fear.

Now Sabio's time was almost up. His child was either going to get the balance of the college money from her father or reenlist for more time in the death zone.

The KUTTHROAT/KAMIKAZE merger was supposed to solve all that.

FYSHBone's death and the ensuing aggression by Bishop had canceled Sabio's ticket.

He was left with no clue how to fix things.

Plus, Slow Mo was now looking to slice Sabio's throat.

Sabio need a smoke. He headed to the dope spot.

The weed was secure in his pocket. Sabio smoked a fat one with his dealer and felt ablaze. He was relaxed. At ease and slow.

It drizzled. The first rain in weeks.

Beautiful.

Microdots floated past streetlamps to make shapeless rainbows. Sabio loved a summer mist.

It was forever since he had gone to Lares. He wondered how high the creek rose behind his mother's house.

Sabio pointed the keyless remote at the Porsche and pressed the Start button.

The car did not start.

He tried again. Nothing.

The passenger window looked smashed.

Aw, c'mon.

He walked toward the vehicle. Broken glass, mostly on the passenger seat. He thumbed the keyless remote to no avail.

Silence.

Some dope fiend must've broken in, popped the hood, and stolen the battery. Terrific.

This was Bushwick, Queens. His father's old turf. Landlocked, at least forty minutes from Manhattan by train. Parts had still not recovered from the '77 blackout. This block was one of them.

Sabio went around to the driver's side, opened the door, popped the hood. He left the door open and went to the rear of the vehicle.

Funny, the battery was still in place. The cables had been disconnected from the battery posts. Sabio's first thought was that the thief had begun his work, thought better of it, and taken off. Probably startled, maybe by Sabio himself when he turned the corner.

He bent to reconnect the battery, then pressed the remote. The engine ignited.

Thank you, Lord.

Sabio let the hood drop.

That was when he spotted Slow Mo. The big man walked toward Sabio like a movie zombie down the middle of the desolate side street. Slow Mo's black SUV idled behind him.

Shit. Slow Mo must've staked out his dope spot.

"Slow? What are you doing out here?"

Slow Mo raised the massive KUTTHROAT AVENGER.

No! Sabio dove toward the open door but saw the muzzle flash and heard the incredible blast and felt when the bullet tore through the Porsche's metal.

The second shot exploded a headlight.

Sabio scrambled to get inside the car. He stretched to stay low and leverage his feet over the gas and clutch.

The third shot spiderwebbed the windshield.

Sabio was doubled over but got showered with glass dust.

He toed the clutch and threw it in gear.

He drove crazily out of the parked position, so low he could barely see over the hood.

Slow Mo stepped aside like a bullfighter. Sabio's car rocketed past him—straight toward Slow Mo's truck!

He jammed the brake and—BAM!—slid right into the SUV.

The airbag socked Sabio in the face like a heavyweight boxer.

A fourth shot—from behind now—exploded the GPS screen.

Sabio pumped, pedaled, and peeled from under the SUV's rear bumper. His vision was clouded by the sting and shock of the accident and blocked by the inflated airbag.

The next shot passed so close Sabio felt it whiz by his ear before it popped the airbag like a ballon. He swerved to miss another parked car.

Slow Mo jumped into the Blazer in Sabio's rearview.

Sabio threw the stick and gassed it but the Blazer still rear-ended him. He banged his mouth into the steering wheel and saw constellations but tossed gears, found traction, got to the corner, timed the turn, and gunned it.

The Blazer remained up his tailpipe.

How is that possible?

Sabio moved fast enough for the elevated track pillars to flicker. Slow Mo's souped-up SUV kept pace.

Sabio made for the Jackie Robinson. "Suicide Road." Famous for narrow, winding turns and savage accidents. It cut through cemeteries and was generally empty late at night.

Sabio banked and leaned into the curves. His tires squealed.

Slow Mo kept up.

A muzzle flash and a loud echo.

Sabio rembered his gun.

On a straightaway he left the transmission in fourth and leaned toward his secret compartment.

The weapon was gone.

Fucker! That was probably Sabio's own KUTTHTOAT AVENGER Slow Mo was shooting at him with.

Sabio's cellphone was dead. He could not call police. He did not know nearby precincts to drive to. No matter how fast he drove, the Blazer would not lay off.

Cat and mouse as they approached the Van Wyck.

I'll go to JFK! The airport's crawling with cops!

The racers hit a straightaway and Sabio opened it in fifth. His sports car finally pulled away. Sabio laser-beamed for the Utopia underpass. He would soon be able to stop a cop.

Two cars up ahead disagreed. They drove slowly, two abreast, like an elderly couple on a Sunday stroll. They filled the narrow road.

Move!

No shoulder. Low concrete walls on either side penned him in.

C'mon!

Sabio's engine raced. He downshifted.

The Blazer rushed from behind.

Sabio glimpsed his daughter's picture and stomped the brakes in a reverse game of chicken to force Slow Mo to rear-end him or whip around.

Slow Mo swerved and was unable to brake his immensely heavier vehicle. The Blazer bore right and hit the low wall at just the right angle. It launched.

Sabio witnessed the vehicle flip through the air over the lane next to him and smash and tumble on the highway with the sound of rolling thunder.

The Blazer ended upside-down, its roof crushed under its own weight. It slid and sparked and spun on the highway and left debris in its wake.

The two slow cars ahead had disappeared under the underpass and did not see what happened.

It was late and no other cars approached.

Sabio froze, but his heart was a piston. The Blazer rested on its back like an overturned turtle. Its wheels spun.

Sabio inched his car closer.

Slow Mo kicked out the tattered rear window and stumbled from the wreckage like a chick poking its way out of an eggshell. He wobbled to his feet in abrupt, clumsy stages and snapped his head in different directions. He staggered toward Sabio's car. His droopy eyes settled roughly on Sabio.

Slow Mo slowly raised the KUTHROAT AVENGER. By Sabio's count he had one more shot.

Sabio ducked.

Slow Mo's head tilted back. His throat had been slashed in the crash. The gash across his Adam's apple was long. His head listed backward. The hole in Slow Mo's neck yawned open in the rough shape of a small but rapidly expanding football.

The gun plopped to the pavement. Slow Mo dropped to his knees. Plasma poured down his chest. He keeled over.

Sabio was in shock. But others would soon come. There was no time.

He jumped out, ran, picked up what could be his gun, and did not look at Slow Mo.

He jumped in his car and sped off.

Ten seconds after he squeezed the Porsche past the wreckage: KA-BOOM!

Sabio saw the flames in his rearview mirror. They reached for the sky.

He took the Long Island Expressway back to Manhattan and crossed at the bridge instead of the tunnel so no toll taker would see him and notice the damage to his car and the fact that his airbag had deployed. This way also no toll camera could prove at precisely what time Sabio left Queens.

Things were getting tighter than ever. He had to watch every step.

CHAPTER 38

Amateur Photography

Cassandra rode the elevator to the fourteenth floor and wondered what the problem was. Moretti had said the police commissioner was on a tear looking for her but did not say why.

Problem with the Marathon Slasher file? she thought.

She really hoped not. Cassandra put her phone on vibrate and walked into the PC's office.

Riley stood next to the window, his back to the room. His view was of the big white Beaux Arts municipal building.

Agent Bollinger sat on a leather couch. There was an unopened FBI file on the coffee table in front of him.

Okay, so this has to do with FYSHBone and Gator. Maybe the FBI had seen her spy on Gator and Sabio outside of the funeral home.

The commissioner chewed an unlit cigar. He pointed at the copper statue of a woman that topped the municipal building.

"*Civic Fame.* Three times life-sized. The laurels in her hair symbolize glory."

The statue had a shield. Her outstretched hands held a leafy branch and a crown.

"One of the tallest sculptures in the city," said Riley. "One time her left arm broke off and crashed through a skylight. Had to be reattached. She's withstood a century's worth of pollution."

Cassandra was not there for a history lesson.

"Sir?"

Riley ignored her. "The woman who posed for her posed for statues all over. Courthouses, libraries, fountains, museums. First female ever to take her clothes off on film. After that she couldn't find a husband. Tried to kill herself and failed and lived another seventy long years in an asylum."

Cassandra shifted. "You summoned me, sir?"

Riley finally turned to face her. The chubby cigar was still in his mouth.

"Maldonado, what is the rule on fraternization?"

"Excuse me?"

The commissioner cited the section from the *Patrol Guide* about consorting with criminals.

Cassandra waited.

"What were you doing in an illegal speakeasy with the target of a federal investigation?"

Oh-oh. This was about Sabio.

Bollinger handed Riley the FBI folder.

Riley tossed it on the desk for Cassandra.

She took it. As soon as she opened it, her heart dropped.

Pictures of her and Sabio inside the club. Drinking, dancing, and flirting. His face in her ear and his hand on the small of her back. Holding hands on the way to the dance floor. In his arms, her eyes blissfully closed.

Over twenty high-definition photos. They looked provocative.

Cassandra's hand shook. She closed the file.

"What does my personal life—"

"Your boyfriend is garbage."

"He's not—"

"Don't speak, Maldonado! Do not speak! Keep your mouth shut."

Cassandra wanted to lash out. She swallowed.

Bollinger cleared his throat.

"Guzmán is just one target of a far-reaching RICO investigation. Corruption in the recording industry. Payola to radio stations. Money laundering. Securities fraud, wire fraud. Loan sharking. And now murder."

What?

"He popped on our radar and we've been tailing him for months."

This wasn't happening.

"You know he's tight with Gator Moses, right? Did you also know he's a pothead? And a degenerate gambler?"

Cassandra shut her eyes.

"And he was in the Bronx at the time and place of the murder. Our agents followed him across the Willis Avenue Bridge until he gave them the slip. If he committed that murder in the furtherance of a racketeering conspiracy it makes him eligible for the death penalty."

No way, thought Cassandra. Sabio? The man she was with last night? The one who spoke about his daughter? The one she had dreamed about? How could *he* be a monster?

"Check the 302s in the file with your pictures, Butterfingers."

FBI agents type 302 reports to summarize interviews with informants. Sometimes the entire narrative of a criminal conspiracy can best be understood by reading the 302 reports generated from the FBI's interviews of turncoat conspirators.

Cassandra could not help herself. She looked.

"A CONFIDENTIAL SOURCE (CS) who is in a position to testify furnished the following information to the below-listed agent based on conversations the CS had with SABIO "SHYSTER" GUZMÁN, an attorney for KUTTHROAT RECORDS and for the label's founder and sole shareholder LEROI "FYSHBONE" EDWARDS III. SA Erasmus Bollinger was the only agent present for the interview."

The report detailed an alleged conspiracy involving FYSHBone, Sabio, and an unknown other to launder contraband money through the label by receiving tens and sometimes hundreds of thousands of dollars a month in illegal proceeds and issuing checks for the same amounts to the unidentified person known as unknown—minus a modest transaction fee.

This was just the tip. The file contained maybe twenty such reports, implicating Sabio in all of the crimes Bollinger mentioned except the murder.

Bollinger said, "My agents fell off after these photos of you were taken. We don't know how the night ends. Did you spend the night with Guzmán?"

"That is nobody's business but ours," she said.

"You better keep a good timeline, Butterfingers, because he may need an alibi."

"For what?"

"FYSHBone's head of security, Slow Mo, bit the big one in one incredible car accident, late this morning."

Cassandra remembered Sabio's across-the-room face-off with Slow Mo at the funeral.

Bollinger said, "They rolled Slow Mo into a body bag, and his head's so barely attached it nearly came off. We have a team going over the burned wreckage of Slow Mo's vehicle. If I find any evidence suggesting foul play and connecting his demise to your boyfriend—"

"He's not my boyfriend!"

Riley said, "Why didn't you 'fess up that you knew him?"

"I didn't. I don't. I mean, not before."

"Really? Because you look awful chummy in these pictures."

"That's how you dance *bachata*."

"Don't give me that diversity crap!"

Go to hell. Cassandra held up the file. "These 302s are just unfounded allegations by an informant. Informants lie all the time. And remember, the Feds tried to make a money-laundering case with the Gottis and their record label, Murder Inc. That went nowhere. This is just racial profiling."

The police commissioner snapped. "Maldonado, are you a defense attorney? Guess what? All your tough talk? Your threats? They don't cut it anymore. You have no credibility. You're back in the bag."

"What? Back in uniform?"

"That's right. Invest in some blue threads. You'll need plenty. I'm sure you'd bust the seams on your old ones. I'm kicking you down to Transit. Have fun in the steam tunnels."

"You're not serious."

"Leave the shiny gold detective's shield on my desk, demotee. Go downstairs, they already got paperwork on a dull white one for you."

"But, sir—"

"What part of 'you're screwed' do you not understand, Maldonado?"

Cassandra's lip wanted to quiver.

Riley turned up his nose. "We'll see what departmental charges will develop from your dangerous liaison. I've already notified Internal Affairs."

Riley popped his stubby cigar and turned back to his view.

Cassandra contemplated a rebuttal. She reached for her shield. She felt its weight, then laid it on the desk.

Outside the window, up in the sky, the gilded copper goddess *Civic Fame* remained on her altar.

Cassandra realized she was holding the FBI folder against her chest like a schoolgirl. She tossed the file on the PC's desk, then headed for the door. Bollinger's glare met her full-on.

Cassandra did not take her eyes from his.

He flinched before she walked out.

CHAPTER 39

Sweet Sorrow

Cassandra felt suffocated. Her heart was on speed. The elevator walls felt as if they were closing in.

Her career. Her income. The stability of her family. Her son's education. Her home. Her sense of self-worth. Everything was in the fire.

Sabio a major criminal?

Cassandra did not want to believe that. But he was the least of her concerns.

Her demotion meant a massive pay cut. She would lose the house. And then what? Back to the projects?

She stopped at HI-PRO to grab her things.

Moretti asked where she was going.

"Home, finally."

Moretti looked sad as Cassandra shouldered her bag. He probably already knew.

"If you need anything, kid."

Cassandra did not thank Moretti or even say good-bye.

She left and climbed into her minivan and drove home, where her son sat on the kitchen floor arranging toy cars. Her mother did a crossword puzzle at the kitchen table.

Cassandra stood in the doorway.

Her mother put the puzzle down and took her glasses off. "What are you doing home so early?"

Cassandra dropped her bag. She went to her mother and threw herself on the floor. She buried her head in her mother's lap and wept.

"All right, *Nena*. It's okay." Her mother passed a hand over her head. "Everything will turn out fine. Have faith."

Cassandra cried and did not tell her mother the terrible trouble they were in.

Mercifully, her mother did not ask.

Cassandra spent the next days alone in her bedroom with the blinds pulled, the door closed, a sheet over her, head to toe.

She slept.

At times she floated.

Even awake she felt dim, low, motionless.

Her son came into her room and Cassandra pretended to be asleep.

She refused to eat.

Sabio left voice messages, which she dumped unheard.

On the third day Cassandra's mother entered without invitation. She flounced in in a floral print dress that would have been just as beautiful in the 1950s.

She opened blinds. Sunlight cracked through.

"Out of the tomb, Lazarus."

Cassandra protested. She wanted to be left alone.

Her mother peeled the bedsheet.

"You'll have plenty time alone when you get old."

"I mean it, Mami."

"Your son is hungry. I'm leaving to the stores."

Cassandra pulled the bedsheet under her cheek.

"Take him out. It'll do both of you some good."

Cassandra and her son ate in silence.

He arranged toy cars. She sat in pink pajamas with a foot up on the chair, the knee to her chest. Her hair hung in a tangle.

"Jason?"

He pushed a car around the floor.

"J?"

"Ah?"

"Do you love me?"

He didn't look. He kept on with his toy.

"Do you love me, J?"

The boy paused, then nodded without looking.

"*¿Papa?*"

"Hm?"

"Can I please have a hug?"

Jason rested on one knee.

"Please, J. Please come over here and hug me."

Jason picked at the car. He seemed to weigh options. Finally he arose, toy in hand. He stepped to his mother, purposeful. He even restrained a smile.

Cassandra leaned. Her little miracle threw his boyish arms around her.

You have come such a long way, baby.

She cried.

All of it was worth it. Her son was worth it. And so was she.

They closed their eyes and held.

*   *   *

They went to the sporting goods store and Jason was well-behaved. He did not run around or make loud noises, but he did touch many things and repeated, "Smiley face!" She could handle that.

It was madness to purchase anything other than the basics for survival at that moment.

Whatever.

She paid cash for a basketball hoop complete with the regulation backboard and on a regulation-height stand. She also bought a basketball and an air pump with a needle. Jason fell in love with a bright blue pair of rubber weightlifting gloves that reminded him of his favorite blue cartoon. They served no purpose, but he had to have them, so Cassandra paid for them.

They took their new toys home and set up the backboard.

Cassandra did not have any illusions that Jason would grasp the complexities of basketball, but he soon understood dribbling, which he had done in other years with other toy balls. He saw her shoot several off the backboard or clear through the rim and figured out the point. He wore his new blue neoprene gloves and wore himself out throwing the large ball up until he finally made one.

How they celebrated!

Jason laughed and clapped and pointed and said, "Smiley face!" over and over.

It would have annoyed anyone else. But he did not belong to anybody else. To Cassandra, her son's voice was music.

She realized nothing important had changed. She would always do whatever was needed to feed her son. So long as she had her wits, she and Jason would be okay.

Cassandra was still concerned about FYSHBone's dog. She called and the pound said nobody wanted Pretty.

Cassandra would try an experiment.

She and Jason took a drive down to the pound. They walked in. Dogs in cages barked and whined and paced and banged their tails against the sides and begged for contact with their eyes.

Jason smiled and laughed and giggled and clapped.

They came to Pretty. FYSHBone's ugly little dog was curled in a far corner of her cage. She looked depressed.

Jason saw her and immediately put his face against the bars and spoke to the dog, calling it by the name of a cartoon. The dog heard Jason's voice and perked up. It stood and ambled over to Jason's face and sniffed him.

Jason turned to his mother. "Smiley face!"

Of course. Cassandra had heard that the dog had a digestive problem and had to be walked often and that meant lots of unpleasant work. Her mother would kill her. But it just felt right.

Luckily for all involved, it had turned out the dog's constant diarrhea was the result of chronic untreated dehydration.

The attendant was happy someone was taking an interest in Pretty.

"Unfortunately, when dogs poop like that people sometimes withhold food and water and that just makes the problem worse. I gave her a sports drink, made a little white rice mixed with unseasoned ground beef, and this dog is good as new."

Cassandra could not believe that stroke of good fortune. Nothing could be done about Pretty's ugly mug. But the other end of her was better than expected. They signed the dog out and took her home.

Cassandra found the last blue uniform she had worn in the back of a closet she rarely visited.

It was musty. She tried it on. A squeeze, but her recent jogging in pursuit of the Marathon Slasher plus a couple of days of not eating had chipped away enough to fit.

She found other uniforms and hand-washed them in the tub. She hung them out to dry in the driveway where her mother hung a clothesline.

Cassandra cleaned ribbons and polished medals, including the Combat Cross. She shined her shoes and oiled her gun.

She thought of Sabio, and pushed him out of her head.

She thought of FYSHBone, Gator, Slow Mo, Tamora, Bishop, Bollinger, blood, money, and lies.

Maybe Cassandra was finished as a cop. Maybe it was time to find something new. A new path. The right one this time. Maybe it was time to chase her dreams.

But what about Jason? He needed his daily bread.

Cassandra would pick up Transit patches for her uniform.

She did not know at that moment where her life was

headed and that was okay. Cassandra needed a steady income and she was not afraid of hard work. That was certain.

For the time being, Officer Maldonado was back on patrol.

CHAPTER 40

Notes from Underground

Cassandra's first day back in uniform, assigned to patrol the New York City subway platforms, was a tumble-dry on high.

The heat was underworldly. It came in waves. Swells of people pushed and moved and pressured for space.

Cassandra rolled with a gang of foul-mouthed rookie cops fresh from the academy. They were stupid about the street, blind to crime. They mostly prowled for free lunch and cell numbers.

The rookies talked about every female as if she was less than a cardboard cutout. They chewed gum, laughed, and eyeballed Cassandra not like a veteran, more like an older cougar they'd bust a nut over given half a throw.

Cassandra kept her mouth shut. She was allowed shades, so she wore dark ones. She kept her hands on her utility belt and leaned against steel girders that ostensibly kept the earth above from collapsing.

The gun felt good in its holster. The cuffs.

Cassandra carried an asp, a retractable baton that she had scored at the police supply store when she picked up her Transit patches. She had used one in a training exercise once and it never left her mind.

Transit Officer Maldonado spent that first day and the ones that followed still numb. She spent most hours skipping eyes from transit rider to transit rider like a slot player who pulls the lever as a reflex, over and over.

This distracted her from the FYSHBone case. It made justice not her problem. She pushed his dead body and his grieving mother and the questions surrounding his demise as far from her consciousness as they would go.

She thought of Sabio. Especially when the loneliness deepened, which it did at unexpected moments, even in the most crowded places.

Cassandra's goal became to keep her head down. To be a worker bee. To do her tour of duty and go home.

Her team deployed to a location just outside subway turnstiles. Since 9/11, police were allowed to set up a table at any point of entry or exit to the system and "randomly" check people's bags.

In the hands of the dunces she now worked with, this meant sexy young women, Arabs, blacks, and Latinos got stopped a lot.

The team searched bags and made comments. Cassandra hung to the side, quiet. She was near the stairs to the street, so her cellphone got reception. It vibrated without giving a name or number, just the word PRIVATE. She answered.

"Maldonado."

No reply. She heard breathing. The connection was bad. "Hello?"

The voice was nervous and low, a whisper. "Detective?"

Not anymore I'm not. "Who's this?"

"Dulles."

FYSHBone's chief of operations.

"Why are you calling me?"

"I'm in a world of trouble."

Cassandra heard what sounded like street noise in the background. The rookies elbowed each other over silicone cleavage.

Cassandra stepped away. "Dulles, what's this about?"

"The books."

"The company's books? KUTTHROAT?"

"I know what they did. What the *real* numbers are. I kept both sets of books. I—Oh, God!"

"What is it?"

"I gotta get away."

"Is somebody there, Dulles? Are they after you?"

"Detective, please help me."

"Where are you?"

"Near the office."

"Want me to meet you there?"

"No. They'll follow me. Somewhere public. I can't let them catch me alone."

The Times Square-Forty-second Street subway station was the busiest in the system, and it was close to Dulles's office. Cassandra was a few stops away.

"Yes, yes," said Dulles. "Go there now. I think somebody's following me."

He hung up.

CHAPTER 41

Grand Pas d'Action

Cassandra clocked out to meal.

The Transit supervisor tried to stop her. He explained the protocols.

Cassandra said, "I'm having woman troubles, all right?" and walked off.

The uptown platform of the Broadway line was hot and teeming. Local trains entered and left the station. Express trains dragged.

Cassandra checked her watch.

What was Dulles going to prove? Financial fraud at KUTTHROAT? The Feds were already on to that. And Cassandra's beat was never white-collar.

A motive for FYSHBone's murder?

Well, it was a lie to say she did not care. Of course she cared. She wanted to know what happened to FYSHBone and she wanted to see the perpetrator brought to justice.

But the FYSHBone file was out of her hands now and not her job. Not her concern.

Cassandra's job was to catch people trying to sneak onto the transit system without paying. It was more serious than that, but that was what it felt like.

Would Dulles implicate or exonerate Sabio?

Cassandra hated to admit it, but this was her main interest. She wanted to know.

The express train finally arrived, sardines. Cassandra pushed her way on. With her blue uniform and weapons and dark shades, people gave her all the space she wanted.

The train made stops. Even though it was tight, there was civility all around. People from every nation, every culture, every religion, every orientation pretzeled together. They touched only when necessary. They avoided one another's breath with discretion.

The train slowed in the tunnel then stopped. Riders fidgeted. Dulles would beat her to the station.

An announcement came over the loudspeaker. The train was being held due to a police incident at Forty-second Street/Times Square.

Cassandra looked up at the top of the train car. *Please don't let that be Dulles.*

Her train jerked forward. It finally moved into the station.

Cassandra exited as part of a human jet stream onto the platform. Commuters crowded and craned their necks toward one end. Cassandra worked her way toward the police action.

Red plastic ribbon improvised for crime scene tape to keep gawkers at a distance. Cassandra approached one of the uniforms.

"What gives?"

"Business guy tried to end it. Tried to jump under the number 1 train and screwed it up. He's wedged between the car and the platform. They can't move either him or the train or his guts will spill out. Right now he's dying of a slow leak. He's down there losing his marbles."

Paramedics, a doctor, transit cops, transportation authority personnel, patrol officers, Emergency Service officers, detectives, and others stood around. Nobody could do a thing.

The uniform said, "Doc says not much longer. Downtown wants us to try to clear the station before rush hour, but we gotta let nature run its course."

Cassandra was tempted to suggest that they send undercovers into the crowd to see if the perp still hung around and to start a canvass for witnesses. She kept out of it.

She wondered if they had recovered the accounting books Dulles mentioned in his phone call.

"Did the guy have anything on him like a suicide note or some documents or something that might explain why he'd take that leap?"

"To my knowledge he dove in hands free."

"All right if I speak to him? I wanna offer a prayer."

"Be my guest. His brain ain't getting oxygen, though, so he's loony."

Cassandra ducked under the makeshift police line and walked to Dulles. She put her shades in her shirt pocket and bent on one knee.

She took his hand. He looked up. His eyes sagged.

"Dulles."

"Mom?"

"No, Dulles, this is Maldonado. You called, remember?"

"Did you tell Nana?"

"Dulles, you didn't try to jump onto the tracks, did you? Somebody pushed you. Who?"

Cassandra knew that if Dulles made a dying declaration, a statement about someone purposely throwing him under the train, if he identified that person, then died, his statement would be admissible as evidence in criminal court.

"Tell me who did this to you."

"Mumsy?"

"No, Dulles. Focus. Why did you call me? It's Maldonado. What did you want to say? About FYSHBone? The accounting?"

A moment of clarity entered Dulles's eyes. But he said something senseless.

"Pièce de résistance."

"Huh?"

"Pas de deux."

His eyes went toward the stairs up out of the subway. The eyes began to fade. The tension in what remained of Dulles's body dissolved.

There would be no more communication. Cassandra held his hand and prayed.

Still down low, Cassandra looked up toward the crowd behind the makeshift police line and happened to catch the strong legs of a woman in shorts and running shoes as she finshed a half pirouette into the crowd.

She knew those ballerina legs!

Oxana! Gator's girlfriend!

The woman carried a metal briefcase, no doubt Dulles's.

Cassandra went after Oxana.

The crowd was thick and sweaty and all faced toward the scene at the end of the platform where Dulles had his final curtain. Cassandra weaved through the crowd like a wolf through familiar woods.

Oxana's blonde ponytail also wove through the crowd.

Cassandra picked up her pace. She would overtake Oxana before the stairway.

Oxana stopped and looked over her shoulder, and Cassandra stopped.

They locked eyes. Oxana's were a frosty blue.

She spun and began to move again.

Cassandra moved also. She began to close.

The crowd forced Oxana to the edge of the platform.

Cassandra followed.

What?

Oxana tiptoed along the edge of the platform, a smooth sideways glide known as *glissade* that Oxana was now using as a getaway move.

Damn.

Cassandra followed in a choppy rendition. It had been a decade since she took dance and longer since she'd been in ballet.

"Halt!"

Oxana leaped from the platform to the tracks.

Oh. My. God.

The woman was such a prima donna that she did not just jump. She did an attitude leap where she became a gazelle. Front leg stretched, horizontal toes pointed, back leg curled behind gracefully.

It was manic, unbelievable, but, God, it was beautiful.

Even crazier: Oxana took that leap off the subway platform down down down to the tracks below. Anybody else would have broken a leg or sprained an ankle.

Oxana stuck the landing. She tore down the tracks toward the subway tunnel.

"Oxana, stop!"

People looked. Heads turned. It was not something you saw every day, not even in New York.

Cassandra looked to make sure no train was barreling into the station, then hang-dropped off the platform old-lady style.

Oxana disappeared into the tunnel with the briefcase.

Ten seconds later, Cassandra followed.

It was dark inside that tunnel, musty and hot. Cassandra hauled into the black.

Oxana's red-and-white-striped blouse bounced ahead in the dim light.

"Stop, police!"

Cassandra immediately decided not to waste another breath on that. She needed to conserve.

So hot.

Sweat oozed. She pumped her arms. Her feet were like bricks in the black patrol shoes.

Cassandra timed her stride between rail ties, through puddles, garbage, and muck. She avoided every rail, not certain which one carried all the voltage.

Oxana ran half a football field ahead. It couldn't last. Even dancers get tired. Cassandra counted on the stamina she had built hunting Marathon.

A tornado approached. The fury of an uptown local vibrated inside the tunnel.

Cassandra leaped to the side, her back against the curved, cool concrete.

The train created wind as it roared super-fast inches from her face. Riders inside were a blur. Up ahead Oxana danced sideways along the wall.

Damn. Cassandra held her breath and kept moving. She unholstered her Glock.

The last car of the train blew past and Cassandra jumped back into a sprint behind it, her goal to not lose sight of the train, to run as fast as the train in order to close the distance between her and Oxana.

The red dot of the train's rear sign faded and left Cassandra in its dust. No sign of the candy-striped blouse.

Cassandra struggled to breathe. She strained and slowed to a trot.

Where did you go, prima donna? Did you leap onto that moving train?

It seemed impossible, but this woman could move. And Cassandra had seen a perp jump down onto a moving train before.

This one would not get away.

Cassandra slowed to a walk, the gun still in her palm. She squinted. Shadows moved. A rat scampered. No sign of Oxana.

Where are you?

Bam!

The woman struck from a darkened recess along the tunnel wall. She karate-chopped Cassandra's wrist, which knocked the gun loose. It flipped and discharged an explosive round, then sparked against the third rail.

Oxana threw a right cross with the metal briefcase that landed on Cassandra's cheek.

Ouch!

Her left fist found Cassandra's ribs.

Oof!

Oxana's knuckles felt like a length of pipe. She clocked Cassandra's temple with the metal briefcase.

Ow!

Oxana wore brass knuckles! She caught Cassandra's chin

Bam!

Spit flew.

Cassandra ducked to miss a haymaker with the briefcase that would have tumbled her toward the electrified rail.

Cassandra covered her head. "Christ, stop!"

Oxana went to work. She battered Cassandra like a hailstorm. She found every opening where the brass knuckles and the metal case could do damage.

Cassandra sprang and deployed the asp, her new collapsible baton. It snapped to its full extension. She threw her arm overhead and held the asp like a samurai sword.

Oxana put up her brass knuckles and raised the case as a shield.

Cassandra paused, then swung the asp around in a clean, quick, perfect circle.

Thwack! *Heavy metal for the side of your neck, bitch!*

Oxana screamed like someone in a horror movie. She turned to run.

Oh, no you don't! Cassandra smacked her across the back so hard it knocked Oxana into a wall.

Rage erupted out of Cassandra. She commenced to beat the crap out of Oxana with the asp the way her father did to her with a belt so many times.

¡Toma! ¡Toma! ¡Toma! ¡Toma!

Cassandra firebombed from every angle. She smacked and smashed. She beat and bloodied. She wanted to break Oxana's bones.

The woman turned to fight and try to swat the weapon

and block with the metal case. Cassandra smashed the case so hard it broke open and sent papers flying.

Shit!

Oxana threw the case and tried to run.

Cassandra caught the woman with force across the backs of her long, powerful legs. The woman's legs felt like Puerto Rico's *balata* trees, which are notoriously difficult to chop.

The earth moved. Another train raced toward them. Cassandra served Oxana one more solid whack.

"Go down!"

That was when Oxana, who had her back to Cassandra, knocked the snot right out of her. She did this by executing a sudden, sharp, perfect *arabesque penché*, meaning she kicked her leg backward and damn near straight up.

Cassandra caught that sledgehammer directly under the chin. She forgot the lecture she had given Moretti about martial arts ballet. She forgot *everything* as the kick relieved her temporarily of all thought and put an immediate stop to her assault.

The dancer dove for Cassandra's gun on the tracks. She grabbed it, spun low, and rose.

Cassandra focused.

Oxana pointed the Glock at Cassandra. She pedaled backward drunkenly toward the concrete wall. A bloody, ghastly grin revealed where Cassandra's asp had hollowed separate spaces for three teeth.

Oxana giggled. She stuck her fingers in her mouth to look at her own blood. She cocked the hammer.

Cassandra read her lips: *"Enchanté."*

That would have been when Oxana fired and ducked out of the way of the speeding train. But she was not fast enough. Her spotting and timing were apparently off from Cassandra's attack, because the number 1 train caught Oxana on the corner of her shoulder and knocked her through the air at an irregular angle.

Oxana's body pinballed off the concrete wall, back into the path of the speeding train, which then kicked Oxana's rag-dolled body ahead of itself and stampeded over her noisily, like a herd of hungry buffalo.

Cassandra turned away, her back against the opposite wall.

When the train was safely past, its noise tearing down the tunnel, Cassandra glanced about to insure that there was no movement.

All she glimpsed was the candy-striped shirt in a bloody heap about ten feet away from where the legs now were. The papers from the briefcase blew all over. Cassandra collapsed her asp and holstered it.

There was no time to freak out. She ran down and picked up the documents she could and did not bother trying to read any, as it was dark and she had to work fast. Another train would soon be along.

Cassandra found her department-issued gun with Oxana's hand still attached. It violated her every instinct as a cop not to retrieve her weapon, so she did.

She went over to Oxana's candy-striped torso. The woman's striking blue eyes were frozen open. Her expression proved Oxana had realized the horror of her final misstep.

Cassandra lifted the collar on the red-and-white blouse. *I knew you would have it.* FYSHBone's necklace.

The diamond-studded pot-smoking fish skeleton sparkled, even inside that dank tunnel.

Cassandra recovered it. Afraid to put it in a pocket where it might slip out, she placed it around her neck, under her uniform, next to her necklace with the special ring.

A slow limp back toward Forty-second Street. Cassandra had sprained her ankle somewhere and it began to swell.

She was hot, sweaty, and thirsty. Armpits totally damp. She felt grimy. She recovered her hat on a rail tie. She found her shades in one miraculous piece.

Cassandra walked toward the light.

Near the mouth of the tunnel, a fresh acrylic mural decorated the concrete wall. A big red bloodshot Salvador Dali eyeball. Graffiti was still alive and underground. The world still turned.

Cassandra put on her shades. She limped into the light.

CHAPTER 42

Smooth Operators

Cassandra climbed out onto the platform without so much as an offered hand.

The first cop she saw she thumbed toward the tunnel. "Better send somebody down there with a body bag and a shovel."

She walked past him and the other cops, detectives, supervisors, white shirts, and others who demanded to know what the hell just happened.

Cassandra was no longer a detective on this case, and she did not feel the inclination to answer to anyone.

She walked past the police line, through the crowd, up the stairs, out of the subway system.

She needed fresh oxygen and light. The noise of the upper world.

The sidewalk outside the station was congested. Media were already on live feed to report Dulles's apparent suicide. Cassandra felt no need just then to correct the record.

She crossed to the east side of Broadway to avoid the crush and bought herself a bottle of water. She downed it.

She sat on a curb in the middle of Times Square with

all of the noise and the flashing lights and the crowds and the tourists and the high summer sun.

Cassandra felt drained.

FYSHBone's necklace felt heavy around her neck.

"Half a million dollars' worth of diamonds," Sabio had said.

Five years of her son's education plus change, she thought.

Nobody knew she had it. Cuca certainly could put Cassandra onto a discreet fence, and would not ask what for.

"Find that necklace and you find your shooter," Sabio had said.

Oxana did not have the murder weapon in her possesion or she certainly would have used it on Cassandra. The gun had probably been disposed of. Even average criminals know not to hold on to the murder weapon.

So why keep the necklace? In this case that tied Oxana back to the homicide just as much as the gun did.

Cassandra found the handful of Dulles's papers that she had recovered from the tunnel.

Copies of certifications made regarding internal audits of KUTTHROAT's financial books, company tax returns signed by Dulles, and the like. None of that made any sense to Cassandra.

She found a letter. It was dated that day and addressed to FYSHBone's mother.

Dear Mrs. Edwards:

   I wish I could congratulate you on assuming ownership and control of KUTTROAT RECORDS. Unfortunately what you inherit this afternoon is nothing more than a house of cards.

I have been chief of operations for the company for several years now and this letter serves as my resignation and as an outline of my crimes.

During my tenure at the company it was my responsibility to maintain and supervise the production of the principal internal accounting documents, including the general ledger and financial statements as well as the submission of all relevant tax and regulatory compliance documents.

Over time I participated in a wide-ranging conspiracy with your son, LeRoi Edwards III, to falsify the company's books, overstate assets, and understate liabilities by over one hundred million dollars. The false books were used, among other things, to continue to secure loans whenever we experienced liquidity crises, which was often.

It was an elaborate scheme where we essentially lied to Paul to get the loan, borrowed from Peter to pay Paul, lied to Paul again for the cash to pay Peter, then restarted the whole deceptive process.

We did this for various reasons. I am sorry to be the one to inform you that one reason was your son used the company to launder profits from criminal activity conducted by unknown associates.

LeRoi would bring in cash in hundreds of thousands, sometimes millions of dollars every month, and the company would issue a check to a dummy corporation for consulting services that were never rendered.

LeRoi's personal spending was also a problem. He had a habit of buying very expensive things, lots of them, always in cash, which he drew down from the company coffers at will. Million-dollar paintings were an obsession.

It may hearten you to know that the crux of the financial problems faced by the label stem from FYSHBone's network of charities. Your son's need to give was so great that it long ago bankrupted what should have been a lucrative, viable, self-sustaining enterprise. Last year alone he gave away around fifty million dollars to all kinds of causes, like building wells in rural areas and combating low birth weight in the Congo. It was FYSHBone's goal to give away one hundred million a year, and he was on target.

When I asked what would happen when this all eventually came to light, he said the people he helped would never allow his imprisonment. He was their Robin Hood. They would storm the Bastille for him. Your son had much naïve faith in humanity.

The reason for my participation in the scheme began with greed. Your son paid well and let me loan myself money from the label, which I then used to make all kinds of disastrous investments. No matter. I just forgave my own debt. My position at the label made it my personal cash cow, and I became addicted.

The reason I notify you now is that I am taking one last shot at doing something right. It is already too late for me. Federal agents have already detained me once and have begun to interview me under threat of federal indictment.

I DO NOT TRUST THE FBI!!!

*I may reach out to Detective Maldonado of the
NYPD—she strikes me as earnest. Your son would
have been the only one for me to turn on with law
enforcement, as he isolated me from whoever else
he conspired with, but he is gone now, so I have
little to offer the government by way of a sacrifical
lamb.*

*I will offer the truth instead, in the hopes that
by simply coming clean I can reduce the penalty,
serve it, and get on with my life.*

*I interrupt the reading of FYSHBone's will
and communicate this now because time is of
the essence. I know you intend to sign the letter
of intent for Bishop today immediately following
the reading. I do not want another person tangled
in the mess left by your son. KUTTHROAT does
not have the value that we represented to Leland
Bishop and KAMIKAZE Vynil.*

*Now that you have been made aware you, too,
will be perpetrating a fraud if you go forward
with a merger. Additionally, the plans to take
the resulting company public would also require
fraudulent representations to the SEC and invite
additional layers of scrutiny and penalties seven
times greater than those for mere tax fraud.*

*It won't be long before Bishop's people discover
the whole thing is a sham. The legal consequences
will be dire.*

*The real danger is whoever your son was in
business with on the street. They will still want to
use the label for their nefarious purposes. I do not*

need to tell you how ruthless they are. I for one am
followed and watched at all times, and I am very
scared.

But I made my own fate.

Now you must take yours into your own hands.
Save yourself. Stay out of the music business. Do
not make the deal with Leland Bishop.

Enclosed you will find some relevant documents
to give you a sense of what we at the company
said was going on versus what was actually the
case. No other executive at the label other than
LeRoi and I participated in these falsifications. I
pressured my subordinates into it, for which I will
accept responsibility.

Please do the right thing.
Respectfully,
A. B. Dulles

Cassandra put away the letter.

Incredible. Money laundering and financial shenani-
gans, as suspected.

Dulles had intended to hand the letter to FYSHBone's
mother at the reading of the will. He put it in writing so
she could digest it in private. Dulles had been headed
there. That was why he wanted an escort. That meeting
was getting ready to start somewhere.

In any case, Oxana killed FYSHBone and now
Dulles. Why?

To protect the other conspirator, the "unknown."

Who was that other conspirator?

Her man Gator? Much more likely.

Cassandra would have said she was certain except for the nagging fact that this theory did not answer every question or explain every piece of evidence. Probably nothing would.

She wondered what to do next. What was the right thing?

Cassandra got out her cellphone.

CHAPTER 43

Last Testament

Sabio got a call from a lawyer who handled FYSHBone's will and scheduled the reading of it. As the record label was part of the estate, and for other reasons, Sabio and Dulles were requested to be present.

The reading was at the DUMBO penthouse in the Egyptian library.

Sabio expected to see Tamora but was surprised to also find Gator, Leland Bishop, and his man Hegel, as well as Princesa.

The library was a starburst of orange, red, blue, black, and gold pigments. Elaborate wall hangings. Tapestries on the floor. The chairs and stools had legs carved to look like lions' paws, alligators' feet, or bulls' hooves.

The group sat in a half circle and waited for the estate's lawyer who had scheduled the reading.

Sabio pulled up a chair.

A creepy black statue stood guard next to the door like a dog at attention. FYSH had told Sabio about it when he acquired it from a dealer in Cairo. Anubis, a human-looking god with a jackal's head.

Sabio sat next to Bishop. His man Hegel was to his

right. Hegel had Sabio's laptop bag on the floor between his legs.

Bishop asked Sabio if he had seen the charger.

"What are you doing here, Bishop?"

"Tough break, old sport, Tamora reached out directly and we have come to terms. I am here at her request to conduct our transaction after today's reading makes her position official. Obviously, my offer to clear your debt," Bishop rolled his eyes toward Gator, "is now withdrawn. You will need to find some other way out."

After they pressured Sabio to act as a go-between, it turned out they never needed him. Bishop probably only wanted to keep Sabio invested in the deal as a pawn of some sort, to feel the situation out, maybe, certainly to smoke out the laptop.

No matter. Sabio was happy to be free of his responsibilities at KUTTHROAT. He decided right then that after the reading he would notify FYSHBone's mother of his resignation, effective immediately.

He was not sure what he would do next, how he would get around Gator. It was impulsive, but Sabio knew for sure that he was sick of this business.

As for Gator, Sabio did not bother to ask him what he could possibly be doing at the reading. At the moment he was square with Gator and uninterested in engaging him.

They waited in silence.

Tamora wore a diamond cross. She busied herself knitting. The sound of the metal spikes click-clicking against one another was like the ticking of some restless clock.

The rest of the party shifted in their seats or played with their phones or checked their watches or yawned.

At one point Princesa made flirty eye contact with Sabio, like, *Now you and I are free to pursue something.*

Sabio turned away and pretended not to notice.

The white-haired lawyer arrived forty-five minutes late. He sat behind FYSHBone's desk next to a large onyx version of the globe that balanced on a pin.

The lawyer sounded as if he was reading, even when he was not.

"We are gathered for a reading of the last will and testament of LeRoi Edwards III. Some of you are here because you are involved in his estate."

The white-haired lawyer gave a sheepish grin.

"Mr. Edwards was one to change his will often. It was his opinion that one should never feel too comfortable, which is opposite, really, to what estate planning strives for. Nevertheless, Mr. Edwards's need to keep the universe, as he saw it, on its toes, made him change his will constantly. Just as well because it kept me and some young associates quite busy."

Sabio realized in that moment that this other lawyer had probably made more money off FYSHBone than he ever could. In the past this would have bothered him.

"What we will hear is the final version, the one that was in effect at the moment of his death. I shall distribute copies. First we should view a videotape with some final messages."

The lawyer pressed a button. The wall hanging behind the desk rose to reveal a large flat-screen TV. The lawyer pointed a remote. FYSHBone's face appeared frozen. One more button and he spoke.

"'Pay no attention to the man behind the curtain.' Ha ha. No, it's me, FYSHBone. *Do* pay attention."

FYSHBone's face was right in front of the camera. He wore big white gliterry Elton John star-shaped sunglasses.

"First, if you are watching this, that sucks because it means I'm gone. I'm sure you already had your moment of silence. The good news is 'I know that my Redeemer Liveth.' I am now in that great recording booth in the sky. And I still get funky! Duke Ellington taught me some new tricks. I'll have plenty of new material when you get here. Hopefully not too soon. Ha ha."

FYSHBone went to a prepared statement. "First order of business: Sabio."

Sabio sat up in his seat.

"Let me say that you are an okay lawyer. At times you show potential. Most times you settle. This is rooted in your self-esteem issues, which have contributed to your addictions."

Sabio sank in his chair a little. He did not wish to have any more of his dirty laundry aired.

"You have problems, Sabio. But they are not insurmountable. Get yourself in a good Bible-based church or become a Buddhist or sign up with a new therapist, but do *something* to face those issues."

That's it.

Sabio was relieved by FYSHBone's tact.

FYSHBone shuffled papers. "Sabio, I bequeath to you all of the paintings that I took from you at poker. First, let me confess that I often cheated."

I knew it!

"Second, I never liked your paintings."

What?

"I understand they're postmodern. But your pieces all

feel soulless. Interesting questions, but no feelings. Too detached. At the time I was trying to teach you a lesson about appreciating what you have, but you seem never to have learned it. The good news? You have a keen eye for market value. I had your pieces appraised. Each has gone up."

FYSHBone grinned at the camera.

"Better still, the fact that *I* owned them is now a part of their provenance, an interesting fact about their history that will further increase their value. Especially now that I died. Taken as a lot, these paintings should suffice to get Gator off your back *and* pay for a college education. Not bad."

What is he saying?

FYSHBone looked up from his notes and looked directly at the camera, which is to say directly at Sabio.

"I could have just taken care of the problem for you, Sabio. But I believe in pursuit of destiny and free will. And I like you enough I wanted to give you one last chance to be the man too many of us, myself included, have failed to be."

Yes.

"Now it is up to you. Please do not think you are on a lucky roll. It is *not* time to double down. In fact, if I were you I would get out of New York and go back to Chicago. There's nothing left to prove. You made it here. By the skin of your teeth, but you made it. You can make it anywhere. Stop spreading the news. Go back to the Midwest and be there for your daughter when she comes home."

Sabio could not believe his ears.

FYSHBone, you arrogant beautiful genius. God love you. Thank you. Sabio's throat swelled at the thought of having the purse to purchase his daughter's freedom.

He wanted to run out of that room and retrieve his paintings and trade them and settle his accounts and leave that very night. He would never gamble again. He would never fall short with his child again. Now he just needed for her to survive and make it home.

Sabio whispered it so all could hear: "Thank you, FYSHBone."

FYSHBone changed the subject. "Slow Mo. You've been a loyal friend. I'll never forget the time you stood up for me in the playground at recess. I always felt big when you were around. Slow Mo, for being such a great friend I leave you my boat, the *Pequod*, where we shared so many memories. Enjoy. Relax. Happy sailing. And please be careful."

The lawyer paused the video.

Now Sabio felt *very* self-conscious, as if everyone in the room could read his mind and knew that he had witnessed Slow Mo's horrific crash and somehow blamed him for Slow Mo's death. Or even worse, that they knew that Sabio had witnessed a massacre on FYSHBone's boat and kept his mouth shut.

The white-haired lawyer said, "Mr. Slopes, who Mr. Edwards refers to as 'Slow Mo,' is actually now deceased. The boat will pass into his estate."

Tamora curled her lip. "That child only had his mother. She still lives across the hall from me in the projects. What will she do with a boat?"

The white-haired lawyer shrugged. He hit Play. Sabio was happy to move on.

"Gator, now you. You are such a special case."

Gator sat up, his reptilian green eyes more alert than ever.

"Gator, you must be wondering why you were called

to a reading of my will. Who were you to me, right? What could there possibly be in this for you?"

FYSHBone paused as if to gather himself.

"Gator, the muscles, the clothes, the cars, the whores are all covers for your nagging feelings of inadequacy. That's why you are such a bully. Your life has never amounted to anything more than a long list of people who hate you. I was among them."

Gator leaned forward in his seat. His eyes turned to slits.

"Don't get heated, Gator. In the spirit of forgiveness I leave you an extra-special gift: my antique Clementi box piano. Manufactured by the master himself. It is downstairs in the center of the ballroom. It does not have as much monetary value as you might imagine, so you should not plan on selling it. But it is *the* sentimental treasure of my life."

FYSHBone took a moment to go to the camera and adjust the view so that they now saw the piano. He sat at it and hit one key right in the middle. He let the note float. The sound was crisp despite the inferior recording.

FYSHBone faced the camera with his star-shaped sunglasses. "Gator. Blood. You can never truly know what this instrument means. It belonged to a great man. It has great power to heal—but also to hurt. It is a gift and a curse. I do not give it to you because you deserve it. I do it because... well, maybe I finally deserve to forgive."

Gator's chest heaved. The garden snake neck vein bulged.

The big bully spoke to the TV screen. "What do *I* need to be forgiven for? I don't need forgiveness. I don't even *play* the piano."

But FYSHBone could not hear him and moved on.

"Princesa, I am sorry to say that you are here merely as a stand-in. I hope you do not feel used."

Princesa sat straight, like a white lily. The sound of her name made her tilt her pointy chin.

FYSHBone's voice caught. "I have spent my entire life searching. I guess we all have. Everybody wants to find that other half. I apologize if this hurts, Princesa, but you were not that person."

FYSHBone waited a moment as if to let the sting subside.

Princesa did not react.

"I have had many romantic moments. I have sired children. What I have never done is fallen in love. Not really."

FYSHBone licked his lips and looked off to the side.

"I carry around too much anger. I am afraid to trust, afraid to make myself vulnerable. That held me back."

FYSHBone held up a book.

"For you, Princesa: a book of love poems. An autographed original, worth a pretty penny. Study it. Make it your goal to make someone feel this way about you. Take it from me, there is no fate worse than arriving at your grave and never having felt the way this guy does in these poems."

Princesa breathed deep, but had no other visible reaction.

FYSHBone now removed his shades and put his face right in the camera. The picture was not of the highest definition, but it still captured the beauty of FYSHBone's hazel eyes.

"The best for last: Momma."

Tamora had long ago put down her knitting needles. She watched the image of her slain son.

"Momma, you are a queen. There is no one in the world like you. You are brilliant. You are beautiful. You are hard-working. The way you sacrificed for me and my sisters growing up. All of my failings as a father and as a man are of my own making."

"However I died, the alienation from my own children is the real tragedy of my life. But I can't blame you. You were a mother *and* a father. I just did not have it in me to become either."

FYSHBone leaned into the camera and lowered his voice. "I know the world is cold. But your smile has been gone too long, Momma. Right now you are hurting. But as I said, I'm good as gold. Go through the grieving process and come up on the other side with a renewed sense of purpose, *please*."

FYSHBone went back to his notes.

"To that end, Momma, I leave you the balance of my estate. It includes all of the goodies. The real estate, the cars, the horses, the jewelry, the music, and all the rest. None of it is mortgaged or on credit."

FYSHBone gave the camera a big, mischievous smile and thumbs-up.

"Now the bad news: The record company is a shambles. But its creditors will never be able to 'pierce the corporate veil' and come after the estate. I saw to that. KUTTHROAT's debts are KUTTHROAT's, not yours. I recently carved all of my publishing rights out of it and what is left in KUTTHROAT is not anything that I care about. The songs have value that may be recovered. You can talk to Sabio about honest, lawful ways in which that can be done."

The part about the publishing rights surprised Sabio.

It meant KAMIKAZE's lawyers would have spotted the missing publishing rights before the completion of the merger and the deal would have been scrapped. Or that after the merger, KAMIKAZE would have discovered that the company it just purchased held nothing of actual value.

Sabio watched Leland Bishop for a reaction but could not tell if he even breathed.

FYSHBone continued: "Momma, Dulles is the accountant. He had been trying to talk me into a bankruptcy. Go forward with that. It will basically be some big banks left holding the bag. With all due respect, Momma, fuck 'em. Dulles will be receiving instructions from the estate's lawyer so that he knows that I want him to be one hundred percent honest with you about the true state of the company."

FYSHBone raised his voice. "You hear that, Dulles? That's why you were invited today. I'm not leaving you anything other than an opportunity to get this mess off your chest already. Come clean with Momma. Tell her everything."

The estate's lawyer paused the tape again to say that Dulles had confirmed for the meeting. Perhaps he had taken the subway. It was a long walk from the station.

Gator shifted in his seat.

FYSHBone addressed his mother. "Dulles knows where the bodies are buried, Momma. Listen to him. And try not to judge me too harsh. You have always been more disciplined than me about money. In fact I didn't name anybody else in the will, my beloved sisters or any of my children, because I want you to determine in your best judgment who needs what. This will give you an opportunity to interact with everyone, get to know my kids, tell them about me, and hopefully be a part of the healing process."

FYSHBone leafed through papers. "That is all for the disposal of property. Now, if you will indulge me, I am going to play one last song."

He stood and went to the piano.

"This one is especially for you, Momma. This was your favorite song once, when we were little. I guess your heart was broken but you thought you might be ready to recover. I hope you still like it."

FYSHBone bent over the piano. He let just the right amount of silence fill the space between his talking and the first note.

Sabio knew the song.

"The Rose." From the Bette Midler movie about a tragic rock star.

The song is a primer on love. How some say love is a river that drowns you. A hunger you cannot feed. The song says love is a seed beneath the snow. Treat it right and it becomes a rose.

FYSHBone was light on the keys to start, louder and with just the right hint of vocal desperation in the crescendo, delicate at the end. He let the final note resonate and listened to it fade.

He was quiet for a moment. He turned to the camera.

"For you, Momma. Because you really are a rose. You have your thorns. God save anyone who gets on the wrong side of them. But you are so beautiful."

FYSHBone choked up.

"Thank you, Momma. Thank you for bringing me into this world. You have been my anchor. I love and trust and respect you. I already miss you. But I am not alone, Momma. The Holy Spirit is with me. And I cannot wait to see you. We'll go down to the river, Momma! Like when we backstroked in the Euphrates and built our huts next to the Congo! Like when we stacked the pyramids above the Nile! Remember? How we were inspired by the sunset over the Mississippi and who cares about the cotton? Oh, we'll go down to the river, Momma! You and me. We'll run down singing! Everything will be sunshine in the house of the Lord! I love you, Momma! Take care of yourself!"

FYSHBone reached toward the camera and shut it off. The screen went black.

Tamora did not lose it the way she had at the funeral, but tears did stream. Sabio choked up.

The screen was dark, but the white-haired lawyer did not shut the TV off. "There's just a bit more."

They waited a few seconds. Princesa looked annoyed and so did Gator. Bishop looked as if he was waiting for the dessert tray.

FYSHBone popped back on the screen. He was now in the Egytian library. The sunglasses were back.

"I almost forgot."

He bent down and picked up his ugly little black dog. She wore a ridiculous little matching version of the white star-shaped sunglasses. She licked her chops.

"This here is Pretty. You all know her. She is one needy little B-I-T-C-H. She has a weak digestive system and needs to be walked many times a day. Beyond that she is an attention hog who demands to be hugged a lot. Whoever takes her into their home and takes good care of her gets one hundred thousand dollars a year up to and including the year in which she dies.

FYSHBone smooched his dog on the mouth.

"Remember: God helps those who help the homeless."

FYSHBone put his finger through her collar.

"And this white diamond collar goes with the dog. Really just a woman's diamond bracelet. Princesa, if you did not volunteer to take care of my dog, this is why you never got any diamonds from me. Enjoy the poems. Whoever took the dog, thank you."

Princesa stood. "He was supposed to love me!" She stormed off.

On the TV, FYSHBone smooched the dog again. He put her on the floor and pointed the camera at the open sarcophagus. He climbed in.

"Now I sleep with the pharaohs."

He lay down and pulled the top down over himself.

The lawyer stopped the tape.

"Well, folks—"

Gator cut him off. "What the hell am I supposed to do with a piano? Can't I trade that for Slow Mo's boat? Or the diamond bracelet?"

"No."

Gator pointed a thick finger at Sabio. "And you better not try to skip town with them paintings."

"Don't worry, I'm gonna settle. I don't want you anywhere near my rearview."

Hegel handed Bishop some papers from the laptop bag.

Bishop got right to brass tacks. "Tamora, if you would just sign here, here, and here, I have the check, and we shall conclude our business."

Sabio did not understand. Had Bishop not heard what FYSHBone just said about the publishing rights? Surely he understood that without those the company had zero value. Nothing but debt.

Sabio wanted to ask Bishop outright, felt compelled to disclose all that he now understood about how fragile the company really was. But Sabio had not yet officially resigned from KUTTHROAT and he still had a technical duty to the label and to Tamora as the new owner. He kept his mouth shut.

Bishop appeared to read Sabio's mind. "It's all about the taxes, Guzmán. I know the company is nothing but a black hole of liabilities. I'm fully aware of its true condition. That is, in fact, the reason I want it. It is to be a tax writeoff for all of our North American activities. That is what the little people never understand about gaming the system. The way we set things up, even when we lose money, we win."

The estate lawyer nodded but did not speak.

Sabio shook his head, but also said nothing.

Tamora Edwards asked for a pen and Bishop handed her a fancy one with a fine tip.

It was against what FYSHBone had advised his mother in the tape. He said pursue a bankruptcy. But again, Sabio exercised his discretion and let Tamora make her own choice.

She scanned the document. She signed it once. She signed it a second time. She was about to sign it a third and final time when the library door slid open.

Cassandra Maldonado stood in the doorway clad in a sweaty, dirty cop uniform. She stood straight with her feet apart as if to dare whoever she had come for to try to get past her. She wore mirrored sunglasses.

The white-haired lawyer spoke up. "Officer? What is the meaning of this intrusion?"

"We'll soon find out."

Cassandra walked in slowly, like a sherrif at the end of any cowboy flick.

"Officer, what are you here for?"

Maldonado looked around at the players assembled.

"I'm here for justice."

"Justice?"

"That's right," she said. "I came to arrest the monster who murdered FYSHBone."

CHAPTER 44

Release the Furies

The circle stared at Cassandra. She removed her sunglasses and hung them in her collar. She made eye contact with Sabio but kept everybody else in the corners of her eyes at all times.

Tamora Edwards sat erect as a cactus. She held a pen. Leland Bishop hovered over her.

"Mrs. Edwards, please finish signing so I can move along. I have my chopper on the helipad upstairs. I'm hopping over to Teterboro where a private jet awaits to ferry me across the pond. I'm scheduled to join the Windsors at dawn. Tommorrow is the start of fox-hunting season."

Cassandra spoke. "Before you sign anything, Tamora, I have something for you."

She handed Tamora the letter Dulles had intended to deliver.

Tamora put the pen down and read. Cassandra watched for a reaction. Tamora played it cool.

FYSHBone's mother folded the letter and put it in her knitting bag.

Strange. Cassandra had expected more.

She reached inside her shirt and pulled off FYSH-Bone's platinum-and-diamond necklace. She laid it on the desk.

"I don't know whether FYSHBone's will mentions this half-million-dollar piece of jewelry, but I know it doesn't belong to me."

Cassandra looked right at Gator as she did this and saw the jolt that confirmed her suspicions. His eyes widened a degree and his muscles bulged. The large vein in his neck throbbed.

Cassandra was not taking chances. She pulled her gun.

"No sudden moves, Gator."

He tightened his mouth.

"You know what it means, don't you? For me to have FYSHBone's necklace?"

"How should I know?"

"Did you know that Oxana kept it? She took it off FYSHBone's neck the night she killed him for you."

Gator daggered Cassandra with his green eyes.

"The murder was for you, wasn't it, Gator? The necklace was for her."

FYSHBone's mother stared at Gator. "What is this woman saying?"

"She's talking crazy. I was in Brooklyn that night."

Cassandra said, "Yeah, and you had the perfect alibi. FBI surveillance at that precise moment. How convenient. Kept me off your scent."

Tamora said, "You're under FBI surveillance again?"

"I can't keep them off me."

"Especially when you're a rat, right, Gator?" Cassandra glanced at Tamora. "I don't know what he's doing here, how he inherits *anything* from your son, but Gator is

an FBI informant who tried to throw your son into a hole
for money laundering."

Tamora's eyes narrowed.

"That's crazy," said Gator.

"I've seen the 302 reports. I know it was you, Gator.
And I know that you were lying to the Feds."

"Why would I?"

"Because you're a congenital liar. And to cover your
ass. The Feds must have something on you. Something
you knew you could never beat. No more witnesses who
conveniently jump to their death the night before jury
selection. Something deeper. So you tried to lie your way
out by offering FYSHBone."

Tamora leaned toward Gator. "Is this true?"

Gator flared his nostrils.

"I know it was you on the 302 reports, Gator. The Feds
tripped over themselves to bail you out of our investigation.
If they need you on the street that bad, you *must* be a rat."

"I don't play like that."

"I know you're lying, because Dulles wrote a confession about what he and FYSHBone were doing. He said
FYSHBone kept him apart from whoever he was laundering the money for. That no other executives at the
label were involved. Your 302 reports claim Sabio was in
on it."

Sabio said, "Gator, you son of a bitch!"

"Fuck you, lawyer!"

Cassandra said, "You said you were good at logic,
Gator. And it was a reasonable guess to imagine the lawyer was involved. Especially when you know he's not
quite right, given that he does business with you."

Cassandra did not look at Sabio and let him react in

private to the fact that she knew something embarrassing and possibly incriminating about him.

"You tell a different story from Dulles, though, Gator. And I believe Dulles, because he had no reason to lie. He was taking all the blame."

"I don't even know what you're talking about."

"Sure you do. And you knew that Dulles was coming here to confess it all to FYSHBone's mother, destroy her deal with Bishop, and come clean with the Feds. That was going to ruin your career as a rat, when the FBI discovered you were lying. Dulles had the documents to prove his version."

FYSHBone's mother said, "Gator, please tell me this woman is lying."

"Documents can be doctored to prove anything, Tamora."

"You know what I don't understand?" said Cassandra. "How you knew Dulles was coming here to set off that bomb. How did you know what was in his letter to Mrs. Edwards?"

Cassandra knew that it was possible that the *timing* of Dulles's murder could be a coincidence triggered not by Gator's knowing Dulles was on his way at that precise moment or his intention to reveal all to the Feds, but rather by the fact that killing Dulles during the will reading provided Gator with another great alibi. Cassandra had only challenged Gator like that to see if he would give something away.

He didn't.

"I don't know squat."

"You did. And that is why you dispatched your assassin to get rid of Dulles."

Cassandra heard Sabio catch his breath. "What?"

"Dulles is dead," she said.

"No!" said Sabio. "How?"

"Oxana pushed him under a train."

"What?" Sabio turned to Gator. "You maniac! Dulles's wife just had a baby!"

"What are you talking about?" said Gator. "I been sitting right here."

"Yeah," said Cassandra. "Except I didn't tell you when Dulles was murdered. So how do you know it was while you were sitting right here, Gator? And the point is not that you did it by your own hand. The point is that you sent someone to do it for you, which still makes you a murderer. Oxana's dead, by the way."

Cassandra wanted a big reaction. For Gator to fall out of his chair with despair. He didn't. The entire process of grief passed through his eyes in the space of six seconds.

"She was a good one."

It burned Cassandra. Oxana was a vicious killer, but she was also a talented woman who had somewhere lost her way. She had given her all under this man's manipulation.

Now Gator acted as if the woman was just a lucky horse that stopped winning. Cassandra wanted to strike him below the belt.

"I know you saw them together, Gator."

His green eyes finally betrayed something.

"You knew they were lovers, didn't you?"

Gator huffed. "I oughta come over there and—"

Cassandra angled her gun at his forehead. "Leave that chair, Gator, and from this distance I will dig a bullet hole through the center of your skull."

Gator stayed in the chair.

"I know it was you up on the train tracks, Gator. Don't deny it. You saw them. Oxana and FYSHBone."

"That's bullshit."

"You pulled yourself up to the tracks by some tree roots, which left them out of whack because you're so heavy. You needed a boost to get up, as I did, and your two bodybuilding groupies gave you one."

Cassandra's confidence in her theory grew.

"You went there from the gym because that was Oxana's special time with FYSHBone, her secret boyfriend. You and your boys spend so many manly hours in the gym. You watch each other flex with your shirts off and oiling one another. Meanwhile Oxana entertained herself at FYSHBone's."

"She was a whore by profession. What do I care?"

"Stop calling her that or I will beat you until you cry out."

Gator contained himself.

"I have physical evidence that you were up on those tracks, Gator. You left blue neoprene wedged into the fractured root. Bad luck for you, I've seen that material. It came from the weightlifting gloves you wore. We matched your DNA from the material you left on the tree to the DNA you left on that gun Moretti wiped against your face when we stopped you."

That last part was a big fat lie, but the Supreme Court has said lying to extract a confession is legal.

"You ever had a man just smack you in the mouth?" said Gator. "Because that's all I can think about."

"I heard your speech the first time. A true pimp. Another man sees your woman's beauty and all you see is the fifty dollars. But it didn't feel so good, did it? To see Oxana with FYSHBone?"

Cassandra changed her tone to a gossipy whisper. "She must have really felt something too, let me tell you, because she broke into their loveshack the night following his murder and rolled around on FYSHBone's bed naked. She left in a hurry when I spotted her up there and forgot her underwear."

"You think her feelings mattered?"

"Yes, Gator, they did. But how did *you* feel?"

"Shut up."

"Oxana liked it."

"Be quiet!"

"FYSHBone made her feel good."

"Shut up!"

"You're not half the man you pretend to be."

"Shut your goddamn mouth!"

"Why did you order Oxana to kill FYSHBone?"

Tamora said, "Gator?"

Cassandra said, "You *forced* her. She didn't want to. But you are such a petty little beast. You ordered Oxana to mutilate FYSHBone as proof she rejected him. And she tried. But when it came time to shoot him in his manhood? She couldn't. She came close to make it look as if she did, but she faltered."

Cassandra did not want to discuss these things in front of FYSHBone's mother, but it was the moment.

"Why did you order Oxana to kill FYSHBone? Jealousy?"

"I ain't answering any more questions."

"It makes no sense as a business move. I would say you were afraid of the merger. That would expose your money laundering to discovery by Bishop's lawyers or federal regulators. But that theory doesn't feel right. Especially in light of the fact that you yourself revealed to the Feds that FYSHBone was laundering money."

Tamora's eyes grew colder. "Did you?"

"She's lying!"

"No, Gator, you're the liar. Your move against FYSH-Bone makes no rational sense. You were jealous. Say it."

"I ain't never been jealous of nobody."

"Oxana was in love with FYSHBone. That made you feel small."

"That commie wasn't worth the effort. She actually thought I would use my connections in politics to bring her kids over here."

Now Cassandra understood the hold Gator held over Oxana. Some promise to bring the woman's children that Gator had never intended to keep.

"See what I mean about you, Gator? You got smallness in your bones. No wonder Oxana felt passion for FYSH-Bone. Who could ever care about you? Who could love you? You must be so selfish in bed. I bet you don't even know how to make a woman—"

"Shut up! Sex didn't have nothing to do with it! It was the look!"

"The look?"

"Yes!" Gator breathed so heavily, his chest heaved like an ocean swell. "The woman made faces I never seen before. Ecstasy. Bliss. And they weren't even doing it!"

Now Cassandra was confused. *They weren't doing it?*

"FYSHBone sat on the floor, barefoot. He strummed his guitar. You know what Oxana did? She danced! Ballet in the mirror. Not even looking at him. She looked at herself. Stared into her own eyes. Loved herself. Pranced around on her tiptoes and jumped and smiled. She *never* smiled for me! I didn't know she was capable."

Cassandra let that ring out. FYSHBone was dead because Gator did not like the fact that his woman smiled.

"So the freedom Oxana felt in FYSHBone's company hurt you so bad you ordered her to kill FYSHBone?"

"He should have left her the way she was."

"How was that, Gator?"

"Alone. None of this would have happened."

Moretti finally walked in.

Cassandra had reached Moretti at his splash pad in Queens and filled him in on what happened with Oxana and Dulles in the subway and the info she had gotten from Dulles's letter. She had already called the record label and determined that the reading of the will was set for FYSH-Bone's library.

Cassandra did not call for the rest of the HI-PRO team because Moretti was the only one she semitrusted. Plus, she was unsure what she would find.

She wished now that the rest of the team was there in case Gator flew into a rage. Moretti would have to do.

Cassandra nodded at her partner. He stepped behind Gator's chair.

Cassandra spoke with authority. "Stand up, Gator."

"What?"

She took a step toward him with her gun pointed.

"Antwoine 'Gator' Moses, you are under arrest for the murder of LeRoi Edwards III."

"You're arresting me? You have no evidence."

Moretti had his cuffs out. "Standing or facing the ground, Gator, but you will wear these bracelets."

Gator eyeballed Cassandra. He looked over his shoulder.

Other members of the HI-PRO team could be heard downstairs making their way up. Moretti must have called them, and Cassandra felt relief.

They were not alone.

Moretti trusted her.

Gator shook his head. "Ain't this about a bitch?"

"C'mon," said Moretti. "Let's do this the silky way."

Cassandra gestured with her gun for Gator to stand.

FYSHBone's mother's mouth wrinkled. "Gator, how could you?"

"I don't wanna hear nothing out of you, Medusa." He looked at Cassandra. "You wanna know who was laundering money at the record label? There she goes right there." He nodded at Tamora. "The crack queenpin of Red Hook. Every rock sold, she gets a taste. Why do you think she don't leave the projects? She controls from within."

Cassandra looked at Tamora, who stared at Gator.

"Witch practices a religion so dark, it don't even have a name. If you were to say it your heart would stop. Your tongue would fall out. Why do you think nobody in law enforcement has ever been able to determine who is at the top in Red Hook?"

Cassandra remembered how Cuca had put it: that the crack structure in Red Hook had always been murky. She and Cuca did a million drug deals in Brooklyn and at one point knew a little something about everybody in the game, yet they never caught a whiff of who ran things in Red Hook.

Tamora stared hard at Gator. She turned her face slowly to Bishop's big contract on the desk. She signed it.

Tamora looked up and spoke directly to Gator, as if the police and the others were not in the room.

"You are blind to the corruption of your own life, Gator. How could you?"

"How could I? How could *he* do that to *me*? That Russian was my best whore."

"You ignorant lizard. If you only knew the truth."

Tamora looked deep into Gator's green eyes and he froze. His mind seemed to travel. For a second he looked pained. His mouth wavered. Then it was gone.

Whatever it was, Gator swallowed it whole. The sinister light returned to his eyes.

"Your boy should never have messed with my property."

Gator spoke over his shoulder at Moretti.

"Take me to Central Booking already. Let's get this over with. I got a lawyer named Richman from the Bronx who's so good, I'll be out before my skanks got time to bake me a welcome-home cake."

Tamora put her hand up in a way that froze everyone in the room.

"If the blood must spill, let it pour."

Gator gulped. He said, "What?"

Cassandra did not hear the rattle of a rattlesnake, but she did see the whole thing go down. FYSHBone's mother leaped from her seat with both knitting needles in her right hand. She struck and instantly punctured Gator's thick neck vein. She struck with such quick precision that she ripped open a quarter-sized hole.

Blood squirted toward the ceiling.

Tamora was in the air again, both arms snapped up with a long sharp needle in each hand. For a second, in the black dress and in that extreme posture, FYSHBone's mother appeared as a giant black bat escaped from some netherworld. She snapped down like a matador to spike Gator in each green eye.

This action burst both eyeballs.

"Aaaahhhhh!"

Tamora really dug the spikes in.

"Waaah!"

Moretti had Gator from behind and spun him around so the blood from his gushing neck squirted away from the others. It sprayed in quick spurts as if from a garden hose, and made red Jackson Pollock designs on the carpet and walls.

Tamora pounded herself in the chest. "You bastard! He was my King!"

Gator flailed and rattled his head and screamed in shock and sudden blindness. He tried to yank his wrists apart from the cuffs to pull out the needles that stuck out of his sockets. That was no use.

"My King!"

Cassandra snapped out of her shock, jumped on Tamora, spun her, bent her over the desk, and cuffed her.

The woman sobbed. "My baby!"

Gator whipped about, but Moretti held and pulled him away from the others. They knocked into the large onyx globe, which fell off the pin on its pedestal, rolled into a wall, and toppled books off the shelves.

Gator and Moretti fell to the floor.

Gator kicked and screamed. The gusher of blood that escaped from his neck slowed its pulse.

He died.

Members of the HI-PRO team ran in and grabbed Tamora, who only wept now.

Cassandra looked around. Bishop and his man had slipped out. The contract was gone from the desk. Sabio was also gone.

They must be headed for the helipad.

Cassandra made eye contact with Moretti.

"Go after him!"

Cassandra ran up the steps to the helipad. Bishop was already in the pilot's seat, starting the machine. The rotors began to turn.

Where was Sabio?

Cassandra ran around to the other side.

Through the open door, she saw Sabio and the German bodyguard in a tug of war over the laptop bag. Cassandra put her hand on the asp and headed toward them, but Sabio pulled a KUTTHROAT AVENGER and put it in the German's face.

The propeller at the top of the helicopter got going. The engine was loud. The skids on the bottom lifted one foot off the ground. Sabio jumped out with the bag, the gun pointed at the German, who leaned out and stared down at Sabio, his tie flapping in the turbulence created by the chopper.

The helicopter rose. Bishop looked down at Cassandra from the controls. He gave the British Royal Navy salute before he rotated the cabin of his aircraft and flew off. Cassandra watched until the black helicopter became a mosquito and slipped behind the curtain that was the Manhattan skyline.

Sabio jammed the gun into the side pocket on the laptop bag. Without looking at Cassandra, he walked straight to the edge of the platform, stood on the end of it, in a position to jump.

They were right at the river.

Cassandra approached Sabio from behind, mindful not to startle him. The sun had barely fallen to the height of the average skyscraper, behind the buildings, west of the city.

The sun peered at them through the spaces between the glass, concrete, and steel.

All that magic light, yet Sabio appeared to shiver. Cassandra stood next to him at the edge.

"You okay, Sabio?"

"No."

Cassandra thought to say, "You will be," but didn't. She wanted to ask Sabio a thousand questions, most of them personal.

They stared straight ahead, each of them, and took in the height and shape of their city. Construction was underway everywhere. Yet there remained an enormous, perhaps unfillable hole near the bottom of Manhattan.

Sabio's hand shook visibly. "People should not have guns."

Cassandra reached for the laptop bag with the gun in the side pocket. Sabio let go.

"What's inside the computer?" she asked.

"I'm not sure."

"What are you afraid is in there?"

Sabio paused. He looked her in the eye.

"FYSHBone ran two sets of books. He intended to defraud Bishop and KAMIKAZE Records. Since there was going to be a public offering, that also means the SEC was in line to be duped."

"White-collar crime. You were part of the conspiracy?"

"FYSHBone never told me about it. I discovered it on my own."

"Was this information privileged? Did you have a responsibility to report it to anyone?"

"I think I had enough influence to talk FYSHBone out of it. But then—"

"Doing so would ruin your big payday."

Sabio tightened his lips.

Cassandra spoke to the ethical lawyer inside him. "Did you help advance the conspiracy, Sabio? Other than keeping your mouth shut?"

He didn't nod. "After my discovery I signed, as general counsel, some documents attesting to the accuracy of certain representations I knew to be false. I let FYSHBone think I was fooled."

Cassandra let that pass without comment. "You visited the studio the night of the murder."

"I did. I went there to tell FYSH that I knew he was cooking the books. To advise him, officially, that this was wildly illegal. To urge him to abort the merger with KAMIKAZE."

"And if he refused?"

"To tender my resignation."

"That's it on the money-laundering, Sabio?"

"Yes."

Cassandra should have known by now that lips like Sabio's were too succulent to trust. She did not even think about it.

She took the laptop by the strap, stepped away from the edge, spun to get momentum and flung the bag with the computer and the .50-caliber gun as far as she could manage into the river. It hardly made a splash.

Sabio looked at her and blinked. "Thank you. I—"

"Don't." She turned her face toward the skyline. "Never speak of this."

They watched white birds float in uneven circles. Debris tumbled in the hot breeze.

Sabio's voice caught. "I'm not sure about attorney-client privilege anymore, but I don't care. I have something to report."

"Go on."

Sabio squeezed his hands together. "I thought about it so much. Made so many arguments. You go in spirals."

Cassandra put her hand up. "Wait a minute. You have the right to remain silent, Sabio."

"I know."

She put her hand down. "Do you really think it could hurt you?"

"I don't care anymore."

"You should."

"On the night—"

"Sabio, don't—"

"—that I met FYSHBone—"

"Please be sure, Sabio."

"I saw three men die."

He left it there.

Cassandra pulled her head back.

"Were they murdered?"

"I can't say."

"What happened?"

"An incident. Men clearly reached for their weapons, and FYSHBone's men got the jump on them. They got buried at sea."

"Why was it not self-defense?"

"The men may have been provoked. I'm not clear."

"Who was it?"

"Three South Africans. It was in the news that their boat was lost at sea. FYSHBone sank it."

"Any idea where?"

"Not really."

"Any other witnesses?"

"I think a couple of the posse members still survive. They all participated."

Cassandra stared at him. "Who dumped the bodies?"

"FYSHBone's men. On his orders."

"And your role?"

"Accidental witness. In a place my mother would have told me not to go."

"Convenient."

"It's been a terrible burden."

"I'm not your pastor, Sabio."

"But you are a cop. And you're a woman. A mother." Sabio looked at her. "And a friend."

Cassandra lingered on that. "How come you never reported this?"

"At first I thought they'd kill me."

"And later?"

"I convinced myself I was prohibited from speaking. Privilege. That there was nothing to be gained. That we were too late to do the men any good. And they were despicable."

"You didn't think about their families?"

Sabio stared into the river. A tear pearled. His mouth went through every twist.

His voice cracked. "Why is my daughter in a war?"

Cassandra did not have an answer.

Sabio's face wilted. "I want her safe. I need her home."

Cassandra wanted to pull the man into her chest. "You'll see her smile again, Sabio. Pray."

Sabio bit his lip and nodded.

Cassandra believed the man's sincerity. It was the first time in a long time she had wanted to believe anyone. She stung from what she had witnessed in the library, the bloodbath, what she had lived through in the tunnel, plus what Sabio had just shared. It had all been so much.

Yet, somehow, Cassandra felt some peace.

She caressed the back of Sabio's neck as he wept. He put his head on her shoulder.

Someday, somebody would be there for Cassandra. For now, it felt good to be needed.

A tugboat led a freighter upriver through the swirls. Cassandra held the man until he no longer trembled.

VISIT US ONLINE
@ WWW.HACHETTEBOOKGROUP.COM.

AT THE HACHETTE BOOK GROUP WEB SITE YOU'LL FIND: